# A SECRET INHERITANCE

# A SECRET INHERITANCE

### Elizabeth Lord

**Severn House Large Print**
London & New York

This first large print edition published 2008
in Great Britain and the USA by
SEVERN HOUSE PUBLISHERS of
9-15 High Street, Sutton, Surrey, SM1 1DF.
First world regular print edition published 2007 by
Severn House Publishers, London and New York.

British Library Cataloguing in Publication Data

Lord, Elizabeth, 1928-
  A secret inheritance. - Large print ed.
  1. France - History - Third Republic, 1870-1940 - Fiction
  2. Large type books
  I. Title
  823.9'14[F]

  ISBN-13: 978-0-7278-7721-5

Printed and bound in Great Britain by
MPG Books Ltd, Bodmin, Cornwall.

# One

In the sumptuous drawing room on the second floor of her Parisian mansion on the Avenue de la Grande Armée, Thérèse Humbert stood gazing silently down on the face of her dead father.

In about ten minutes from now the *entrepreneur de pompes funèbres* would arrive. She would move aside for the lid of the coffin to be screwed into place then follow at a respectful distance as it was solemnly borne from the room and down the wide marble staircase to the waiting hearse.

Crowds were already lining the route to the church of St Honoré d'Eylau, the church itself filled by the wealthy and elite of Paris come to honour the Comte d'Aurignac – people who ten years ago wouldn't have given him house room. Only his family and a few very close friends knew of his humble origins as plain Auguste Daurignac.

Earlier they had filed quietly past the body, exactly as if it were lying in state, to pay their respects and offer hushed condolences to the family. Thérèse Humbert's full lips twitched into a small, contemptuous smile.

What they were more interested in was what

lay in her father's mysterious strongbox. At this moment, securely locked, it lay behind closed doors on the third floor of this establishment, its contents so secret that a close friend of the family had arranged to mount guard over it with a revolver while the family attended the funeral.

People had now left for the church. A few close friends and members of the family down in the reception hall were waiting for the coffin to pass before being conducted to their coaches. The house had fallen silent. In the room where the coffin lay, only four people remained: herself, her two sisters Marie-Louise and Maria, and her lifelong loyal friend, Catherine.

Thérèse glanced down again at the elderly face of her father. Eighty-five years old. In death the lines of age seemed to have been ironed away. His face now bore only the serenity of good living.

Again she smiled. Her mind's eye was seeing the house in which they'd once lived, in Aussonne, a village fifteen kilometres from Toulouse. Not large by any means but in its rural way comfortable. Built from local honey-coloured stone, its walls left to weather naturally in the heat of Languedoc summers like all the houses. She remembered it being shaded by fruit trees. There had been a paved courtyard and a good sized vegetable patch. There had been a couple of goats, chickens, a small pond for ducks and Toulouse geese for the table or for barter. There was a little horse that pulled the buggy taking her mother into Toulouse, where her shop sold high-class lingerie in the most fashionable quarter of the city.

Thérèse's smile faded. She'd been fourteen when her mother died. Everything had changed. She'd had to grow up quickly. As the eldest of six children she became the breadwinner, her father having sunk into himself after losing her mother and doing nothing but spin the stories he loved telling. He'd been a wonderful storyteller. They had been so real to her, those tales of distant places and a far more romantic life than the one she had then known, of an ancestry stretching way back in time and a rich inheritance her father vowed would be his some day. She'd truly believed it.

'They should be here for the coffin in a little while.'

Catherine's voice, from where she was sitting by the door, stirred Thérèse from her reverie. She nodded and smiled, not wanting to be taken from those far distant memories of hers. Just a while longer, her mind said.

Papa was well into his fifties when she was but a toddler. He'd been fifty-one when he married in 1852, her mother only half his age at the time. Born around 1801 as far as he could tell, he'd been a foundling left in a Toulouse church tower and brought up in an orphanage. Given the name of Auguste, he'd been taken on by a priest who eventually put him in charge of the church vestments and taught him to serve mass.

'It was said that the priest was my father.' She remembered the sneer in his voice. 'That isn't true. My father was a nobleman but dared not acknowledge me as he and my mother were unwed. He was said to have been Portuguese and owned vast estates and a fine chateau overlooking the deep Atlantic. He had no other issue but myself, so his wealth and property is rightfully mine and one day I shall prove it.'

She loved relating the tale to her little friends who listened wide-eyed. It didn't bother her that if he hadn't proved his right to his inheritance by then, he might never do so. An elderly man by the time she first heard the story, he'd acquired the name Daurignac in his mid-thirties, he said, when a local widow had claimed him to be her son and given him her maiden name.

'Her husband was a watchmaker,' he'd told Thérèse. 'But when I finally trace my true father and come into my inheritance, we will all be rich beyond dreams. No more scrimping and scraping for us, my little one.' By that time scrimping and scraping had become a way of life for them; her mother dead, her shop taken, the mortgage left to fall disastrously behind.

It was her mother who'd kept the family. A strong, resourceful woman, she too had been born out of wedlock, her natural father a rich farmer who seemed to have begotten a whole string of bastards in his time.

'But not a single sou did he ever give your mother,' Thérèse's father had told her. 'Though he must have had a change of heart, for he eventually left everything to one of his daughters, your Aunt Dupuy, who gave each of her sisters, including her sister Rosa your mother, a dowry of a thousand francs. Your mother bought this house with it when I married her.'

Gazing down at her father's body, Thérèse felt her lips curl. Yes, her mother, not he, had been the mainstay of the family. Taking a mortgage on the house she had bought her shop. Being in one of the best parts of Toulouse it had cost her a good deal, but the expense had been necessary in order for her to sell her fine lingerie.

The shop had prospered. Life had been pleasant. Her father, forever dreaming of his inheritance – the proof, he said, was in the old documents locked in his strongbox – had sat back and let his wife do the earning. His only contribution to the family income had been as a faith healer and bonesetter, with a bit of fortune telling thrown in. What little he did contribute to their income soon fell apart when she died in her early forties, reducing them to poverty in no time at all.

Thérèse shook her head at the corpse in its ornate casket. 'You old rogue,' she murmured mildly, for it was a long time ago and the bite of it had long since faded. 'It didn't take you long, did it, to get through what Maman left? You, with your mad schemes, letting everything be taken from us, the shop, the house, reducing us to begging from friends and neighbours?'

The sound of her voice in the quiet room made the others glance up in her direction. 'Did you say something, dear?' Marie-Louise asked.

Thérèse shook her head. 'I was thinking of the bizarre ideas our father resorted to when we were children to earn a living for his family.'

Marie-Louise clicked her teeth with impatience. 'You call what he did earning a living –

9

everything from bone setting to necromancy, giving people to believe he was a visionary? They only gave him money because they were scared of him and his prophecies. They were afraid he might cast a spell on them if they upset him.'

'I remember,' Maria said quietly, gazing down at her small black-gloved hands. 'He would put on such airs in his frock coat and top hat, but not two sous to rub together for all his efforts. He saw himself as lord of the manor while our debts mounted and mounted. If it hadn't been for our mother when she was alive —'

She broke off as their brother Romain came into the room, the door opening so silently that his sudden presence startled them all.

'It's time,' he said in a low, full-bodied voice.

In the church of St Honoré d'Eylau, Thérèse Humbert gazed at the ornate splendour of gold all about her and thought again of her humble beginnings.

With the voice of the priest droning on, extolling the virtues of the deceased during the drawn-out service, it seemed she could hear her mother's sharp voice calling to her – almost as though it were yesterday.

'Thérèse, child, stop those stupid stories of yours! Come in here and help me. This minute!'

Another snippet of memory. 1864. She'd be around eight years old. Small – people said she was petite, that her dark eyes were always bright and lively and that she had a pleasant, rounded face, hands always gesticulating with everything she said, and that she charmed everyone who saw her. She supposed that to have been true, for she'd had no enemies then.

She could see herself now, sitting on the doorstep of her mother's house, which was called L'Oeillet. Mid-morning, a hot summer sun blazing down upon baked brown earth as she sat cross-legged on the paved courtyard shaded by the trees, surrounded by a ring of children. Their expressions agog at the tale she unfolded, so enthralled as to be oblivious to the heat on their faces.

'The chateau rightfully belongs to my father,' she had been saying to them, already enlarging on what her father had told her. 'One day it will be his. It's called the Chateau de Marcotte in the eastern Pyrenees. It's built on green slopes and looks down into the deep blue Atlantic Ocean and has marble terraces and orange groves and flower gardens.'

As she told of it, for her it really did exist. 'And one day my family will leave this dusty little village and go and live there. My mother will never again have to travel to Toulouse to her shop because she'll have lots of money.'

Even though the shop kept them in modest comfort, her father's heart was always dreaming of the fabulous inheritance that would one day be his.

She believed because she wanted so much for it to be real, a far cry from the flat, baking farmland around Toulouse, the only open water the quietly flowing Garonne, the Tarn, the Lac d'Aussonne with its swans and ducks and herons

11

and the tree-lined Canal du Midi. She longed so often to gaze at the cool expanse of the Atlantic Ocean.

She had been engaging her small listeners with her idea of the place when her mother abruptly ordered her inside. At the sound of that sharp voice, they leapt up from the dusty ground and hurriedly dispersed. Madame Daurignac was known for her fierceness.

A small woman, but determined like Thérèse, and with a good head for business, she had never displayed tenderness for any of her six children. No cuddling when they hurt themselves, just ointment and a bandage slapped on the hurt place if needed, any display of tears thrust aside with 'Stop making a fuss, it will soon heal!'

The funeral oration was still going on, but Thérèse Humbert hardly heard it, her thoughts wandering way back in time.

There was no option but to obey her mother's command and follow her into the cool, dim interior of the house. But the moment she entered the kitchen, she was rounded on.

'You sound exactly like your father! When will you realize that by telling tales until you practically believe them yourself, people will begin to see you as a born liar – or mad, just as they see your fool of a father?'

'But, Maman, they're true. He's told me they are.'

'And take that for impertinence!' The sharp retort was followed by a thump on the head with the metal ladle her mother had been using to stir the cassoulet in a large terrine to which she'd

12

been adding pieces of pork, sausage, and white beans that would become a golden brown when done.

Ignoring Thérèse's cry of pain, she handed her the ladle. 'Now finish this off for me while I feed the baby.' Maria, the youngest of her six children, was still suckling. 'And let us have no more of your silly chatter!'

Her dark hair splattered with bits of bean and onion, she fell silent, while she stood on a chair, the easier to stir. She wasn't allowed outside again until after lunch – cheese, onions, olives and bread, wine for her parents, water for her. Emile was seven, Romain five, Louis three, and eighteen-month-old Marie-Louise; little Maria was at the breast as the family ate.

Thérèse's task that afternoon had been to weed the vegetable patch beside the house, her mother believing no child should be idle even if it were only eight years of age.

The August heat had grown in intensity. Her mother had gone off to Toulouse as she did most days, not trusting her shop assistant to manage alone though the woman was capable and honest.

Maman trusted no one. Sharp-eyed, people said, almost too sharp. Businesslike and dogmatic. How Auguste Daurignac the highly imaginative dreamer had come to take her on, much less endured her as a wife, was little short of a miracle, people said. Except that on his own he would probably have faded away, so it was plausible that he should have wanted to marry someone like her. And besides, she had money then.

Her mother's absence left Thérèse to herself. There were still chores to do but none of them hard – see the cassoulet didn't burn, keep an eye on Louis and Marie-Louise and feed little Maria the surplus breast milk her mother had expressed into a bottle.

Papa would take her into Toulouse in the cart and fetch her home again after the shop closed for the day. Meantime he'd enjoy a few hours of peace and idleness with his village cronies under the shade of the trees in the village square, maybe tell a fortune or two.

Her head still sore, Thérèse went on hoeing any weeds that might have secreted themselves between the growing plants. No time for self-pity. She must watch that Louis did not wander off. At the moment he was being good, sitting on the house step playing with some coloured stones. Maria, in her crib with a full tummy of milk, might wake and become fretful and she'd have to go and comfort her. She could at least take heart from the surreptitious cuddle her father had given her, asking why she looked so crestfallen, while Maman had sat in the cart waiting for him.

'Never mind, little one,' he'd whispered when she showed him the little lump on her head. 'She loves you, in her way.'

'But they are true, the stories you tell me?' she queried.

His cuddle had grown momentarily tighter. 'If you choose to believe, then they are true. You believe in Our Lord and in His miracles,

14

don't you?'

'Yes.'

'You believe in the stories told in the Holy Bible, do you not?'

'Yes.'

'Then never doubt what you believe in, little one. Grow up believing.'

He had let go of her the instant her mother called out from the cart, 'I'm waiting, Auguste!'

But Thérèse had felt that her sore head didn't really matter as she thought of her father, of the wonderful tales he could tell. He would never lie to her.

She saw Catherine Fuzie coming towards her. Daughter of the bailiff, a close friend of the Daurignac family, Catherine was sixteen, eight years older than her. Thérèse couldn't remember a time when she'd not been there to take her under her wing, as an older sister might.

Coming up to her, Catherine frowned as Thérèse rubbed the raised bump on the top of her head, her dark eyes screwing up at the tenderness as she touched it.

'What's the matter, Thérèse?'

Her friend's look of concern brought a smile to her full little lips. 'I made my mother angry.'

'That's easy enough,' Catherine said. 'What did you do?'

'All I said was that Papa's stories were true and she tapped me on the head with her ladle.' At Catherine's chuckle she scowled. 'It hurts,' she snapped and Catherine became immediately grave, bending to put an arm about the smaller girl.

'Then tell *me* a story. About palaces and princesses and hidden treasure.'

At her urging Thérèse forgot to scowl and as they went and sat down on the house step, little Emile edging closer, she lowered her naturally high voice to a more intriguing tone and let her imagination flow.

'There *is* hidden treasure. I know it. In the strongbox Papa keeps by his bed. It's locked, and chained to the bedrail to stop anyone stealing it. It's been there for years and Maman moans every time she cleans around it for he won't let her move it.'

She saw her friend's narrow eyes widen even though she'd heard the story often.

'He says it holds what he calls bonds that will turn into gold one day when he comes into his inheritance.'

She wasn't quite sure what an inheritance was, knew only that it was important enough to be kept securely locked away and worth lots of money and that they'd all be rich one day.

'He calls it his Portuguese inheritance. He really is a nobleman, or should have been if he hadn't been swindled out of all he had. One day he'll claim back his inheritance and we will live in a splendid palace. He says I shall be a princess.'

As always her tale grew steadily in step with her imagination, and as other children began to gather the story became more vivid and freer. She told again of the beautiful chateau, of magicians that came to perform when he was there as a child and how they taught him every-

16

thing they knew, of how beautiful was his mother before she was banished for some wrong-doing, finally to pine away and die penniless except for the great chest whose key she had mislaid, of how when her father became a man he'd had a key made for it but never dared allow anyone to see inside in case they wanted to steal the wealth it held. Not even her mother had ever seen inside that chest.

It was only as little Marie awoke and began crying that she was forced to break off her story and attend to her. The circle of listeners drifted away, their minds full of wondrous visions. Finally Catherine too departed as it was growing late.

On her way to attend to Marie, Thérèse crept into her father's room. His fabulous strongbox stood by his bed. Lifting the cloth covering it, she touched the rough wood. It felt so warm, as if the gold and jewels it held beside these mysterious bonds emanated a heat all their own. With reluctance she came away as the baby's cries for attention became more persistent.

Her parents would soon be home. Papa, having spent his afternoon playing boules in the shade, no doubt intriguing his friends with the same stories he told her, would have torn himself away some time ago to fetch her mother home in the dogcart from Toulouse.

A soft rustle sweeping through the congregation startled her. The sound of people rising as one for the last hymn, the coffin about to be conveyed from the church, brought her back to the

17

present.

Striving to gather her scattered thoughts, she too rose from where she had been sitting in the front stall beside her husband Frédéric, their only daughter, her brothers and sisters with their spouses, preparing to lead the solemn procession in following the coffin.

Her father's stories had been his real legacy, stories she would carry on with.

'You were quite an old rogue in your day,' she whispered again. Smoothing her skirts of deepest black silk, black fan dangling genteelly from her gloved hands, her hat, the largest to be seen in Paris, delicately balanced on her piled mass of dark hair, she walked with slow dignity behind her father's coffin, the rest of the congregation making ready to fall in behind her.

# Two

Catherine Parayre, who'd been Catherine Fuzie before her marriage, gazed around the gilded salon of the Humbert mansion. Clusters of guests stood chattering like magpies, as if relieved that the funeral itself was over. Every corner of the place was now filled with noise and laughter, more like the celebration of a wedding than the quiet reflection of a man's life.

In one room people were helping themselves

from the mountains of delicious food. In ante-rooms and vestibules they surveyed the awesome gun collection belonging to Thérèse's husband, Frédéric Humbert, gazed at his collection of musical instruments and the fine display of modern paintings and old masters.

Only one area lay silent, forbidden to guests. On the third floor, behind locked doors, sat the famous chest. Catherine's husband was still standing guard against any who might succumb to curiosity. She was proud that Armand was so trusted. Proud that she was too, the only one allowed to dust and polish the strongbox said to hold a hundred million francs in bearer bonds. As Thérèse Humbert's closest friend since childhood, what else would she be but trusted?

Across the salon with its elaborate décor, silk upholstery and window drapes, deep-pile carpets and hand-embroidered tapestries, bronzes, antique carvings and costly enamels, she caught a glimpse of her friend. A small woman with a tendency to roundness, Thérèse's face was lit by a charming smile as she gazed up at those towering over her and with whom she was in conversation: an ambassador, a banker, a member of the cabinet, and their elegant wives. Richly dressed as she was, no one could call Thérèse herself elegant, but she had a way of captivating any who met her and her laughter came flowing towards Catherine over the babble of conversation filling the room.

She was completely at ease with her present audience, holding them spellbound. No one would have thought that an hour ago she'd been grieving over her father's ornate casket as he was laid to rest in his place of honour.

But Thérèse was a fighter, had always been a fighter. As far back as Catherine could recall, she'd never let herself be bowed by grief or adversity. She would bounce back with a courage Catherine admired, still as reckless as she'd been as a child, oblivious to the consequences of the stories she told, convincing everyone with her make-believe, her apparent innocence. But Thérèse had always known exactly what she was about.

Catherine watched with interest as an eminent *Monseigneur* joined the little group. Thérèse turned to him with a small inclination of her head, then instantly passed some remark that had the man's ample stomach trembling with laughter.

She feared no one. Yet she constantly needed the loyalty of two totally different men – her husband Frédéric and her brother Romain. Without them Catherine wondered if she'd have got as far as she had. Frédéric was a small and bespectacled man, seldom stepping into the limelight of his wife's exciting social life, though with a sharp, legal brain, he was always there to smooth her path should any difficulty arise. Difficulties there seemed to Catherine to be in increasing numbers lately; quite a few times Thérèse had come close to disaster. But Romain was always there to grapple with awkward customers, to a degree that had Catherine worried at times.

He was a thug at heart. She remembered him

as a boy; even then there had been the promise of the violent and hard man he would become. Hardly ever out of some fight or other, he'd give back as good as he got. He was like Thérèse in this, fearless, determined, though without her vivid imagination. There he was now, over by the window, his champagne glass held firmly though he hardly touched its contents. Handsome, dark-eyed like the rest of the Daurignac family, like most people of the south of France.

As he chatted amiably to the man next to him, those dark eyes seemed never still, surveying the room for any sign of trouble. Should such a sign become apparent, he'd ease through the throng, a smile fixed on the thin lips beneath that narrow moustache, a word or two quietly uttered in the potential troublemaker's ear. The man's upper arm in a firm grip, he'd be discreetly conducted towards the door while Romain nodded at any protest the man might make. Catherine had seen it all before.

If a woman made a scene, he'd take her hand, lift it to his lips and before she could recover, draw her from the room. She would return flushed and subdued. A man seldom returned to show his face, professing to be a little under the weather or suddenly recalling an urgent appointment elsewhere.

Whatever was said to either, Catherine could only guess, enough to make her blush or gnaw her lip. An unprincipled ladykiller with an easy charm, even so she wouldn't wish to cross him, and was often left wondering about those who did.

He had truly come into his own when his mother died and he was eleven years old. Catherine remembered an occasion, only two days after his mother's death, when he had fought and floored a boy nearly twice his size for calling his sister a born liar.

Thérèse had tried to face up to her loss by referring to her father's strongbox yet again. The older boy had sneered at her. 'How many times have we heard that tale? Why hasn't he used some of his so-called treasure to buy this so-called chateau of his? He's an old windbag. And you're a young windbag.'

'He's not a windbag!' Thérèse yelled back, her young chest heaving with anger. 'His father was a nobleman and so will he be once he can claim his inheritance.'

'Some nobleman!' the boy had scoffed. 'Your mother kept him – that's how noble he is. What's he going to do now she's dead?'

In a sudden explosion of fury, Thérèse leapt up and was at him, clawing for his eyes as he caught her wrists to defend himself.

It was then that Romain came flying out of the door, throwing her to one side. Before she could scream at him, Romain, his head down like a charging bull, had butted the boy full in the stomach.

As the boy went down under the impact, Romain was on him in seconds, fists punching at his face in fury. Thérèse's small audience turned from her to urge on the fight, girls leaping up and down with excitement, boys punching empty air as if they were the fighters.

Over and over they rolled in the dust until villagers came to separate them, a cuff about the ear of each. The injured lad, holding a hand to a bleeding nose, cried out, 'I'll get you for this, Daurignac!'

Catherine never remembered him carrying out his threat. Romain was given a wide berth from then on and other young people felt it better never again to challenge Thérèse's stories. Surrounded by the guests at this huge funeral reception for the wealthy Comte d'Aurignac, Catherine smiled sadly at her recollection of that day.

Having asked his sister if she was hurt, Romain had marched off without a backward glance, accompanied by some of his mates, worshipping him like a hero as they taxed him on what it was like to hit someone so hard as to smash a nose and make it bleed like that.

Catherine had gone to comfort her small friend, to find her with her head lowered, her dark hair fallen each side of the face and hiding silent tears. She looked up as Catherine stooped down beside her.

'I'm all right,' she managed to smile. 'I'm not upset over my mother. I never liked her. I'm upset because I'm going to miss you.'

Thérèse was fourteen at the time, Catherine twenty-two. Eight years' difference might have seemed too much for friendship to develop, but it was more akin to mothering, and Thérèse was such a sweet child.

Catherine was soon to leave to marry the young schoolmaster of the little town of Beauzelle. One day she would have children of her own to care for, but she vowed never to forget Thérèse. And she hadn't. Years later they were still together.

For the daughter of the bailiff of Aussonne it had been an excellent match. She was very much in love with Armand Parayre. Sophisticated and so very handsome, his short, soft, dark beard and rimless spectacles added to his good looks. Each time she thought of him she'd been overwhelmed with excitement at the coming wedding.

She remembered so well kneeling awkwardly beside the girl, in her long tight skirt and bustle, and putting an arm about her shoulders. 'I shall make sure to visit you often. You've your brave brother to look after you.'

Thérèse shook her still bowed head. 'I don't care about him,' came her sharp retort. 'He'll always be getting into fights, if not over me then over something else. I don't want him to look after me!'

'Emile then,' Catherine placated gently. 'He's older than Romain and more placid and trustworthy.'

Thérèse lifted her eyes to look straight at her. Catherine was surprised to see that the dark orbs held a dull gleam of desperation.

'Romain and Emile will always be all right. But what about me? I'm fourteen. How am I going to care for this family?'

Catherine wished she'd bitten her tongue. She should have thought more carefully. But Thérèse was still speaking.

'What am I going to do?' The tone was pleading. 'Emile has no fight in him. He's too gentle. Romain has too much fight and will land us all in trouble. There's only me to look after us now.'

It sounded like an accusation – her friend was about to go off to get married, leaving her all alone to cope.

'You have your father,' Catherine offered lamely, knowing how inadequate that must sound.

Thérèse's lips curled upwards in a sad, resigned gesture. 'Papa can only dream and does nothing. What we need is money coming in, real money.'

It wasn't said disparagingly, it was merely a statement. What little her father brought home – a small portion of cheese, a pat of butter, supplemented by a few eggs from their fast dwindling livestock – came only from his fortune telling and faith healing. People did believe what he told them, superstitiously had even begun to fear that if they didn't he might cause them bad luck.

'You still have your mother's shop,' Catherine said encouragingly, but was confronted by those soulful dark eyes.

'Maman took a mortgage on the house a long time ago to buy it. We're already falling behind with the payments. Papa spent most of our money on a grand funeral we couldn't afford so that people wouldn't look down on us. There's little left and he is hiding in the house in shame. It only leaves me to look out for us.'

'Couldn't *you* carry on your mother's shop?

Wouldn't her assistant help you?'

For a second Thérèse's eyes blazed. 'I've only just turned fourteen. What can *I* do? What do I know about selling lingerie?'

'You could learn.'

'And who's to look after Louis and the girls while I'm away?'

So vicious was the retort that Catherine realized how foolish her solution must have sounded. The two girls were still only five and four. Louis was now ten, Romain eleven and Emile nearly thirteen, but boys couldn't be trusted to keep an eye on toddlers. It had been a silly idea. Her father had to be getting on for seventy, too old to find proper work. The family's welfare now fell solely on Thérèse's young shoulders.

It was a hopeless situation. 'I wish I could help,' she sighed.

To her surprise Thérèse lifted her chin. There was even a small smile. 'I shall manage,' she said so lightly, suddenly so confident that Catherine was taken aback.

'How?'

Thérèse's smile grew cunning. 'I have ideas,' she said secretively.

That was all she would say, shaking her head to Catherine's efforts to discover what these ideas were. She came away convinced her friend had no plans at all and was merely putting a brave face on things for her benefit.

Days passed before Thérèse finally let on to what these mysterious plans were. 'But you are not to tell a soul.' She made Catherine promise before she would go on.

'I'm going to contact my natural father.'

'Your natural father!'

Thérèse was looking straight at her. She even smiled.

'Papa isn't my real father. Mine was someone my mother met before she married Papa. His name was Crawford. She never told Papa she was already pregnant. He thinks I'm his. If he found out, it would kill him. And you wouldn't want that to be on your conscience, would you, Catherine?'

Catherine almost choked on her intake of breath. It was close to a threat. But there was a look in Thérèse's eyes that, having known her all these years, made Catherine wonder. Another of her tales, made up in her head since they'd last been together? Yet, uttered with such conviction, it could be true. She solemnly nodded confirmation of the girl's question.

It had to be true. Otherwise Thérèse's face would have been creased with worry virtually over where their next meal was coming from. But here she was looking serene and bright-eyed, almost excited.

'How long have you known?' Catherine asked. 'You never mentioned it before.'

'I've known for years. And I've never mentioned it because ... well, because it's not the sort of thing you talk about. I'd almost forgotten about it myself, until now. Now everything is changed and we need money urgently.'

Her tone became less confident. 'He was an American millionaire, but he had to go back home on urgent business and had no idea that my mother had fallen pregnant. She never told him. He wrote but she didn't reply, because by then, being so desperate, she had already accepted Papa's proposal of marriage. I've already started making enquiries and when I find him I will claim my inheritance.'

Now where had Catherine heard that one before? A family inheritance, a locked box containing bonds worth thousands of francs once his heritage could be proved. 'But it takes money to get money,' old Monsieur Daurignac would say darkly. 'We do not have that kind of money. I will find other ways. But it takes time.'

He could bring tears to people's eyes when he spoke of his mother, shamed and cast out to bear him all on her own. It left people wondering if the tale hadn't some grain of truth in it. Catherine had come to believe it long ago.

Now here was Thérèse with a tale so reminiscent of his that she no longer knew what to believe. She'd known Thérèse for fourteen of her own twenty-two years, had held her in her arms a few months after Thérèse was born. A true feeling of affection had grown from that. Now this little sister was being forced to fend for herself as well as a large family – and at such a tender age too, needing someone to trust. Of course she would have kept a secret like this to herself all these years. It stood to reason. Very well, she could tell a tall story with conviction, but this one Catherine couldn't help but believe. One look at the girl's face was proof enough.

# Three

Four months on and Thérèse, who had now turned fifteen, seemed not to have got very far in her search for her real father, despite her initial flush of determination. If she had tried, nothing appeared to have come of it, and Catherine was growing increasingly concerned about the declining state of the family.

'I've been trying so hard to find him,' Thérèse replied to her questions, her tearful smile wrenching at Catherine's heart. 'I did contact the American Consulate in Paris who said they'd try to find the person I was looking for.'

'Perhaps you should contact them again,' Catherine suggested kindly.

'I did,' came the immediate reply, uttered with a tremble of that full lower lip. 'Three times I've written. I don't know what else to do.'

The way Thérèse's voice shook as she spoke convinced her that the girl was thoroughly frustrated. It wasn't as if her letters were badly written, fit only to be dropped into a waste-paper basket. In fact she was rather well educated for someone raised in a rural environment. Taught at home by her father – who himself was far from short of knowledge, having been educated by the priest who'd taken him in as a child – she was no

29

untutored idiot.

'Never mind,' Thérèse said suddenly, lifting herself to her full small height, the brave soul Catherine had always known. 'I shall let it rest for a while and try again some other time.'

It left Catherine at a loss to help, short of offering to see what a letter from her might do. And she refrained from that. If they'd ignored a girl trying to trace her father, they'd pay little heed to interference from a mere friend. The matter was put aside. Thérèse never mentioned it again. It might have left Catherine doubting whether Thérèse's story had any true foundation, had she not had other things on her mind at that moment.

In a few months she'd be marrying Armand Parayre, the handsome young schoolmaster in Beauzelle. They'd met several months ago when her father visited the village as bailiff to welcome Armand to his new situation.

Love had blossomed from the start. Both sets of parents declared that the two young people made a handsome couple, Armand tall and upright, with eager dark eyes, and she what people called a striking beauty.

'My dark-eyed queen,' he liked to call her, melting her natural reserve that those who little understood the hidden passionate nature of southern women might mistake for haughtiness.

She'd be sorry to leave Thérèse, of course, the girl she'd known from a baby. But in time she would have her own babies to love. She'd never forget Thérèse Daurignac, her wonderful accumulation of stories that never failed to enthral her

30

no matter how many times she heard them. She would always be her friend, intended to visit her regularly and see her grow to womanhood, for friendship cemented in deep affection is not easily broken.

Six months since Catherine was last here. At first she'd visited at least every month, apologizing that it wasn't more often. As winter came, her visits became a little less regular.

'I'm so sorry, Thérèse, but as the wife of a schoolmaster it isn't easy to get away,' she explained on one occasion. 'I've so many duties connected with his work. They take up every waking hour.'

Her visits had dwindled even more of late. She now had a two-month-old daughter and there was even less time to come over to Aussonne than before. Her family now visited her rather than she go to them, especially as her father – whose income as bailiff was far greater than that of a struggling schoolteacher – had his own private carriage.

Thérèse had thought she would miss her more but her own time too was taken up, in her case with caring for her family as she continued to do in her own fashion.

This evening she was returning home with a few eggs, a pat of butter and a portion of cheese, as well as a few coins given her by Madame Tulard, wife of the village barber. For half an hour she had mesmerized the woman and her two grandchildren with a dark and sinister tale of a great-aunt of hers, who had so frightened her as a child but had undergone a change of heart in her final days and by all accounts had now mentioned her grand-niece in her will and left her quite a substantial sum of money.

She had half terrified the two children telling how her great-aunt, clothed all in black with a thick veil over her face, would creep into the house when Thérèse herself was only four years old, frightening the life out of her with her thin, shaky, menacing voice.

'I regret now being so terrified of her,' she'd said, leaning back from the awed children to resume a more adult posture, while Madame Tulard had leaned forward, her eyes wide with interest. 'Because at this moment we are awaiting word from the solicitors. There are a few legal matters still to be dealt with which might take a few months yet, but when all is settled we'll be able to repay all our debts and live with dignity again.'

She'd allowed her lips to quiver as Monsieur Tulard came in from his shop while she said this. Touched, he'd offered to loan them a small amount for a short while to help tide the family over.

'So that you won't need to be subjected to the indignities of relying on the dubious handouts of others, while you're waiting for the legal wheels to grind,' he'd said kindly. 'I'll go to my bank tomorrow, see what I can do.'

It had been her second conquest of the day.

Earlier this morning she had approached Madame Angine, the baker's wife, spending some twenty minutes telling of a wealthy godmother of hers who'd recently written to her, quite out of the blue.

'I'd almost forgotten about her,' she'd said brightly. 'But yesterday I had a letter from her, which was such a surprise. She wrote that she often thinks about me. She wanted to know what sort of person I have become. She married a Dutchman, you know, and has now been living in Holland for a good many years. That's how we lost touch with her, you see. She says her husband is tremendously rich with a very prosperous shipping business.'

She'd gone on to describe how the two had met, her godmother a poor widow at the time, told of the adventures they'd had living in South Africa before, on finding gold, they had returned to Holland, the land of his birth. There he had invested in several merchant ships with the gold he'd discovered.

'She wrote that she didn't want to lose touch with *her goddaughter* again.' She had let her voice drop as a hint at some future monetary promise and took delight in seeing the woman's eyes widen with keen interest.

Madame Angine wasn't known for her generosity or gullibility, but Thérèse must have convinced her, coming away with a new loaf baked this morning, her promise to pay tomorrow readily accepted for once.

'Lord knows we need some luck,' Thérèse had said, tears gathering in her eyes as she made to leave. 'I've had to spend what I had on boot leather for my poor father. Unless you would prefer I bring a couple of eggs as a payment,' she went on, her dark eyes glistening hopefully. 'I can give them to you this evening, I promise.'

Many in the villages were used to bartering at times and she was relieved that her offer had been accepted. Having now handed over two of the eggs given to her by Madame Tulard, leaving four for her own family as well as the other food and money she'd wheedled from her, she felt pleased with herself as she made her way home. Even more pleased after what Monsieur Tulard had said.

She hoped the loan would be more than just a few francs. People in the village understood her family's plight since the death of Madame Daurignac. They were all sympathetic and Thérèse intended to make sure that sympathy wasn't going to diminish.

She was becoming a real actress, able to cause the tears to spring to her eyes at a mere signal. Her full lips would tremble while her smile showed bravely through her sorrow for her mother. It was enough to break the hardest of hearts.

Her small stature helped. There had been a time when she'd hated being small, but not any more. Now she was making it work for her – a diminutive young girl trying to care for her family, she appeared so very vulnerable. Little did they know how far from being vulnerable she really was. She knew what she was about and was growing to know it more and more with every passing month. She was fifteen now, a young woman with an attractively slim waist, a pretty, rounded face. She had perfected a way of looking at people, oblique yet innocent; had practised a way of holding a pose and a studied walk she knew captured the hearts of all the young farmers around. In fact she was certain that half of them were ready to give her the earth for just one look in their direction. Without even having to try, she was beginning to assert herself and make a decent living from it.

This evening she'd had Madame Tulard believing every word she had been told. Her delicate, expressive hands, gesturing to every sentence, had added colour to her story. Papa had shown her how to use the sleight of hand that he utilized when doing tricks. Learning to put that to good effect, she even had Monsieur Tulard, a strong-minded man of business, believing her. Beguiled by her, he'd often slip a coin or two into her hand, aware how hard up the family was. But this present promise of his sounded wonderful.

Her feet hardly touching the ground, she turned at a run on to the dusty path to her house, her ill-gotten gains from the story she'd told threatening to spill out of the small basket she carried.

Situated at the far western end of the village, her house was similar to many in the locality. Square, two floors, few windows, every one shuttered against the summer heat to keep the interior dim and cool. It stood on a substantial plot of land that since her mother's death had become sadly neglected. She'd always grown her own produce, raised her own livestock for the table or for barter, but there were few animals left – half a dozen chickens that laid very irregularly and the goat that no longer gave milk, no money to pay to have her serviced. Their only income now was from what she managed to wheedle.

Monsieur Tulard's promise of a small loan might be a godsend, if only for a limited time. She just hoped it would prove generous enough, perhaps would enable them to buy seeds for the vegetable garden, or a couple of Toulouse geese, maybe some ducks to fill the deserted pond. At least they might be able to get the goat serviced and have their own fresh milk again, their own cheese. Monsieur Tulard's loan might help solve a lot of their problems.

Her hopes high, she skipped along. It didn't once occur to her that she'd have to pay back the loan. Her only thought was that she wasn't going to rest on her laurels. Perhaps she could persuade others with money to spare to contribute a loan.

Not in Aussonne though. In time they'd begin to see through her and her stories, and one shouldn't over-milk a cow. There were the surrounding villages, the young farmers, to impress with her wonderful tales as she smiled bravely through her tears. She'd continue to plead poverty despite Monsieur Tulard's loan, so long as it didn't get back to his ears.

She might even extract another – hopefully sizeable – loan elsewhere. If she could do it once she could do it again. She could pay him back little by little without too much suspicion. She could try for several loans, repaying each lender in turn bit by bit, keeping back enough for herself. It was an attractive idea. She wondered why she hadn't thought about it before.

Thérèse shaded her eyes against the glare of a sinking April sun. Crimson clouds along the low horizon gave the weathered sandstone house walls a pinkish tinge. They'd once been kept in moderately good repair, as far as hot Languedoc summers allowed. But since her mother's death the work had been neglected, her father withdrawing into himself and doing little but dream of the wealth he insisted he'd been cheated of so long ago.

People knew about the inheritance, but it had been spoken of so often, without anything ever seeming to come of it, that they'd grown tired of it, saw him as a rambling old fool. But she was romantic, blessed with such a vivid imagination that she revelled in the stories she wove around it, and in which it seemed sometimes that she was the only one who believed. Time and time she had spoken to him about opening his beloved strongbox, taking a peep at the documents he said lay within to see if by now he had any chance of his claiming his inheritance. All he would say, listless and lethargic, was that the time wasn't yet right.

'If only it were, little one,' he'd murmur so pitifully that she couldn't bring herself to push him further. It left her at her wits' end how to pay the mortgage still owing despite the loss of her mother's shop to creditors. Though now, her head buzzing with new ideas, there'd be no need to worry. She had the solution. She could hardly wait to tell Papa.

To her surprise he was there. She hadn't expected him to be. The last time she'd seen him had been this afternoon. He'd been sitting in the shade under the sparsely foliaged, stunted trees of the village square, crouched over a thin-legged table, playing checkers with a few friends of his own generation.

'Don't be too late home, Papa,' she'd called to him as she passed on her way to see what she could get out of Madame Tulard. He'd already been in the shop having his thin hair trimmed, with a promise to pay next time he came in. Monsieur Tulard always indulged him, an old, old friend.

Her father had looked up. 'No doubt I shall be in before you, little one,' he'd quipped and returned to his game.

She had doubted it, but he must have gone by while she had been entertaining the barber's wife and her two grandchildren.

As she entered the large kitchen, savouring its dim coolness, he was sitting at the table reading a tatty newspaper, around him the debris of what he'd been eating – the skin of an onion and the crumbs of yesterday's loaf to which he'd helped himself, not waiting for her to prepare supper.

She felt instantly annoyed. The onion would have gone to make soup. But within minutes her annoyance had melted away.

It seemed Monsieur Tulard's offer of a loan wasn't as simple as she had imagined.

At her entrance her father had come to an

upright position on his chair, his normally benign features swept away by a deep frown. 'What do you think you were doing?'

The question was sprung on her, leaving her at a loss, but before she could ask what he meant he surged on. 'I've been speaking to Monsieur Tulard. He says he has offered to loan you money. Did he tell you how much?'

Thérèse shook her head, wondering why her father was looking so angry. 'I thought you'd be pleased.'

'Well, I'm *not* pleased!' came the astonishing rebuke. Her father was the last to admonish her for bringing in a few coins; in fact he was her mentor in the art of playing on the sympathy of others. 'I am not at all pleased,' he went on. 'The man is no fool, Thérèse. What made you think he would transact a business deal with a mere girl?'

What was he talking about – transact a business deal? She hung her head, not in shame but in disappointment. Monsieur Tulard had generously offered to lend her a little money to help her out. Now it seemed he was going back on his word and it had obviously angered her father.

'What made you think he'd hand over cash as easy as that?' When she shrugged, not knowing how to reply, he rushed on. 'He called me over after you left his wife and said he was willing to loan me two hundred francs on the strength of this legacy you told her was coming to you from this great-aunt.'

Two hundred francs! Thérèse's eyes popped. She mentally apologized to the man for thinking so badly of him. Never in her wildest dreams would she have expected such a huge sum – it was almost foolishly generous. But her father was still looking far from pleased.

'To be paid back as soon as we receive the legacy – failing that, in twelve monthly instalments. How are we going to repay two hundred francs in that short time? We've no resources. Why couldn't you leave well alone? You've no idea what a problem you have landed me with, girl. Did he not mention the word interest to you?'

Interest? She'd heard of that – something to do with what her father was having trouble with since losing her mother. Her mother had spoken of paying interest on the mortgage for the shop she'd bought. She had used this house to obtain a mortgage. Since the shop had been seized after she died, Papa had steadily fallen behind with the repayments. The premises not having covered the amount owing, he was being required to scrape the money together to prevent the house too being claimed. It was a terrible worry to him, to them all. Her father was still holding her gaze.

'He is asking five per cent interest, so long as the loan is repaid in full as soon as our money comes in.' He laughed bitterly. 'Money! What money? Your story must have been convincing indeed for an astute businessman like Tulard to be duped. Did you not give any thought at all to the trouble you could be bringing on us?'

'I didn't think I was bringing any trouble on you, Papa,' Thérèse defended, feeling angry at herself and near to tears that this time were genuine. 'I was so excited. He seemed so kind.'

'He *is* kind, generous and kind, a kind man and an old friend. But first and foremost he is a businessman. And don't you forget it. Take what is given you by housewives and suchlike but watch those who offer to loan you large sums of money.'

'I didn't think it was to be a large sum. I thought he meant just a few francs. I thought he was being generous.'

Her father wasn't listening, his gaze wandering past her. 'But if we have to repay in twelve monthly instalments – and that's what we'll have to do unless I go back to him and lie that we can do without it after all, and look a complete fool and lose what little dignity is left to me – the interest on the loan will go up to ten per cent. We haven't twenty francs, much less two hundred. We exist only on what you and Emile and Romain and myself can bring in by the good will of others.'

His gaze lifted suddenly, riveting on her. 'Now do you understand what you've done? Did you really expect him to *give* you the money?'

'I didn't ask him for anything,' she protested. 'He offered.'

'Of course he did. Greed. It is in us all, good and bad alike. He saw money coming to us and thought to trade in on it. Anyone would.'

His voice had lost its anger, now sounded sad. 'I'm not blaming you for trying to help this family out of its present situation, but you still do not understand the ways of the world, little one. Tell your stories by all means. You have a

41

rare gift for it. Take what is offered in produce or a few coins. But do not get out of your depth with something you do not yet understand.'

Romain and Emile could be heard coming up the path, talking loudly to each other as young boys do – as if conversing at a distance of a mile or more from each other. The rest of his brood, Louis and his two little sisters, had come to stand at the door, wondering when supper would be ready.

Auguste got to his feet as if a weight hung on his shoulders and went out, looking suddenly tired and far older than his already accrued years, leaving her to get on with supper for the family.

Caring for a family of seven with no help from anyone was hard on a sixteen year old. None of her brothers would dream of doing woman's work even if she asked them, and the two girls were too small to be of much use. There was no point asking her father's help. The house could fall down for all he seemed to care as he idled his days away with other old men of the village. There were times she would feel angry over his lack of help, but tonight she felt only chastened, so seldom did he rebuke her.

# Four

Despite his surly attitude over the loan, her father had accepted the terms laid down, in fact opting to repay the amount in one lump sum. 'The very instant my daughter's legacy arrives,' he lied to Tulard, who blithely settled for that.

It was now autumn. Not a single sou had been repaid and the man was beginning to lose patience, confronting her father whenever he happened to clap eyes on him. Auguste gave him as wide a berth as possible, avoiding him whenever he could. Thérèse always cut his hair these days to save money so there was no need to go near the barber's shop. Thankfully, so far Tulard hadn't come to the house to enquire when he could expect his money, but Thérèse felt it wouldn't be long before he did.

'I know it won't,' she said, starting to feel desperate.

She was now spinning her tales in surrounding villages, reaping a modest harvest. She'd always loved seeing amazement on people's faces, but now it had become a serious business although she still took pleasure from it.

Rotating her jaunts to other villages kept the same stories going while others were added from time to time. Her present favourite was a distant

43

cousin of her mother's who'd gone to America and made his fortune. Replying to a letter she'd sent him, he'd said he must send his favourite aunt's children something – in the form of quite a substantial sum of money, she would add, using that confidential sideways look of hers. She had managed to secure several loans on the strength of the money that was supposedly coming to her.

Taking from one to repay another at a lower rate of interest than Tulard had demanded, slowly she'd accrued a small profit. But it was still nowhere near to covering what was owed to Monsieur Tulard and time was running on.

'What will happen if we can't pay?' Small debts didn't matter but this one was huge, enough to bring a bailiff down on them sooner or later. Her father's reply was an indolent shrug as he sat listlessly at the kitchen table.

'Why didn't you offer to repay bit by bit?' she cried out angrily. 'Then you could have dodged an instalment or two with a promise to pay later. I'm sure he'd have let you. He's been an old friend of yours for years.'

Why he had agreed to repay in a lump sum she couldn't say, unless he had been persuaded by the lower interest asked – or more likely had convinced himself that money would miraculously appear. It had been an agreement Thérèse hadn't been happy about and had made her feelings very plain, though it didn't once occur to her that it was she who had started this in the first place, no matter how innocently.

Now he gave her a confident grin. 'I spoke to

him last week, told him the will was taking longer to finalize than we expected. That can happen.'

He sounded as if he believed there really was a will.

'I might get in touch with your mother's sister, your Aunt Marie-Emilie in Toulouse. Perhaps she will advance the money until things are settled. She and her husband are comfortably off. As a professor at Toulouse University he'll not miss a few francs. And you *are* their niece.'

Thérèse's laugh was bitter. 'That side of the family did nothing for us after my mother died. They knew our predicament and never lifted a finger.'

'There comes a time when they must,' he said sternly. 'Families must help each other. I'll ask anyway. No point approaching her sister, your Aunt Dupuy. It will be a waste of time. With all that money she has, she clings to every franc of it. As tight as maid's...' He broke off, about to say something obscene, but remembered she was only just sixteen and as far as he was aware knew little of such things.

Thérèse smirked grimly as she went out into the courtyard to cool her anger at him. Sometimes he treated her as if she were a child. But she wasn't a child, she was the main bread-winner of this family. She knew what the young farmers were after. She would entice them just so far, accentuating her small waist and wide hips in a well fitting skirt, her sideways glances making them lick their lips. She used them for all her worth and they'd give her little presents, hoping for greater things.

The gifts she would sell to other people to keep her family going, holding a little of it back to buy something nice for herself. If you don't dress well, she told herself, who is going to believe in you enough to swallow stories of wealth coming to you, of how your lack of funds is only temporary and you solemnly promise to pay back any loan with interest?

One or two farmers had even proposed to her. It could have been a way out of poverty, but she didn't fancy any of them, they were an uncouth, rough lot. She dreamed of far better things for herself when the time came – someone with fine manners, a learned man, someone like Frédéric Humbert, the son of her uncle, Professor Gustave Humbert.

She remembered Frédéric as a small boy, young children growing up together. Even then he'd been nice looking. As he grew older and was sent to a fine school by his parents, they'd lost touch. He'd be fifteen or sixteen now.

Until she met someone like that she would continue to keep her family together. But her father was right about her aunts. Wealthy, living in a nice part of Toulouse and seeing themselves as above the Daurignac family, it was true they hadn't lifted one finger to help when her mother died and money had dwindled. They seemed to forget that they too had once been poor before that wealthy old farmer, Duluc, father of many bastard children as Thérèse had been told, had eventually left his money to his favourite child, her Aunt Dupuy. She had turned out to be as much a skinflint as he had been, despite having given a share to each of her sisters all those years ago. Perhaps there still was a tiny spark of generosity somewhere inside her. Papa should go and see her.

She went thoughtfully back indoors, ignoring her father as she passed him. The sisters had all put their share to good use. If he'd been given such a sum, he would have gone through it like wildfire through dry grass, whereas her mother and two aunts had done well to invest it. Had it not been his odd ideas of supporting his family, they might still be as wealthy as them and wouldn't be in the predicament they were now in.

He *was* an idle good-for-nothing dreamer, fit only for tricking people with his so-called necromancy, frightening the life out of them by pretending to be in touch with the other side, giving them to believe he could lay hands on them, soothe a stiff neck, a rheumatic joint, a poorly healed fracture. But he could charm and she loved him, loved his stories, an art she had inherited from him. *Inherited*, yes.

Of course he was her real father, but if she wanted to she could at any time have others believing that an American millionaire was her natural father. She had convinced her old friend Catherine well enough. That story had come in use many times since, helping to keep the family's head above water. This borrowing from one to partly pay back another was working well. So far she had managed to keep things ticking along. But if Monsieur Tulard was to get his money before he lost his patience entirely she must try even harder.

In her room she changed into a riding habit. One thing she made sure of was a good wardrobe. One must always look nice when carrying out a transaction, as she liked to call it. No more begging. This was business, and for that one had to look smart and not appear in need of anyone's charity.

She'd gone to Toulouse two weeks back to buy the outfit. It was still unpaid for but what did that matter? She'd learned that if one entered a high class establishment with a moneyed air there was virtually nothing a proprietor wouldn't do to make an important sale. The story she'd spun of waiting for a large amount of funds to come through had his eyes goggling.

She had indeed flourished a purse of cash, loaned earlier on a sincere promise that it would be paid back with interest within two weeks. The contents of the purse, however, had not been enough to cover the purchase of the riding habit. By the time the proprietor grew concerned at the non-settlement of his bill, she'd have enough to pay him in part, just enough to keep him at bay. It was a ploy she was beginning to handle and was so far working quite wonderfully. The riding habit was now an essential part of her wardrobe and made her seem older and more mature than she was, confident and certainly wealthy.

The reason for buying it had been the high-stepping little mare one of the young farmers had grandly given her as a gift in hopes of reaping his reward at some point. She hadn't been above readily accepting it.

She'd known for some time that Paul Millot – having lost his wife last year in childbirth, along with the baby – had her in his eye. He was comfortably off, so it was said, but she had no fancy to take the place of his dead wife. He had met her on the road outside his farm. They had passed the time of day and she had asked how he was faring since losing his wife.

That was when he had broached the subject of the horse, suggesting she take it, give it a good home. It was sad to see him so pleased when she'd accepted the gift of the dainty little animal, but if he wanted to give it to her, who was she to turn down the offer?

'It was my wife's,' he said, causing her a small stab of superstition that made her draw back. Something belonging to a dead person! She had even shuddered inwardly.

'I couldn't!' she blurted, hanging her head, but he'd been persistent.

'I feared you might say that. But the creature reminds me of my loss and I've no use for her. And I could never *sell* her. I would feel so much easier in my mind if you took her. I know she will be well treated and cared for. Please, I shall be hurt if you refuse.'

She'd smiled sweetly, her face lowered slightly to hide the covetousness that might be showing there, wanting the horse more than anything.

'I would never wish to offend you, Monsieur Millot ... Paul,' she'd said softly, a little flirtatiously. 'But it seems too great a gift for any man to give a woman he only sees on chance

49

occasions. I don't think I should...'

'You must take it, Mademoiselle Daurignac ... Thérèse...' He had begun to move towards her. 'I have the deepest regard for you, the deepest admiration for how you, one so young, are managing to cope with your adversity. And, may I dare, my deepest affection...'

She had held up her hand, halting his words before he could say more, knowing instantly what he was leading to. He was regarding her so ardently that she thought it better to leap in before he committed himself and her. Her flirting had gone too far. She gave a tinkling, flippant laugh.

'One might almost see such a generous gift as a forerunner of a proposal of marriage, if I wasn't so young – too young as yet for marriage.'

He had stood back from her, a dusky blush spreading across his sun-bronzed face, on which life in the open air of heat and rain was already starting to trace deep crevices, promising that the strong, handsome features would look old before their time.

'Of course.' He gnawed at his lips. 'I am sorry. I apologize.'

She had remained smiling sweetly at him. 'Please don't.'

She'd let her gaze fall longingly on the mare. 'It is such a beautiful little animal. I am so tired of riding my rickety old donkey cart. It's simply falling to pieces and I so need to get from one place to another. Without it I think my family and my poor father would starve. He is too old to turn his hand to work these days. I am the only one he can rely on to keep him and my family now.'

She made her face lengthen prettily and her eyes glisten. 'But how can I accept such a lovely gift? I really shouldn't...'

'Take her!' he burst out impulsively. 'Please, Thérèse, Mademoiselle Daurignac, please take her. I would be so honoured. And she is very gentle.'

As if on impulse, she had nodded, hardly able to stop the excitement from showing on her face as he gave her a sidesaddle and the rest of the tackle to go with it, even a mounting block. He had no need of any of it now, he said, still looking hopeful.

'One day she could be back in her stable and you under my roof, who knows?' He had spread his arms, lifting his hands as if in surrender to fate, and as they parted had even clumsily kissed her hand.

The next morning he appeared at her door, having ridden over from his farm on a great plough horse with huge feathery fetlocks, leading the neat little animal by a rein. The mare looked so tiny against the other brute.

The man too looked huge and uncouth on the larger creature. Even as she thanked him, smiling her deep gratitude at his generosity, she was very aware that after biding his time he intended once again to propose marriage. The very thought of ever consenting to become his wife made her feel a little sick, she being so trim and he so hulking – like the slightly built mare submitting to the great weight of the animal now towering over her.

She had been heartily glad when Paul Millot left, waving farewell until he was out of sight. She had spent days on edge, fearing that he might have taken her responses as a promise of her hand in the not too distant future. After all, next spring she would be seventeen, a marriageable age, God forbid! But the friendly way her father had chatted to him had her feeling uneasy for weeks afterwards that this could be her fate.

Since then she had skirted the Millot farm by another route if she had to pass in that direction on her way to other villages. But the mare was lovely – very gentle, just as he had said, and a joy to ride. She felt as proud as a peacock when people watched her pass by, quite the mistress of some fine chateau.

She had plenty of feed for the animal, whose name he had said was Fleur, given to it by his wife. The feed had been bought on credit with a promise to pay as soon as next month's allowance arrived from her wealthy uncle. Wearing the expression of wide-eyed innocence and trust at which she had become adept, she had even handed the man a small down payment to prove her sincerity and keep him happy for the time being.

Dressed in her new beige riding habit with its high collar, the skirt sporting a fine bustle, the hat she wore as dainty and fashionable as any in Toulouse, she rode off at a leisurely pace, as might any lady of breeding. A good horsewoman, she held the reins loosely in her gloved hands, the bridle jingling merrily as she made towards Saint Roch. She would visit that little boutique, choose herself a few more nice clothes. She hadn't been there for several months.

She had left her father brooding how he was to pay Monsieur Tulard back the two hundred francs, perhaps dreaming of one day regaining his beloved inheritance. For herself she could see only good things ahead as her mount cantered through the flat golden countryside on a golden afternoon that matched her mood.

She had her choice of villages but always made sure to vary them so that no one village would see her for several weeks. She would test the welcome she received and if it was not too hearty would keep away for a while. It was never wise to neglect small things like that. Today it was Saint Roch.

The seamstress who ran the boutique appeared at her shop door the moment Thérèse drew rein. She knew she'd been noticed. Who could not help but notice her, sitting side-saddle, proud and erect, her tweed skirt elegantly draped, sure of herself as any fine mistress of some great estate. The seamstress's young lad even came hurrying to place a box for her to dismount, his bright young face creased with pleasure as Thérèse grandly dropped a coin into his hand, aware that her gesture made her look the part. The woman actually gave a small bob as Thérèse entered; rumour of her recent legacies must have reached here, she guessed.

She referred to her most recent legacy as she looked around at what was being displayed, casually letting drop the fact that a sum of three thousand francs, bequeathed to her by an elderly relative, was to be settled on her any time now.

She was a little taken aback to see the expression on the woman's face alter to one of scepticism, and knew she must tread carefully. Without hesitation she fished out her purse from her skirt pocket and opened it, seeming to accidentally let a huge ruby ring – a fake gem kept for such occasions – fall to the floor.

'Oh dear!' she cried in a tone of alarm, snatching the precious thing up. 'I mustn't lose that! It was a present from my aunt's husband in Holland. He's an Amsterdam shipping magnate and he is always sending me expensive presents like this. They have no children and so they dote on me. Such a pity they are so far away.'

She lifted the ring, enough for the woman's eyes to glitter avariciously, and dropped it back into her purse. 'It's worth quite a lot of money, but it's too big for my little fingers so I am going into Toulouse tomorrow to have it made smaller.'

It was a delight to have the woman hurrying about the tiny shop, eager to find whatever she was looking for. Thérèse chose wisely. Too much would have been unladylike. She finally selected a smart bodice, knowing she meant to come away with something. She always did.

She was seventeen. Almost a year since Tulard's loan and very little of it had been repaid, the promised legacy apparently still unsettled. Tulard was surprisingly long-suffering. Generous man that he was, he'd agreed to its repayment by instalments, at the same interest agreed for full payment.

'We are old friends,' he'd told Auguste. 'A friend doesn't kick another friend's backside when he is down.' But so far only two payments had been forthcoming and even he was beginning to fret a little.

Debt had been steadily accruing all year. She was having to go further afield, often as far as Toulouse, in order to separate people from a handful of francs with stories of a legacy or inheritance that would soon get her back on her feet but was being held up by some delay.

Nearer home, creditors were starting to call on the Daurignacs to settle up soon, or else. Romain tried to come to her aid, dropping a subtle word or two that should any legal action be taken against his family, claimants might easily find something odd and unpalatable happening to them.

Some laughed. A boy of fourteen, threatening them! But it was a little disconcerting and most claims were withheld for the time being, each creditor apparently waiting for another to make the first move, just in case. Threats had their uses and Thérèse was deeply grateful to him. Romain was her champion, unlike Emile who kept well out of it, being of a gentler nature.

Catherine Parayre had come over to see what she could do – which was very little, her husband as a humble schoolmaster being far from wealthy. She returned home to Beauzelle more than a little worried.

'I tried to warn her that she could be spelling ruin for the whole family, but she will not listen,' Catherine told her husband, who smiled philosophically as he adjusted his pince-nez, the better to see the small print in the radical newspaper he was reading.

Armand was an idealist by nature with an instinct for reform. He had no interest in Thérèse Daurignac's fantasies. Yet he had to admire the way she tried to keep her family together, even how she could convince other people so easily with the wildest of fantasies. What sane person could believe some of them? Yet people did, in no small numbers, and there lay her talent.

'In my opinion that young lady will always know exactly what she is about,' he said, glancing up from his paper. 'She will always come through no matter what.'

But others were not so sure. 'She is bringing disgrace down on us all,' her Aunt Dupuy in Toulouse said angrily to her sister as they sat over cups of coffee. 'She should be stopped. Handing them money is no answer.'

So it was that when, in total desperation by September, Auguste – accompanied by his whole family to add weight to his plight – paid his in-laws in Toulouse a visit, he was met with a chilly welcome and came away with exactly nothing.

The trickle of creditors that had already begun to hammer on the door of the Daurignac household with their demands would soon become a deluge. Something had to be done to convince them there was money coming. Within a month Thérèse had the solution.

'I am going to *make* them see that we *do* have money,' she said without hesitation, her belief in herself utterly rock solid.

# Five

While the proprietor nodded attentively, Thérèse explained the exact style of bridal gown she had in mind.

'The finest your seamstresses can produce,' she was saying. 'The best, the most fashionable, the highest quality material, silk I think. I want it to outshine any gown you have ever made. No expense must be spared.'

'That will be done, Mademoiselle, with no bother whatsoever.'

'I shall want it to fit my small frame perfectly.'

'But of course. Mademoiselle will need to return for several fittings. Everything that is re-quired will be done expertly and to perfection.'

'Of course,' Thérèse replied, turning to wander around to see what else the place had to offer. The proprietor followed closely, pointing out all those accessories a bride marrying into wealth might need.

As well as being polite he was cautiously sym-pathetic, uncertain how to behave. He'd listened to her tale of woe and had secretly concluded that were his daughter in this young woman's shoes, she'd be over the moon with such a rich marriage, not lamenting the fact that she did not love the man she was marrying. Some people are never satisfied, he thought as he hurried to display a line of excellent lingerie for his esteemed customer.

He did not know Mademoiselle Daurignac, as she had announced herself with great dignity. She had never set foot in his shop before. Yet the way she had confided in him, he might have been a close relative. In truth, he felt most honoured. Select though his establishment in the high class district of Toulouse was, it was small compared to many. But it was his she'd chosen, had even shared her troubles with him, a complete stranger.

Thérèse had gone into Toulouse happy enough, having persuaded Catherine to accompany her. They had hired a carriage as if money was no object and had put on their best clothes. 'You shall be my companion and we must look as wealthy as possible,' she'd said, but Catherine wasn't at all happy.

'I hope you know what you are doing, Thérèse. I know you need to make it look to everyone that you've come into money, but don't you think this is going a little too far?'

'It's what I must do if I'm going to get my family back on its feet before it's too late. The trousseau will be sold in some other town well away from Toulouse. I shall make up a story to break a trader's heart. We need the money. We've creditors banging on our door at all hours of the night.'

It wasn't quite true, but it was near enough, and she was, perhaps for the first time, becoming a little alarmed. But she had the answer.

It had taken a lot of persuading for Catherine to come round to her argument. Catherine was as loyal a friend as ever. Having found a local girl as a nanny for her two daughters, she'd been able to visit Thérèse more often and their old friendship had been re-established. It would not be long now before Thérèse reached eighteen and they seemed more equal in age, talking woman to woman, the difference in their ages no longer an issue.

'I know what I'm doing,' Thérèse said to Catherine, who was still biting her lip in uncertainty.

'But none of it is true.'

'How do you know it isn't?' Thérèse had rounded on her. 'It can be as true as one wants it to be. And I do have an admirer. He proposed to me only a month or two ago. He has a large farm and lots of money. He can afford me. It is only that he's a bit older than I and I don't love him. So in a way it *is* true, or most of it. The rest I can embroider. It's the only way to keep the bailiffs off our tail – if it were to come down to that – for a little while longer, just until we can get our heads above water again.'

She said it so confidently that Catherine finally agreed to take part in the charade and go with her to Toulouse to assist if necessary.

With Catherine staying in the background, still

not a completely willing party to what she had in mind, Thérèse had entered the little shop as she'd entered others with all the confidence in the world. Only when she gazed on all the beautiful gowns on display did tears began to fill her eyes.

At first the shopkeeper looked embarrassed, but curiosity had got the better of him. He came forward holding a hand out to her, stopping short of actually taking her elbow. 'Is something wrong, Mademoiselle?' he enquired cautiously. 'Can I be of some help?'

Thérèse turned to him. 'Oh dear, I am making such a fool of myself. I'm sorry. And I meant so much to be brave.'

This time he did take her elbow and, with his other hand so lightly on her back as to be hardly touching at all, gently guided her to the little cane-back chair placed at the counter for regular and privileged customers to sit whilst being attended to. Quickly he summoned his assistant to bring the young lady a glass of water. When she shook her head, he placed it on the glass top of the counter in case she needed it. Catherine he totally ignored, perhaps taking her for a paid companion, standing so far in the background.

'Is there anything I can do to cheer Mademoiselle?' he enquired.

Thérèse waved away his concern. 'Nothing.' She gave a tremendous heave of her bosom and smiled bravely up at him. 'I do apologize.'

He looked thoroughly relieved. 'Please. I am glad to see you recovered. Now in what way may I be of assistance?'

With a second deep breath, her hand lifted elegantly to her throat, she explained she was looking for a trousseau for her forthcoming marriage to a young man of a wealthy family in Bordeaux, his father a shipping magnate.

That she omitted to say his name was of no business to the shopkeeper. Only too overjoyed that such a person had chosen his establishment for the purchase of her wedding gown, he didn't press her. Though he remained curious as to why she should appear so upset by what should be a time of great happiness, especially for a young woman about to marry into wealth.

Of course, young women about to marry are apt to be overcome and emotional, but this young lady had been genuinely unhappy. What he didn't know was that this same scene had been enacted in several high class establishments across Toulouse, as the hitherto impoverished Thérèse Daurignac's engagement was spread across the city.

'My future father-in-law is paying for everything,' they'd been told. 'My trousseau, the wedding breakfast, everything.'

As in each of the other establishments, she had begun to weep such copious tears that it wrenched at the proprietor's heartstrings, not knowing how to comfort this distraught young woman except by the offer of a handkerchief.

'I'm sorry to behave this way,' she had sobbed, dabbing the tears as he ineffectually patted her shoulder, again offering the glass of water.

This time she accepted, gratefully sipping a little of the contents before looking up at him with large, dark, soulful eyes and hesitantly explaining the reason for her misery. It sounded like a fairy story, yet it had the proprietor's eyes popping with wonder.

'His father and mine were old friends but lost touch when he became wealthy and my father sank into poverty. When I was a small child they were very close. His son and I grew up together. Our fathers made an agreement that we should marry. I met him again months ago and he declared himself in love with me and proposed. His father is making a settlement on his old friend, my father, as soon as the marriage takes place. What can I do? For my father's sake I must honour the agreement. But the young boy I knew has grown gross and fat and ugly. I can't love him yet I must marry him.'

The same tale, told in half a dozen other shops, had enabled her successfully to order hose, shoes, gloves, the finest hand-embroidered lingerie, chemises, nightdresses and dressing gowns, drawers, camisoles, petticoats, corsets.

Catherine had stood in the shadows, aghast at her friend's astounding, almost insane, cheek as she ordered millinery, hand-made shoes and boots and a variety of morning dresses, afternoon tea gowns, evening gowns in the very latest Paris styles. Now, her tears on the very verge of overflowing, she was seeing about the most elaborate bridal gown, one that was enough to overshadow every bridal gown in the whole of France.

Catherine was heartily relieved that this shop was to be her friend's last stop. Thérèse finally left, an esteemed customer. A very happy pro-prietor beamed from ear to ear, having promised to procure all the necessary materials and have the completed gown, lingerie and accessories sent to her home in Aussonne as soon as possible, assured that the bridegroom's wealthy father would be footing the entire bill.

'How do you expect to get away with it?' Catherine asked as they came away. 'You can't pay for any of it. It's not as if you will get all your money back even selling it in some other town. What do you expect to gain?'

'Prestige,' Thérèse answered promptly. 'Every-one will believe I am marrying into money and they'll be falling over themselves to gain fav-our.'

'And what happens when they discover there is no marriage?'

'I'll worry about that when the time comes,' Thérèse laughed light-heartedly as the coach they'd hired took them back to Aussonne. With the same carefree air and a sweet smile, she told the coach driver on their arrival that she could not pay at this very minute.

'I'm afraid I and my companion spent all of our money this afternoon. I can give you a promissory note. My fiancé will send your money first thing tomorrow morning with a generous tip for your bother, if that is all right?'

What could he say? Surly, but intoxicated by the number of parcels being dragged from his vehicle and by his passengers' fine clothes, he could only agree and whipping up his horse, drive off.

Thérèse was thoroughly triumphant as she and Catherine sat drinking coffee and eating the cream cakes they'd bought. There were just the two of them; the children were not yet due to come home from school and her father was no doubt idling away his time under the shade of the trees in the square.

Thérèse was still full of excitement over the day's events. 'With luck our creditors will stop harassing us. They'll even want to loan us more, at a high rate of interest of course. That's the trick, Catherine. The promise of high interest can work wonders. People are so greedy!'

She felt utterly confident and within a few weeks everything she had ordered had been delivered, the shopkeepers practically bending backwards to please. Even their creditors were content to wait a little longer for their money.

Auguste Daurignac sat slumped at the table in the main room like a doomed man, staring at the mountain of bills in front of him.

'I don't know what we're going to do this time.'

'We'll do what we've always done,' Thérèse shot back, sweeping half of them on to the waxed floorboards with a single angry swipe. 'We'll fob them off.'

'This time I don't think we can,' he said glumly.

'We need to make one or two of them sweat a little,' Romain said, his expression as pugnacious as any boy coming up to fifteen could muster. Emile glanced at his younger brother

64

and sighed.

'It'll only make things worse.' He bent down and began methodically to gather up the bills his sister had hurled on to the floor. 'We need to come up with a better idea than that.'

Quiet and thoughtful, at sixteen Emile was fast growing into a level-headed young man, totally different from his forceful brother. It was he who now ushered the younger children from the room to play outside in the winter sunshine for a while to give their older siblings some peace in which to think.

Thérèse wished she felt as cool and collected as he appeared to be, though she was sure that under that calm exterior he too was worried. She should have been aware that people were endowed with only so much patience.

At least the family had managed to hold their creditors off throughout the winter. And at least, with the money that had been loaned to them, they had been able to pay off the whole of the two hundred francs owed to her father's old friend Tulard, who was friendly towards them again. But it had drained them almost dry.

Using all her skills Thérèse had managed to put off a few by using loans from others. It was a good strategy so long as people didn't see through it. But that was exactly what had now happened.

She scolded herself for failing to see it coming. In truth she'd been so carried away by her success that she'd forgotten that when her wedding to a millionaire's son didn't materialize, of course retailers and tradesmen would grow suspicious. Maybe she could have held them off just a little longer, but what she couldn't allay was their painful embarrassment. The fact that a slip of a girl had managed to dupe them, make fools of them, hard businessmen that they were, accentuated the need for redress. The family now found itself faced by a mountain of demands that if not settled immediately would be followed by the bailiffs.

Though perturbed, Thérèse remained unbowed. One valuable lesson she'd learned at least – that she *could* fool even the toughest businessman. In the future, that knowledge would stand her in good stead and she certainly didn't intend to let this small setback destroy her, even if her father looked as though it was about to finish him. What she had done in Toulouse, she could do again.

'I'll think of something,' she said firmly.

By that evening she had. The next day she set out again for Toulouse, already bold and confident, sure that her plan would work. She persuaded Emile to go with her lest she needed someone to back up her tale of woe.

She'd have loved to ask Catherine again. Two women would have been more adept at convincing men, but she had already imposed on her friend once and Catherine was back home in Beauzelle. But she needed someone with her and Emile was the best choice. She didn't even consider her father, and Romain might turn ugly if a shopkeeper became awkward. It was the last thing she wanted.

'I'm not happy being an accessory to these

lies,' Emile said. But she was adamant.

'All you have to do is stay to one side. I shall do what's necessary.'

'I still don't relish it.'

She turned on him. '*Do* you want us to lose everything, our home, everything, if receivers are called in? Well then,' she added as he shook his head. 'Trust me.'

With Emile's protective arm about her shoulders if needed, she visited each establishment that had delivered the orders, meekly suffering the anger of the owner before breaking down to weep piteously that she'd been jilted.

'I am suing for breach of promise,' she managed to say between grief-stricken gulps. 'I don't know how long it will take. But I *will* win! I've been treated shabbily and any woman in my situation has the court's sympathy. And you'll be paid handsomely for any inconvenience caused. Forgive me.'

So convincingly did she speak that she almost had herself believing it, her heart aching with grief, the tightness in her chest almost unbearable, her tears those of one who'd been cruelly left virtually standing at the altar.

It wasn't as though love had blossomed, she sobbed, for the heavily built bulk of the man she was being compelled to marry still haunted her. She had indeed felt an enormous sense of release. But she had been deeply humiliated, a humiliation intensified by the absence of any hint of apology from him or his wealthy father. She had been made to feel utterly cast off, insulted and distraught with grief.

Yet despite all, she detected a certain wariness. With most of the orders having been made to measure, she was told, her trousseau, gowns, shoes, outfits, none were easily returnable. They were sorry but she would still have to pay in full. Her tale was sad and they were sorry for her but that did not mean they should be out of pocket because of what had happened.

'But I will pay,' she sobbed. 'As soon as I receive damages for what has been done to me, I will settle everything in full. What more can I do?'

Before this tearful promise they'd little option but to grudgingly agree to wait a little longer for their money or else look inhuman. But they would not wait too long.

It was all that she needed for the present. By the end of the day she came away from Toulouse so thoroughly drained by her own imagined grief and devastation that it took all her effort to return to reality. But she had gained time and that was what she had been after.

Then someone astutely making enquiries discovered that no suit had even been filed. Word spread like wildfire and patience finally ran out.

# Six

Thérèse gazed at the scrap of paper thrust into her hand by Madame Tulard.

'I thought you should know,' she said as she hurried by towards the fountain in the square with its stone parapet in front of the red-tiled church of Notre Dame de Bernadette. 'A customer who was having his beard trimmed told my husband by chance. No one should lose their home, no matter who they are.'

Thérèse resisted the urge to run after her. The woman wouldn't thank her for being seen as an informer, though by now half the village must know.

'Bailiffs coming tomorrow morning to claim your house and goods,' the note read, nothing more, but it was enough to fill Thérèse with alarm.

Crumpling the note between her fingers, she turned towards home, trying not to look too hurried though her heart was racing. Certainly they owed a substantial amount, but not enough to have their house seized.

If that happened, and she kept telling herself as she hurried away that Madame Tulard must have got things totally wrong, where would they go? Who would offer to take them in, even if they felt sorry for the plight of an old man and his six children?

More than likely they would be glad to see the back of them – old man Daurignac with his strange talents for foretelling the future and, as some believed, the power to cast a spell on anyone who offended him, and she with her stories that they'd been fool enough to believe.

She should have seen this day coming, the inflow of final demands threatening to take the family to court, hints of putting it into the hands of receivers. Especially when her tale of having been jilted, her fiancé's father refusing to honour his promise to pay for her expensive trousseau and she taking them to court for breach of promise, hadn't worked.

She'd been surprised that it hadn't as the demands began to pour in calling for the goods to be returned, along with recompense for the trouble they had been put to, or for payment in full. These demands came on top of others from those who'd loaned them money. Together it must come to a thousand francs or more, impossible to pay back as things stood at the moment. Once again, creditors had even started to come in person to claim what they were owed, sometimes several at once.

To beat them off, her father declared himself bankrupt, though it was hard to admit that her bright idea of raising money with her tale of marriage to the wealthy heir to a fortune had been a failure. She had loved dressing up in her trousseau, still child enough at nearly eighteen to enjoy parading about in it at home, relishing the feel of real silk lingerie against her skin, of fine shoes on her feet, cooling herself with a huge and gorgeous ostrich-feather fan even though winter was nowhere near warm enough for such an item.

'You must get rid of all that stuff as soon as possible,' her father told her in his deep, mesmerizing voice. 'We will sell it in another town and raise some money.'

That had been her plan anyway. She and her father had gone off to Albi, far enough away not to arouse suspicion. The entire trousseau, however, realized far less than it had been bought for. They managed to pay off several larger bills but what was left owing was still accruing interest. They were nowhere near clearing their debts. For some time a threat that their affairs would be put into the hands of the receiver had hung over their heads. They'd evaded it so far, but now it was here.

Word of the imminent repossession of the Daurignac property was already going round even as Thérèse reached her house, less than half a kilometre beyond the village. Speculation was rife.

Madame Duler, sweeping the two steps up to her house, had seen the odd exchange between Edith Tulard and Thérèse Daurignac and descended on her with questions. What could Edith tell her friend and neighbour but the truth?

'What will they do if they are turned out?' asked Madame Duler.

'I don't know. But I feel sorry for the children and for that Thérèse. She's so young.'

71

'Not so young as to wheedle several chickens out of my trusting fool of a husband last year. And nothing ever returned, in kind or anything else.'

Going back indoors she could hardly wait to tell her husband. And so it spread – from mouth to mouth. By the time everyone retired to their homes and beds that night there wasn't a soul who didn't know and hardly a word of sympathy for the unfortunate family.

'People get what they deserve, I say. When I wouldn't lend him some money Daurignac told me my dog would die. And though the animal was healthy enough at the time, it did. He put a curse on it.'

'His daughter is no better, swindling little minx.'

'Anyone who fell for her sob stories won't see their money again.'

'We'll see what the bailiffs turn up tomorrow.'

'What of those bonds they say Daurignac keeps locked away? Must be worth something. Deeds to some great estate, he told me, in Portugal, he said.'

'That's just stories he told so people would believe they'd see the money back they've been fool enough to lend.'

'I'm not so sure. He's a miserly old devil – keeps it locked, they say. What if he really is proved to be heir to a fortune? His daughter has vouched for the truth of it more than once.'

These words were met with a sneer. 'We'll find out the truth soon enough when it's seized. She's as big a liar as he is. And I for one am wise to her, if people such as you aren't.'

'She took you in, around eighteen months ago, if I remember rightly!' came the affronted retort, leaving the other to hurry off home in embarrassment.

Thérèse was very aware that tittle-tattle wouldn't take long to circulate. Aussonne was a small village. By tomorrow morning there wouldn't be a soul who hadn't heard. For the first time in her life she felt utterly helpless, but her audacious nature refused to let her succumb to the fear that clutched at her. Even as she turned on to the path to her house her mind was already churning over several possible solutions. None so far were practical but she'd think of something. It had been she alone who had kept this family together this far. She would continue to do so.

As she entered the main room, her father was sitting at the table. He had removed the velvet cover, revealing the walnut surface, its deep-grained pattern glowing golden in the rays of the sinking sun that poured through the window. The glow belied the air of gloom hanging over the room itself.

The table had been her mother's pride and joy. Every day of her married life she had insisted on it being polished. She'd paid a good price for it and the set of matching dining chairs at the same time as she had bought this house. Soon it would be someone else's pride and joy, along with all the other furniture. Thérèse felt her heart fill with tears despite her resolve not to despair.

Despair was on her father's face as he sifted

73

through the official-looking papers spread before him. 'It's come at last,' he said as she went up to him to kiss his forehead.

'What has?' But she already knew.

'These,' he said concisely. 'We are going to have to think quickly.'

'Madame Tulard put a note in my hand about it,' she said. 'But we could still put them off. We always have.' Even now she firmly believed in her own power of persuasion.

'Not this time,' came the disconsolate reply. 'If we had the means to pay most of what is being demanded, the courts might relent. But we haven't a quarter of what we owe, let alone enough to pay bailiff's bills and court costs on top.'

'What if we ask Monsieur Tulard for help? He's a good friend. He was so patient about that loan. I'm sure he'd—'

'I've asked him already,' her father cut in. 'He said he was sorry but couldn't help with such a large sum. I don't blame him. But I shall thank him for his timely warning. He has been a good friend to me.'

'If we can't pay,' Thérèse asked, 'what else can they do?'

He looked at her, his dark eyes sad.

Finally he said, 'It isn't only our goods they'll be taking, child. It will be the house as well. They'll take everything we own.'

So it was true. It could happen. Even though she knew it was so, she had always believed they would surmount this final difficulty.

'Since your mother passed away it's been hard

meeting the mortgage repayments,' her father was saying. She knew that too.

'When did you last pay any at all?'

'Not for several months now. There's never enough money.'

He said it so calmly. 'Why didn't you tell me?' she burst out. 'I might have been able to do something about it.' She was sure she could have. But his next remark cut right through her as he looked up at her.

'Do something about it, child? It's your talk about a fine marriage that has got us into this trouble.'

Now she was really angry. 'That's unfair, Papa! I've been left to fend for this family, trying to make enough money for us to live on, trying to keep us together while you sit in the square playing your games, telling your own tales, idling away your time. I know you bring a little in, but it has been left to me to keep us solvent. My last efforts might have gone wrong, but I do my best.'

There were tears in her eyes, genuine this time, stinging, her throat tightening. But already he was apologizing.

'I know you do your best. But you are still a child.'

She wasn't a child. Already she felt the weight of the disgrace, being watched by the entire village as they left with nothing but what they stood up in, trying to muster as much dignity as possible. As if being thrown out of one's home had any dignity to it. Yet within her there was still a spark of belief that something must turn

75

up. It just had to.

Beyond that she felt anger against those with no heart, impervious to their distress as they took every last thing they owned. Angry too at herself, that she could have done more. But especially at him, in letting things go this far and not telling her how far behind they'd fallen with the mortgage. He'd even kept the notary demands from her, leaving her in the dark, all the time thinking she'd been doing so well. It broke her heart.

'My mother bought this house!' she burst out as Romain and Emile came into the room, both already aware of the situation. She glared at them as if it was partly their fault. 'How can they take her house, a poor dead woman? She made this home for us, sacrificed herself for us.'

In her eyes, her mother had suddenly become the saint, the beloved, the tender, loving Maman – that hard soul she had known, swept away.

'They will not see it that way,' her father said gloomily. 'Though we had to sell your mother's shop when she died, we still owed money on this house.'

Thérèse turned on him. 'And you've let everything she worked for slip out of our hands, allowing the repayments to mount up and never a word to me. I'd have worked something out. If only I'd known. If only you'd told me.'

She had begun to gesticulate, her clenched hands beating at her temples, her small foot stamping in anger. 'Why didn't you say? It was left to you, the man of the house, to take care of such things. I took on the task of looking after us all. That sort of thing is something a man should deal with. But it seems you haven't.'

He noticed her anger. 'I'm proud of my little one, for all she has done.'

She could hardly believe how calm he sounded.

'But we've only ever just about kept our heads above water,' he went on as though talking to himself. 'Borrowing from this one to pay that one, never enough to keep up the repayments on this house. Never enough.'

Suddenly he startled her by leaping to his feet, the chair legs scraping on the stone-tiled floor.

'No more time for crying over spilled milk.' His voice had grown urgent. 'We must move quickly. They mustn't find my strongbox. They will force it open and take what is inside.'

Thérèse's wits came together too. She didn't care what lay inside his strongbox. There might be untold wealth to be realized. On the other hand, there might not be. It was the moment she was interested in. 'They'll take all my lovely clothes. I can't let them do that.' And the lovely little mare her hopeful farmer had given her. And her handsome little two-wheeled chaise.

She had come by it some time ago, from an elderly man in need of funds in the nearby village of Trescats who wished to sell the thing. She had put down a deposit on it, managing to persuade him to let her take it away with her, signing a promissory note for the balance to be paid within a week. He would probably be one of those sending an official to the door; word that the bailiffs were coming tomorrow, as ever, would travel swiftly.

'Don't worry, Papa.' Romain was ready to make for the door to his father's bedroom. 'We'll load everything we possibly can on Thérèse's chaise and hide it all somewhere well away from here. They won't find much to take by the time they get here tomorrow morning.'

Thérèse jumped. 'No, Romain! It will break if you overload it.'

He stopped and glared at her. 'Damn your chaise! And your precious fancy clothes! It's everything else, the furniture our mother bought. They're not taking that!'

With a shriek, Thérèse sprang at him, her hand up to slap his face, all her pent-up emotion and hollow sense of personal guilt behind that shriek. It was Emile who stopped her, stepping in front of her so she almost collided with him.

'Let me pass!' she screamed, but he remained standing there.

'We'll take only what we can carry ourselves,' he soothed. 'Whatever clothes you wish to take, the children's clothing, my books. The strong-box is the only awkward item. We can sit on top of it once it's in.'

'It's not a cart!' she yelled back. 'It's—'

Her father broke in, his voice strong. 'We must leave your mother's possessions. If we take all of it, the authorities will become suspicious and start asking questions. We could find ourselves charged with theft.'

Tears flooded Thérèse's eyes, genuine tears, not those turned on to support some tale of woe. Her father had lived his life hoping something would turn up. Now all he was left with were his dreams of his inheritance. And at this moment even she couldn't find it in herself to believe in it.

'Then we'll barricade the door,' Romain was saying belligerently, his fists clenched, his feet firmly spread. 'And secure the shutters. See if they can get in here then. And if they do, we will fight them.'

Her father rounded on him. 'No we won't. Our life here is finished. We'll go to Toulouse and look to the good nature of your mother's sisters. They cannot see us with no roof over our heads and with the winter rains on us.'

His expression had never before looked so decisive. 'Tonight we will get out of the house whatever Thérèse's little vehicle can carry in the time we have. I must take the chest. My inheritance lies in that box. If they find that, I'm done for forever more. They must never get their hands on that.'

'We'll start now,' Romain cried, going to the door. 'Find somewhere to hide it all until they've gone. But I'd like to have got in one swipe at them.'

Emile's face was calm but glum. 'Tomorrow morning everywhere will be alive with creditors and bailiffs. Word will spread before we know it and people will be clamouring to claim what they can.' He smiled. 'Too many for you to confront, brother. We must start moving what we need and be quiet about it. We can't wake the others. You know what children are like. They could say something tomorrow and give the game away. We can't risk that.'

He took his brother by the arm, Romain slowly calming down. 'You and I will start with Papa's strongbox. More than anything else, that must be got away.'

Thérèse saw her father's old eyes cloud over in profound gratitude that his three older children still believed the story of his inheritance.

She vowed that she would do her utmost to see they would never be poor again, that when his time came to leave this world, she would give him a funeral to stun the whole of France, or at least the whole of Paris, for that was her dream – to live in Paris where everything happened. But before that day she would install her father in the most splendid house to be found in Paris itself, where he would hold his head up with the most splendid of society.

It was the vow a young girl not yet eighteen might dream up, to be instantly laughed away, but she knew that one day that dream would come true. She was utterly determined that it would.

# Seven

'The first thing we must do,' said Auguste as he and Thérèse made their way towards Toulouse, 'is to visit both your aunts. They may help us.'

They drove her little chaise with his strongbox under their feet and her lovely clothes tucked in all round her. The rest of the family followed in a small mule cart provided by a kind neighbour named Petit.

'After all,' the man said when advised to let them get on with it, 'how can one be so uncharitable as to see them in such a situation and not offer some kind of help, especially when there are small children involved?'

Fortunately, not being one of those owed money by the Daurignacs, he had no axe to grind and could afford to be magnanimous. His son Pierre had agreed to drive the cart the fifteen kilometres to Toulouse with the three boys, the two little girls and what pitiful possessions the family had been able to bring away with them. Leaving them there, he would make use of his time in town buying a few items his family needed before returning home with the empty cart.

The bailiffs had stripped the Daurignacs' home. The house and its contents would be auctioned. After the huge wagon carrying every

81

last stick of furniture had trundled off, followed by a ribbon of creditors like a funeral procession, none so far having received a single sou of what was owed, Auguste and his children had climbed into the mule cart and left.

The seized goods would go under the hammer, much of it good, sound stuff. The proceeds would go to the main creditors. What was left, if any, would then be shared out between the others, though it seemed likely that not every last one would recoup his losses.

It broke Thérèse's heart to watch everything they'd owned dragged unceremoniously from what had been her home with no care for her mother's beautiful furniture. She was glad when they'd driven away.

Though she vowed not to look back, she hadn't been able to resist. What she saw – her lovely house standing forlorn in the winter sunshine – broke her heart all over again as wonderful memories came flooding back to her. The courtyard full of children gathered around her, wide eyed as she brought to life worlds totally different from the one they knew, or devised plays for them all to act in, or arranged picnics and escapades, or entertained them with small conjuring tricks that her father had taught her, or got them all to dress up and parade around pretending they were rich. She would never forget those happier times and knew that those whom she'd endowed with the gift of dreams would never forget them either, not for as long as they lived.

By the time the house she'd so loved had

disappeared from sight, her throat ached with unshed tears. But as she turned her back on Aussonne, she had already vowed that come what may, this wouldn't be the end of them. Her father still had his strongbox with its mysterious contents and she still had her lovely clothes, allowing her to continue the illusion of wealth and so helping earn them money. She still had her pretty chaise and Fleur, her little mare, which they'd retrieved from the place where both had been secreted away.

The young lad's eyes had popped in bewilderment when told to take the road leading away from Toulouse; popped even more when he found what had been hidden from the bailiffs. Romain had taken off with them last night and, having spent a chilly February night on guard, was in no mood to trifle.

'Breathe a word of this,' he'd snarled, his face close to young Petit's, 'and I'll come back and slit your nose.'

Romain's voice had broken not long after he'd turned fifteen and was aggressively low. His victim, vigorously shaking his head in compliance, was released from the vicious glare and Thérèse and her father had climbed into the chaise. With Romain, his brothers and two young sisters clambering into the mule cart among the few valuables they'd managed to hide, they'd set off at a brisk pace.

In Toulouse, despite all Auguste's hopes of melting his sister-in-law Madame Dupuy's stony heart to sympathy, there was no joy to be had from her.

'You've brought shame on us all,' she stormed after she had very begrudgingly allowed him and his eldest daughter over her doorstep, leaving the others on the other side of the abruptly closed door. She had no such grudge against her younger nephews and nieces, though what she had to say was not for young ears, but Thérèse was as bad as her father.

'My sister Rosa would turn in her grave if she knew to what depths her family have sunk. I've no time for you, Auguste Daurignac, much less money to throw at you, and consequently into the gutter. For that is where it would end up.'

'If not for me,' he pleaded, 'it's for the children. They are of your flesh and blood. You can't stand by and see them starve?'

'They wouldn't be starving had you been a man!'

'After my wife, your poor sister, died...'

'You weren't much of a man even when she was alive – and working to keep you, more fool her. God only knows why she married you.' She had continued to rail as they stood in the centre of her second best room, without so much as the offer of coffee or a glass of wine, or even an invitation to sit down in one of her comfortable armchairs.

'You were useless even before that – a foundling, an idler, a leech sucking from others with his lies and his fortune telling and his sleight-of-hand tricks. Not a decent day's wage earned, ever! I warned her but she would not listen. She and I and Marie-Emilie were of a kind. We were resourceful and strong-minded, and made a

84

success of all we did. But you dragged my poor sister Rosa down with you, and for that I can never forgive you, nor would I raise a finger to help you. I have nothing but contempt for you, Auguste.'

She'd totally ignored her niece in all this. Now Thérèse broke in, but warily, not wishing to antagonize her aunt any more than need be. 'Surely it doesn't mean that all my father's children must suffer for his mistakes?'

Her aunt gave her a lengthy look, at first scornful but then with something like thoughtful admiration.

'It does not mean that at all,' she said slowly. 'You and your father's two older sons are big enough to find work. But this much I will do – for the younger children's sake. I shall arrange for young Louis to go to a Cistercian school. Trappist monks will teach him respect rather than how your father would see him raised, forever scrounging off others. As to Marie-Louise and Maria, I will put in a word for them to be placed in an academy for young girls. That is as far as I will go. Their school fees will be your concern and may encourage you to find honest work in order to keep them there.'

Coming away empty-handed for the first time in her life, Thérèse felt chastened, unable to find any affection for her aunt. But Auguste didn't seem a bit put out. He even had a smile on his lips. 'I'm sure your Aunt Marie-Emilie will be more helpful,' he said lightly.

Her aunt had a gentler nature than her sister. 'She may be guided by a strong-minded husband,' he said. 'But she is more open handed than her sister, more like your mother, though all three were hardworking women in their day.'

Thérèse had been told often enough how her aunt Marie-Emilie had earned her living, keeping house for Gustave Humbert in the Rue de Pommes in Toulouse. He'd been a young law teacher when she had eventually married him. Thérèse learned that her mother, who was her aunts' half-sister, had lived there too. She and Aunt Dupuy had sold lingerie from the ground floor room, as her father had said, all of them resourceful and industrious.

Gustave Humbert, who had strong political ambitions, had become a professor of Roman law at Toulouse University and had recently been elected socialist deputy for Haute-Garonne, as a respected member of the Third Republic.

'He's done well for himself,' her father often begrudgingly remarked. 'Your aunt knew what she was about when she married him.'

Marie-Emilie's home was in the small village of Beauzelle, where Thérèse's friend Catherine lived. Too far for the Petit lad to take them now they were in Toulouse.

'How are we to get all the way to Beauzelle?' Thérèse asked.

Her father didn't hesitate a moment. 'It'll take no time at all if we use your chaise. You and I can go. We'll leave the others here in charge of things and when we return we can find somewhere to stay the night. And tomorrow, with what your Uncle Gustave lends us, we can look for decent lodgings.'

He was rambling on in his customary way, certain all would come right. Thérèse though was being practical. 'We can't leave two boys alone in charge of their sisters. I can't trust Romain not to keep out of trouble.'

'He had better!' Auguste began, then paused thoughtfully. 'The girls had best come with us then. There'll be room.'

But he wasn't prepared to leave his treasured strongbox in his sons' charge, nor was she willing to leave her precious dresses behind. It made a squash in the dainty little chaise, but Fleur didn't seem to notice the extra weight as they drove the twelve or so kilometres through low countryside along the straight road towards Beauzelle.

They arrived just after midday. Her uncle met them cordially enough, but it was expecting too much to assume he'd finance them even after he'd heard their tale. Her father's natural indolence was against him. But he agreed to give them enough to pay for temporary lodgings and food.

'Were I to give you more, Daurignac,' Gustave Humbert said gravely, 'you'd fritter it away until it was gone, doing not a single day's honest work to feed your family. It may sound harsh, but you cannot continue to rely on dreams of something good turning up. I've seen you ruin your family and I despair of you. When your wife died I thought you might rally and support your children, but you never did.'

Auguste was somewhat taken aback. 'You can't mean to consign your own brother-in-law's children to a life of poverty?'

'Not so. They are welcome in my home any time. Your sisters-in-law and I have seen this coming for some time and this much we will do for you.'

He laid out the plan for them exactly as her Aunt Dupuy had. 'The older boys will find employment. But Thérèse...' His eyes turned to her with a knowing glint. 'No doubt you will continue to do only what you are best at.'

She had to agree, understanding instantly what he meant, but she felt no animosity towards him. It was almost as if he were condoning her actions.

She suddenly felt strong, ready to face the future. 'We'll survive,' she said to her father as they came away. 'Now we must find somewhere to live.'

'With what that stingy skinflint gave you?' Romain scoffed when he heard. 'He must be rolling in money. What he gave you, Papa, won't get us the corner of a yard, let alone a roof over our heads.'

Their father didn't reply. He seemed to have lost all heart. Seeing him like this tugged at Thérèse's heart. She put her arm through his. 'We are a family, Papa. We'll be strong! We need no one's help and we never shall.'

The weeks following were a test of that strength. The lodgings they finally found, all they could afford, were no more than a garret. When the woman who owned the house, decently dressed with neat hair though she was as fat as butter, showed them up to the couple of rooms, they were shocked.

'We can't possibly live here!' Romain burst out as though he were head of the family. His brother hit at his hand.

'What do you expect on the money we've got, a palace?'

It was the only time Emile had ever spoken without thinking. His father looked as if he'd been struck between the eyes, though he said nothing. Thérèse felt she could have killed her two brothers at that moment and came to his side, taking his old hand in hers. 'This won't be for ever,' she said softly. 'Just temporary until we get back on our feet.'

He didn't reply, his silence forcing her to look at their surroundings through his eyes, although to her own it was bad enough – the few bits of broken furniture, the dust and dirt and rubbish piled in the corners, one tiny grimy window that she already guessed couldn't be opened. The uneven wood floor was bare and there was no curtain at the window, though being so high up who would need curtains? The view was of roofs and church steeples, with not one tiny glimpse of the wide, blue Garonne that flowed through the city.

There was a table, one leg of which was supported by a block of wood, four old chairs, a scratched and stained sideboard with broken door hinges, and in one corner a bed with a grubby mattress – a place unfit for even a dog.

The other room held two sagging double beds with equally appalling mattresses, a cupboard and two cane chairs. Thérèse had already worked out the sleeping arrangements; she would be in the main room, her father and brothers in the other one, and she'd have to find bed linen. It wasn't going to be easy with so little money, but soon they'd move somewhere better than this.

Weeks later, although she had managed to procure some bedding, the wages her brothers were bringing in weren't nearly enough to keep them and pay the rent being asked, much less enable them to find better accommodation.

Romain had found work as a draper's assistant. The pay was insultingly low, since he was young. But he did manage to filch a few bits and pieces that could be resold to help the family's coffers.

Emile secured employment as a piano sales-man, being mild tempered and suited to per-suading people to buy. It left Thérèse hoping he might yet have something of his father and herself in him. But his wages too were pitiful and in his case there was nothing to steal and bring home.

'Why couldn't you find a more lucrative job and contribute something useful?' scoffed Romain, depositing a pair of gloves on the table while Emile looked on.

But Emile wasn't made that way. Hardworking like his mother, he was dependable, honest, and without her sharp impatience. He had his father's gentleness, thank goodness. But at this moment, his brother had riled him.

'Eventually I intend to start a business,' he

retorted. 'While you're still bowing and scraping to lofty customers I'll be bringing in good money.'

Romain gave a laugh that sounded quite ugly. 'Bow and scrape? Me? They'd better watch out. I'll give them lofty when they least expect it.'

'Stop it, you two!' Thérèse snapped at them.

Romain turned on her. 'You can preach! What have you done to help us since we came to this cursed city? Nothing so far!'

Thérèse squared up to him, eyes glaring, but it went no further. He was right. From the moment they had set foot here in Toulouse her talent for beguiling people with her stories seemed indeed to have fled. She'd been so confident that any story she wove would be instantly lapped up. All she had been faced with so far had been scepticism and suspicion, even amusement.

Never had she met such open opposition. It was impossible that she could have suddenly lost her touch. Yet she had dried up and didn't know the answer, her powers of imagination strangely undermined. Was it that village people had been more gullible, swallowing her tales easily, leading her to believe she was invincible?

City dwellers were a different sort of people. Instead of their mouths dropping open, they grinned at her stories. She could read their thoughts – a young woman with an over-imaginative mind, they had little time in their busy lives to stop and listen to far-fetched stories. Here her guiles were not working.

The worst was that she'd begun to doubt herself. Had it merely been sheer luck that she'd managed to dupe those hardheaded Toulouse tradesmen and shopkeepers with the tale of marrying into wealth? Or was it that word of her had spread among others of the city's tradesmen?

If the latter, she'd have her work cut out to get anyone to believe any tale she spun. If the former, there was nothing she could do. She kept telling herself she was just being silly. But what if her talent had died completely? Who would pull this family together? Once it had all been a game. Now, with real poverty staring them in the face, it was no longer that.

She was starting to feel as bleak as her father looked. It called for a tremendous effort to pull herself together, to recover the spark she'd once had. But, if they were to escape the situation they were now in, then she must. In desperation she'd even sold her beautiful little chaise three weeks ago and Fleur the following week, in genuine tears at parting with her.

She did get a good price for both, helping towards the exorbitant rent. With Romain and Emile's earnings they ate well for a few days, but even that failed to disperse the cloud hovering over her. It wasn't like her to be down and defeated.

One small encouragement as spring came was that she found herself being welcomed in the Humbert household, though her father kept well away, knowing what his reception would be.

She'd go there alone. Her aunt Marie-Emilie was friendly to her, her uncle too when he was there. His days were mostly taken up with politics, but when he was at home he was surprisingly warm towards her. She began to see more of her cousin Alice too, though her brother Frédéric mostly stayed in Toulouse where he was reading law at the university.

Her father's name was never mentioned when she was there, which was a little hurtful. But she was constantly asked how her brothers were doing, she suspected in the hope that if the Daurignacs got back on their feet they might no longer be a burden to the Humbert family.

It made Thérèse smile that no one ever asked what she was up to. Knowing her, they probably already guessed, but while it wasn't put into words it could be ignored.

Finding no joy with city tradespeople, she had turned her attention to the more gullible souls of the suburbs, housewives who could be easily duped. But it was hardly bringing in a fortune. Nor did it challenge her imaginative skills. While almost any tale of woe could separate the out-of-town naive from a few coins, it threatened the very sense of romance she had always enjoyed in her storytelling. Had she gone in rags to such women's doors she was sure she'd have been handed as much as she made from the stories she wove.

Nicely dressed, holding herself upright as a lady might, her ploy was to pass the time of day with a likely woman browsing at a stall; she would fall into conversation and have the woman marvel at her knowledge of the world. Having got her victim's interest she would lift a delicate lace hankie to her lips and begin a tale of a recent descent from more fortunate times. It might be a drunken father who'd brought a good family to ruin, or one who'd gambled away their fortune, or someone her family had trusted who'd run off with their life savings.

She would tell the saddened woman that she vowed never, ever to let poverty show on her, which was why she was trying to look as neat as possible in the circumstances. Her bravery as she drew herself up with dignity would inevitably wrench a soft heart, and a hand would delve into a purse.

Thérèse would recoil as if affronted and push away the offered coin. She was after more than a single franc. She'd appear thoroughly pained and flustered and more often than not was rewarded by the woman befriending her.

It could take days but patience was the essence of this game, the gradual manipulation of a victim. They might sit at a restaurant table in bright spring sunshine over coffee and gateau. She'd tell of how her family had fallen on hard times – which was no lie in her case. With a brave but tearful smile she would talk of creditors demanding that their bills be paid immediately or the law would be brought in. Again she could rely on first-hand experience. Then would come the fabled legacy, a recently deceased aunt, the interminable legal processes, and all the time creditors baying at her mother's door, refusing to wait a moment longer.

'The world can sometimes be harsh indeed,' she would say, dabbing away tears. 'The law has no heart. We could be stripped of all we possess,

94

even as we wait for the law to take its time over a simple legacy. My mother's lovely, treasured old heirlooms will be seized and sold with no hope of reclaiming them.'

With wide, appealing eyes she would mesmerize her victim. 'There is no kindness left in this world. And I am sure my mother has become a little deranged by it all. She cannot see that there must be some light at the end of the tunnel and I am at my wits' end to help her. She frightens me with talk of suicide.'

Her lips would tremble, her eyes mist up, and she almost believed it herself. 'If only I knew where to obtain a small loan for a few weeks. We are strangers to moneylenders and I should feel so humiliated to approach one. I am afraid of them. I'm not concerned by the high interest they charge. When our money comes, the size of the interest will be no bother. To stay out of their clutches I'd pay over any percentage a professional money lender would ask.'

It always worked. Though the offered loan might be small, she'd ask that it be done properly. A promissory note would be drawn up, signed and witnessed; she would give her address, authenticated by a false receipt she always managed to find on her person. With tears of gratitude, a promise to repay the money with interest the moment the legacy was settled, she even went so far as putting out an invitation to her home once the legacy came through. It wouldn't be taken up, of course – the false address would see to that.

None of it was ever as fulfilling or as much fun

as once it had been in her old village, where her true seat of power had lain. But here, while finding herself out of her depth for what had seemed an alarming length of time, practising on these suburban folk was helping regain her confidence.

She wasn't ashamed of what she did. These quiet women in their nice homes could afford to lose a little. Their only pain would be to be denounced as weak and gullible females by their husbands when the truth came out. Small reward now, but it would grow. Next year, 1876, would become her jumping-off point, would see her reaping the benefits, prospering.

With the passing of spring she was slowly getting back into her stride, rediscovering the pleasure to be had from it. But she was taken completely off guard when on one late spring day, visiting the Humbert home, her uncle suddenly asked, 'And what exactly are you up to these days, my dear?'

There was a knowing look in those steely blue eyes, giving her the impression that he knew exactly what she was up to. Here was a man of law who could forbid her to practise her art ever again.

Staring up at him from her small height, Thérèse Daurignac felt her world beginning to crumble.

# Eight

Put at a disadvantage, Thérèse thought quickly. Probably best to lie.

'The person who owns the property where we live pays me to keep house for her. She likes to see it kept tidy.'

She was safe enough saying this. The Humberts were never likely to come visiting and see the squalor her family was forced to endure. What really concerned her was the cunning expression in her uncle's eyes, that sideways quirk to his lips within his trim, greying beard, the way he said, 'Then I wish you luck, my dear, in your ... venture, shall we say?'

It spoke of his perceiving more than she felt comfortable with.

He had never offered her monetary help for her family, nor did she ever push for any. Something always stopped her, a small sense of dignity perhaps. Certainly it wasn't that she'd feel ashamed in asking. More loathing to have him see her family still so flat broke.

There was always more going out than ever came in. Rent, food, clothing took almost all they had. School fees for Louis and the girls had recently rolled in for the first time. Not that they had paid them as yet, requests for payment were to be fobbed off as every other request in the past had been. What the boys brought home wouldn't keep them in shoe leather, and with her gift for procuring worthwhile sums of money having virtually dried up things were going steadily downhill all over again.

And the rent was once again due, and nothing to pay it with. If they were thrown out for non-payment, where would they go this time? The thought scared Thérèse, she who had always been confident of falling on her feet, never letting the future frighten her. Unless it was that she was growing up and saw ahead more clearly.

In Aussonne they'd at least had a decent house and means to grow a little of their own food if they tried. Here they had nothing to fall back on. She would often take the public coach to her old village, popping in for a chat with her father's old barber friend, Monsieur Tulard and his wife. She always made sure to put on a bright face for them, entertaining them with accounts of her city life.

'We are doing well enough,' she told them, animatedly describing her two brothers' work, how well the youngest boy Louis and the two girls were doing at school.

'They're very good schools. My uncle insisted they be well taught so that they would emerge as fine young ladies.' Then she would pout. 'But the fees are so high. Rent takes up much of what the two boys and I earn. And there is food and clothing.'

She'd make sure to dress modestly to verify her story, her bonnet and gloves would be of the cheapest material and there was not a bustle to be seen. 'There is so little left at the end of the week, no matter how hard we try, that my father cannot even afford wine with our food so we drink mostly water. Our eviction weighed hard on him and added to his years. He cannot work any more.'

She skimmed over this quickly in case the question dawned on them as to when he had ever worked, apart from fooling people with his fortune telling and faith healing.

'And he seldom leaves the house now. We children need to look tidy to go to work. So, paying out for clothing, rent and food and schooling for the children, we are just about surviving.'

She would summon up a cheerful front, smile and now and again give a little laugh, end her tale by saying, 'We do our best, so no need to fret on our part.'

It invariably worked. Tulard was a kind-hearted man, and she could always be sure of coming away with a few coins, a chicken or two and some vegetables from his own plot of land.

Her other source of help was Catherine. She didn't need to tell her tall stories to receive kindness from her. Catherine did what she could willingly and without coercion. 'As long as we are friends I will always help,' she said.

It inevitably re-established Thérèse's old confidence. She would thank Catherine from the bottom of her heart, for once with total honesty.

'We shall not always be in this position,' she'd say time and time again. 'You give me such strength, Catherine, and I thank you so much for your friendship. You make me feel I could move the world. And one day I will, I promise you, and you will be beside me, both you and Armand, and I promise you will both be rewarded. Handsomely. I promise. But don't tell my uncle what you do for me, please.'

If her Uncle Gustave knew just how she was reduced to having to take money even from her closest friend, surely he would help her out. But no, she was not going to demean herself by asking.

Her Aunt Dupuy ignored the family altogether, and Thérèse knew that her talk of schooling the children hadn't been her idea but Uncle Gustave's. In her heart, Thérèse felt grateful to him for his benevolence. He could so easily have ignored the plight of her family as her aunt had done. As a consequence she found herself drawn closer to him and his family than she had ever felt towards anyone.

The Humbert family was having a celebration meal in Beauzelle.

Gustave Humbert, socialist deputy for Haute-Garonne, had been made senator of the Upper House. Thérèse was surprised that not just she but her whole family, including her father, had been invited. Catherine and Armand Parayre were there too.

She saw a lot more of Catherine since visiting Beauzelle. Soon after her marriage to Armand, Deputy Gustave had seen what a talented young man Catherine's schoolteacher husband was, engaging him as tutor of Latin to Alice and

Frédéric Humbert. Lately Armand had also become his confidential secretary, and of course they were invited to the party.

Catherine looked very prosperous in deep green, with cuffs and fichu of Chantilly lace and a fetching little bonnet to match. What struck Thérèse most was the bustle, or lack of it – half the size of last year's styles, whereas hers was full blown. Despite the fashionable shade of beige that set off her dark hair she felt conspicuously out of fashion, and vowed to do better next time.

When the invitation arrived, she'd purchased suits for her father and the two boys, flourishing money borrowed from another naive soul. For herself, she had chosen the beige dress with its sizeable bustle, lightweight boots, bonnet and accessories, determined on this occasion that no one was going to see her family as the poor relations. The best part was that all her purchases had been bought on credit, by virtue of the stories that were suddenly coming to life in her at last. From somewhere all her old skills had sprung up like mushrooms, as if out of nowhere, leaving her to wonder where they had been hiding.

More than that, she seemed to have acquired more poise, her stories were stronger, more believable. It was as if she had suddenly grown up, become a woman of the world. From now on she would learn to keep one step ahead of her creditors, not letting a moment pass when she wasn't concentrating on how to get money out of one in order to pay another, but this time keeping it going so that no one person's suspicions were aroused.

'And how are you going to do that?' asked her father, whose curiosity had at long last been pricked.

'I'll work it out, don't worry,' she told him brightly. Just how, she dared not pause to think. Despite all, they were still poor, still living in squalor. How could she ever hope to fulfil those dreams she was dreaming?

But the solution was just around the corner, though she didn't know it then as she and her family drove off to Beauzelle in a hired coach with the hope – no, the certainty that someone else would kindly pay the fare for them at the other end.

In Senator Gustave Humbert's impressive grounds, a long table had been set up under gnarled olive trees whose grey foliage provided just enough shade while allowing flickering splashes of sunlight to play across the food and the faces of those gathered there.

The guests comprised his immediate family, those more distant relations, one or two dignitaries, colleagues of his and several of his closer friends. All in all it was quite a gathering.

Thérèse and her family sat at a little distance from her Aunt Dupuy, who every now and again shot them sour looks of disapproval and managed not to speak to any of them throughout the party. Thérèse wasn't interested in her aunt or her opinion of them. Her mind was on her cousin, Frédéric, son of her uncle. He sat with his sister Alice halfway down the long, cloth-covered table.

She noticed that Emile had somehow found a seat next to them and was in deep conversation with Alice. His other cousin was talking to Romain, who had gone to sit there beside him as if he were already a man and could position himself wherever he liked.

Thérèse pouted, the joyful babble of conversation about her receding. It was easy for them to wriggle themselves into whatever company they chose, male or female. But decorum dictated that a woman must wait until invited to speak to someone of the opposite sex.

It wasn't as if she didn't know Frédéric Humbert well. As children they had seen a lot of each other, she and Alice and Frédéric, but after her mother's death they had grown up and drifted apart.

Since then she had seen Frédéric on only one occasion, when she'd been here visiting her uncle and aunt. That had been at Easter time. He usually resided in Toulouse where he shared university rooms with fellow students, but had come home for that important festival. His family had taken up most of his time whilst she was there that Sunday. But she had sat next to him during the late morning service at Beauzelle's ancient church of Saint Julien. She had been very conscious of the warmth of his arm against her sleeve. The only real chance they'd had to talk together alone had been when he insisted on driving her back to Toulouse in his mother's pony and trap. It had been a little embarrassing. Fearing to let him see how she truly lived, she had persuaded him to drop her off before her home, saying she needed to visit a friend of hers and would probably be staying quite some time.

A thoughtful, studious young man, she had heard him spoken of as scholarly and boring, but what she saw was a very good looking young gentleman, his thoughtful expression only adding to those good looks.

Perhaps to others he wasn't the most scintillating person in the world, but when she met him at Easter, his conversation had intrigued her. She found him learned and interesting. His father had helped in establishing the newly founded Third Republic and they were of the same mould. She could actually feel him taking pleasure in explaining it all to her as they rode back to Toulouse.

Perhaps her interest was captured more by the fact that when he gave her a hand to get into the little vehicle, it had been warm and smooth and firm, and when he put the rug about her knees, his arm going momentarily about her shoulders to make sure she was safely in her seat, she'd yielded to an impulse to lean against him and it had felt so good. He had smiled down at her and that had felt good too.

The rest of the way home she had listened, enraptured, to a potted history of how the Third Republic had come to be, the war between France and Prussia, the numerous mistakes made by Napoleon III. 'People said he was a buffoon, though he did a lot of good for industry and the railway and made Paris what it is today, demolishing the slums to make way for the beautiful city it has become.'

She knew this from the newspapers when she'd been around thirteen. Her father had read snippets to her mother, who hardly had time in her busy life to read. She knew of the siege of Paris, the humiliating loss of Alsace and Lorraine to Prussia five years ago after France had declared war on Prussia. When Napoleon III and his army surrendered to the Prussians in the Sedan, revolutionists overthrew his empire. He died an exile in England, and a provisional republican government was established. Its president, Louis Thiers, had resigned two years ago. But Thérèse had her own problems to deal with and Paris was a long way off, its troubles little affecting most people in the quiet isolation of south-west France.

The Third Republic having been declared this year, Frédéric had been full of it at Easter as he rode with her back to Toulouse. She didn't find it at all boring and in fact became thoroughly enamoured by the intent expression on his face as he talked. It was a look that brought back memories of their childhood when he'd given her a ring fashioned from a piece of tin, solemnly placing it on her finger and saying it was a pledge to marry her when they were old enough. She had laughed but she'd never forgotten it.

At this celebration party she wondered if he remembered that childish gesture. Perhaps he did. Finding herself unable to take her eyes off him, she saw him look up every now and again from where Romain was talking to him at the long table to glance in her direction, a shy smile on his lips beneath the moustache he was gradually cultivating.

Every time she returned the smile he would look down as if instantly flustered. It gave her a wonderful sense of satisfaction to guess the effect she was having on him. Such a reaction must spring from something more than mere cousin love.

Later she did her best to approach him, but with all the people there was little chance of catching him on his own. He was either talking to others or else someone was demanding his attention. But several times she caught him glancing over towards her through the throng.

Some time later she suddenly noticed him on his own, wandering off between the trees away from the others as though glad to be alone for a moment.

Giving herself no time to think, she started after him, her heart in her mouth lest someone else should reach him first. She was halfway to him when a voice hailed her.

'Ah, my dear. Thérèse!'

She turned to see Catherine Parayre hurrying towards her. Reaching her, Catherine puffed, 'Honestly, my dear, these parties are all the same. The moment you go to talk to someone, another stops you.'

She had no idea she was as guilty as any. Thérèse cast a glance at the diminishing figure of Frédéric and gave herself up to her friend.

The only time she saw Catherine these days

was when she came to Beauzelle, always making a point of visiting her friend and her two little daughters; they even called her aunt.

So far she had managed to avoid inviting Catherine to her own home, if one could call it that. Not for the world would she have her see how low they had sunk, especially since she was always dressed in her best when visiting so as to give the impression that she was doing well. Despite her resolute determination to force Lady Fortune to smile on them eventually, there were moments when she felt she would never realize her dream of riches even though she cast them aside almost in the same instant.

As Catherine chattered on, Thérèse was only half listening, her eyes going constantly to the distant figure. Suddenly she was aware that her friend had fallen silent, the silence dragging back her attention.

'I'm sorry,' she apologized. 'You were saying?'

Catherine smiled, her eyes following the track of that previous glance. 'Young Frédéric Humbert?' she said slowly, with an understanding nod. 'Is he becoming the light of your life?'

Thérèse came abruptly to herself. 'Don't be silly!' she bridled. 'We're cousins.'

'So then?'

'Well...' Thérèse began, then let her voice fall away. Should it matter that they were cousins? The look in Catherine's eyes echoed that query.

'I do like him,' Thérèse admitted. 'Very much.'

'Then, so long as he is of the same opinion about you, I cannot see any obstacle. It all depends of course on what his father feels about it, and your father too.'

'I don't care what *my* father thinks!' Thérèse burst out. 'My father hasn't thought for years. When we lost Maman he stopped thinking. I had to do it all, think for our welfare, and so far I've done a good job...'

She broke off. Had she done a good job? They were reduced to living in two attic rooms, while she was still not adult enough to put her true plans for them into action...

She lifted her head defiantly. 'Why then do I need to ask his opinion of the man I'd like so much to marry?'

Catherine was still smiling. 'It's as serious as that?' she said simply.

'Yes, it is.'

Thérèse looked away from her, but refusing to look in the direction of Frédéric, gazed instead at her brother Emile talking to Alice, Frédéric's sister. They were standing a little way off but even from here she could see how attentive her brother was to Alice, bending close as if her words came from heaven itself. They appeared quite wrapped up in each other.

Hardly sipping their wine, they ignored the delicacies left on the table after the meal for people to pick at, seeming to have eyes just for each other, oblivious to other guests moving past them to help themselves.

The evening was developing into a golden one. As the sun sank behind the trees, its glow reflected off a blush of elongated high clouds, adding a romantic air to the gardens below. Lanterns were being lit, guests becoming mellow. An accordion was playing gentle tunes as befitted such an evening.

It had been a long, happy day. One or two guests were contemplating the time. Those living nearby lingered with no need to hurry home; a few with further to go would eventually summon their coaches, their drivers standing by to hitch up horses. Thérèse noticed her Uncle Gustave in deep conversation with Catherine's husband. Catherine, a half-empty glass of wine in her hand, was also taking note, both women lost in their own thoughts.

Thérèse almost leapt out of her skin as Frédéric's voice spoke her name, practically in her ear. She hadn't seen him coming towards her. Now he was by her side. She turned and stared up at him, not knowing what to say. Having called her name he too seemed lost for words.

Catherine touched her arm. 'I see I am not wanted here,' she said amiably with a small, amused laugh. 'I will see you later on, Thérèse.'

Left alone, Thérèse raised her eyes to Frédéric's and gave a shy smile. She had to say something.

'I noticed you walking on your own away from everyone else and I was thinking of asking if you would object to my company.'

'Were you, then?' he returned.

'Yes. But then my friend, you know, Catherine Parayre, spoke to me. I couldn't very well ignore her.'

'No, of course not,' he said formally. Then, unbending a little, he became more chatty. 'My father is very taken by her husband, whom he sees as a radical, very much like himself.'

She was glad to hear it. If her uncle, an influential man already high up on the political ladder, saw some fine potential in Catherine's husband, then Catherine would rise with him. It was possible that as Catherine's lifelong friend she too would go up in the world alongside them. The thought conjured all sorts of possibilities, and why not? With such relatives and friends in high places it had to follow that her family would be looked up to again, even envied.

'I'm very happy for her,' she murmured absently. 'She is a lovely person and deserves every good fortune.' And so do I, came the thought.

'I shall be going back to university tonight.' Frédéric's voice broke through her reverie. 'I could accompany you and your family back to Toulouse and perhaps spend the rest of the evening with you.'

Thérèse turned on him almost vehemently. 'No!'

He looked bewildered. 'The university is only a stone's throw from where you are living. Rue du Tair, that *is* where you live, isn't it?'

'Yes, but...' Her words died away.

The Rue du Tair was in quite a respectable district, graced by the large edifice of the church of Saint Sernin in its large open space, the imposing Palace d'Esquiral and Notre-Dame du Tair, along with many of the buildings of pink stone that gave Toulouse its other name, the

Rose City. Lining the road on which she lived the tall houses were clean and attractive if you looked at them from ground level. What lay unseen to a passer-by were the garrets hidden away under the rooftops. She dare not let him see the way she lived.

'We've already ordered the coach that brought us here to come back for us.' Her uncle had paid the fare and would doubtless pay for their return. They might be his poor relations but his pride wouldn't let him allow them to walk the twelve kilometres back to her home through the twilight, even though anyone with little money saw it as only a step.

But she wasn't *anyone*. If a coach could be had, she'd have it, by one means or another.

'Then I will accompany you in yours,' he said brightly.

Wisely, Thérèse ordered the coach to drop him first, at the university itself where he shared rooms with two friends. Standing ready to alight he bent and kissed her hand, lifting his gaze to hers. The rimless spectacles emphasized the smouldering darkness of his eyes enough to make her tingle all over. His lips felt gentle against the back of her hand.

'May I see you again, Thérèse?' he whispered as the other occupants concentrated on rearranging themselves on his seat. She heard Romain's giggle and gave him a sharp look.

'That would be nice,' she said quietly.

'Wednesday?' he suggested quickly. 'Five o'clock? Let's say the Place Saint-Pierre?'

It was near the university and just far enough

away from where she lived to be safe. Eagerly she nodded, and watched him as he alighted nimbly from the coach, thanking her father for allowing him his company.

'I look forward to it,' he said simply, but it was enough for her.

She ignored her brothers' titters, her father's enquiring look as the coach moved away. In seconds she had made up her mind. This was indeed the man she intended to marry. But what if his father refused to countenance a match with his talented son, not only because they were cousins, but because she hadn't a penny to her name except that which she made by her wits?

What was needed was a carrot. A golden carrot. Something to make his father's eyes all but pop out of his head. She would become an heiress in her own right, with a fortune just waiting for her when she attained the age of twenty-one. Already Thérèse Daurignac's head was buzzing with ideas. That wondrous inheritance her father so often spoke about would become hers, so long as she got her story right.

It was of the utmost importance that she did. Frédéric Humbert must not slip through her fingers. She had fallen in love with him. And by the way his eyes had lingered on hers as he kissed her hand he in turn had fallen in love with her.

# Nine

With little else to do on such a wet Sunday afternoon, Emile sat at the table, playing dominoes with Romain. Only the four of them were here in this small room; Emile himself, his father dozing in the large chair they'd bought some time ago, Romain intent on his game, and Thérèse, gazing pensively out of the window.

Young Louis seldom came home for weekends, being at boarding school some way from Toulouse. He only returned when the Trappist monks who taught him allowed it during the short school holidays.

His young sisters too remained at school during the weekends. He'd got used to them not being around. But it wasn't like the old times in Aussonne when everyone was forever in and out of the house. The days had always seemed to be sunny there. He missed those days. But if they hadn't come here he might not be walking out with Alice Humbert.

The girls could have come home by public transport, but that cost money and it was better to keep them there. Though if they didn't pay the fees soon, they might be sent home for good anyway. And that would be admitting to the family's lack of money, lowering them in the eyes of those who had arranged their education when they'd first arrived here.

Thérèse with her glib tongue had fobbed off the authorities with promises to pay the fees at the end of term. Terms had come and gone and so far she had managed to evade each demand as it came up. But those fees were mounting.

A domino idle in his hand, he glanced over at his sister. She was sitting by the window gazing vacantly out across the wet rooftops, obviously begrudging every minute of being forced to mark time. She was dressed for going out but the rain had developed into a steady downpour that promised not to let up for hours yet. He could guess what she was feeling. Fortunately he wasn't seeing Alice today and could forget the weather. He and Alice had been seeing each other just over a year now – Thérèse and Frédéric for a little longer. She was very much in love with her handsome Frédéric, as he was with his beautiful Alice.

'Wouldn't it be marvellous if we had a double wedding?' Thérèse had suggested a while back. Emile hadn't so far had the courage to formally propose to Alice, but he knew she was already thinking along those lines.

'We'll see,' was all he'd said to Thérèse's suggestion.

It sounded a good idea. But how could he even think about marriage on what he was bringing in, living in this hovel and no likelihood of moving on to something better? Every week he tried hard to put aside a little of his earnings but with rent and food to buy, it was sometimes impossible.

Thérèse made a modest amount in her own fashion but needed to buy things to look presentable for what she did. To find somewhere nicer to live, somewhere that would impress the Humberts, was an obstacle high as any mountain. Neither he nor Thérèse had as yet allowed their sweethearts up to their shabby home, using every excuse not to.

Their father had at least snapped out of his depression and had begun to seek out those who yearned to hear their future told for a few centimes. But what he brought in was only just enough to keep him in tobacco and a glass or two of wine with friends he'd made. Elderly, like himself, they'd meet every day in a small nearby café where he no doubt regaled them with tales of lost wealth and romance.

'Are you playing or not?'

Romain's deepening voice at seventeen broke through his thoughts and he quickly turned to select the required dominoes, their spots hard to see in the dim candlelight necessitated by the overcast sky beyond the single small window.

'Why does it have to rain today of all days?' came his sister's voice.

'What's so special about today then?' he asked, his eyes on the game.

'Frédéric was going to drive me out into the country. I was so looking forward to it. He was hiring a cabriolet for us especially. I wish I still had my pretty little chaise and my darling little Fleur. I wonder how she is.'

It was probably the only thing she really

regretted in her move here from Aussonne. Not the state in which they lived, nor that city dwellers were far more sceptical than village folk, making her job all the harder, but her dainty little mare. If Thérèse loved anything at all, it had been that animal. She had given up the creature for the good of her family, and Emile felt constantly sorry for her and as constantly indebted to her for the sacrifice.

It had also got her going again, enabled her to buy something really stylish to support her stories. Though she'd said she had never made much headway, as far as he was concerned she had. But for her, God knows where they'd be now. She was unstoppable. Adversity never got her down for long. After each setback, up she would bounce and off she would be, squeezing money from the tightest purse. He had to admire her tremendous audacity.

'How can I get there in this weather to tell him I can't be there to meet him?' she fretted.

He couldn't resist a grin. Strange logic, but that was exactly what beguiled people into believing everything she said. She had a natural and innocent way of expressing herself, even when she related the most outrageous stories in her husky, hesitant voice with its merest suggestion of a lisp. People just felt they had to believe all she told them.

There came another rather uncomfortable thought: that, as she grew older, she would learn to employ it to even better advantage. He wasn't sure whether he'd like to see his sister turn that professional.

'In God's name, do you want to play this game?'

As Romain's irate tones invaded his brain there was a light tapping on the door. Emile got up to answer it, to find their landlady standing there.

'A young man downstairs,' she said. 'Name of Humbert, asking for Mademoiselle Thérèse. He says he has a cabriolet waiting outside for her. Quite a presentable young man, I'd say. Her young man, is it?'

'Thank you,' Emile said evasively, giving her an abrupt smile and closing the door. He turned to his sister. 'It's Frédéric.'

'Oh God!' Thérèse's small hand flew to her mouth. 'He's come here?'

'Obviously. He knows where we live if not the conditions we live in. Don't worry. It looks a smart enough address from downstairs.'

'But he mustn't come up!'

Thérèse was on her feet. Without a word of goodbye to anyone she rushed from the room and down the stairs, her face glowing with joy, the rain forgotten.

Things couldn't go on this way. Something was going to have to be done.

She and Frédéric wandered the path beside the Canal du Midi. It was quiet now; as the day came to a close the barges plying their loads between Toulouse and the coast had been moored for the night, their owners gone home to their supper.

The evening was fine and warm, not a cloud to

be seen. The May twilight lingered, a canopy of fading colours, dull red blending to translucent green, turquoise, purple, fading to an eastern horizon of indigo. Frédéric had his arm about her waist. She in turn leaned against him as they strolled in silence, lovers relishing the romance of such an evening. But her mind was on other things.

The first time Frédéric had asked to keep company with her had been at that celebration party in August 1875. It was now 1877. Almost two years seemed simply to have flown by. Frédéric had hinted at odd times on the question of marriage when he finally graduated from university. Not exactly a formal proposal as yet, but she knew it would come. But what would happen when he discovered she was an impulsive concocter of wild stories that she used to support herself and her family? She was proud of what she did, but would he be?

Lately, with love and romance on her mind, her stories had begun to reflect that more than ever before. Luring people's hearts with tales of romance, seeing their eyes dilate with greed as she spoke of the riches awaiting her from some ardent lover, or from a long lost father about to bequeath his fortune to his natural daughter, was a joy to her.

Her father's mysterious chateau had begun to come to the fore again – the beautiful, marbled Chateau de Marcotte. That fabulous inheritance now stemmed from several sources, each of which might have been genuine: after a chance accident years ago, the wealthy Portuguese owner of the property, cared for by her mother after he'd fallen through her shop window, had subsequently become her friend; he had willed his property and money to her young daughter whom he suspected to be his own. Since he was reported to have recently died in Lisbon, the legacy would be coming to her at any moment.

Such tales were always good for a loan to be repaid at a very enticing rate of interest. She had learned how to do the thing properly; no longer relying on the old sob stories of being poor, instead she made a business deal of it. She had begun to frequent small banking houses, to seek out serious investors looking to make a handsome profit. No one was aware that the profit they made came from some other loan.

Her business, as she now called it, still remained modest but in these last months she was beginning to see it grow. What she had made so far she was keeping to herself, saving carefully. Within a year there would be enough for the family to move to a decent address. But she couldn't wait that long. She needed to impress Frédéric now, not in another year's time. What she needed was more backing. Making money out of something she enjoyed doing was so wonderfully satisfying, but how would he see it? She was going to have to think very, very carefully how to go about it.

Frédéric glanced down at her. His arm tightened about her slim waist. 'You're very quiet and thoughtful this evening,' he murmured.

Thérèse looked up into his face. 'I'm sorry, dearest, I was miles away.'

'Anywhere I can be too?' He smiled.

'No, not really,' she began. Then, before she could stop herself, she had said absently, 'I'm worried for my father, fretting over his inheritance.'

'Inheritance?' he echoed. 'What inheritance is that?'

Something seemed to snap inside her, propelling the story from her. Before she knew it she was repeating the tale her father had always told her, how his mother had been forsaken by the man she had loved and, cast out in disgrace by her family, had borne her illegitimate son alone, how her father had discovered in his later years that the family was without an heir but for him, the rightful claimant of the family's wealth.

She told it brokenly. The story had always moved her to tears. It was so poignant, the tale of a woman forsaken by all, she couldn't help but believe in it. As she did equally the love story of her mother and the man from Portugal. Often she wondered if her father's version hadn't been told to cover up the fact that she had actually been the child of his wife and her lover. There could have been some truth in it. But why did the name Crawford creep into her stories sometimes? Somewhere, in the deep recesses of her mind, that name had stuck as if there really was some truth to it. Sometimes he was an American who'd lived in the USA, other times an American who'd gone to live in Portugal. Sometimes more chaos lay in fact than in fiction and she could never be sure. But for now she told her father's version of this mysterious inheritance.

Frédéric listened in silence. When she'd finished he remained silent for nearly a whole minute, leaving her to fret as to what he might be thinking about her. She was almost prepared to hear him announce that their relationship was at an end.

Finally he said, 'And you've never seen a single sou of this.'

'No,' she responded faintly. Shock almost made her frame go weak, causing her to hold on to him for support. But his arm held her. The next moment, she was being pressed to his body, his lips hard on hers.

Standing there with no care for the world around them or the looks from others strolling along the canal path, they remained with their bodies locked in embrace, their single reflection fixed on the still water of the canal, melting into the dull reflection of the trees beneath the translucent light of the evening and of the yellow glow of lamps that now lit the way.

'We'll have to look into all this,' Frédéric said as they walked towards her home. 'I am becoming well versed in the law. My father is a politician. He is acquainted with more than a few men of good standing.'

It was dark now and he couldn't see her eyes widen with anxiety as he went on, 'How could your father allow this to go on for so long and do nothing about it?'

'We had no money to make enquiries,' she said lamely.

'But you have me now to fend for you. And for

your unfortunate family, though I hasten to say they will be fortunate when this thing has been finally settled. I've little money of my own, I admit. My father insisted I stand on my own two feet, which I agreed was a wise decision. But I know he will help us in this.'

He seemed so eager to join the fray. Though he was gentle, almost timid, in this his voice sounded adamant in the dark. She'd have a champion for a husband. But at this moment he was a champion for reasons she didn't want and she didn't know what to do. It certainly was a good thing that no one knew where exactly the Chateau de Marcotte was.

At home she told her father. He listened until she was done and then without a word got up from his chair and went to where his strongbox still lay locked beside his bed.

Sitting with her brothers here in the living room, she stared vacantly into space as she heard the scrape of the iron key being turned in the lock in the other room, the leather straps being undone, the creak of the hinges. One could hear every sound in these rooms with their thin walls.

Her father came back holding a legal-looking scrolled document.

'Title deeds,' he said simply. 'Show this to your Uncle Gustave. Unfortunately the location of Marcotte is not indicated.' There was a sly look in his eyes. 'There must be other papers that show it, but I do not have them.'

Thérèse had a momentary vision of a large and beautiful chateau, its white marble glowing in the twilight but its terraces and lawns, orchards, vineyards and orange groves all overgrown, the house empty and forlorn, deserted these many years, just waiting for someone to bring it back to life. She almost wanted to weep but kept her eyes on the documents.

'Our proof?' she queried, while Romain and Emile stared in disbelief that after so many years in which they had believed their father merely to be living his pipe dreams, it had to have been true all the time.

'Our proof,' he said slowly. 'Be careful in showing these to anyone,' he added, his throaty voice holding a tone of warning. 'To the sceptical they may not be all that you want them to be. When presenting these to your uncle, be on your toes. Think before he does. Work out carefully what you need to say.'

Looking into her father's eyes, Thérèse saw the truth lying deep within. While her brothers capered about in excitement, she knew instantly to what he alluded. For a moment she wilted. Then her lips tightened. She knew exactly what to do. She wouldn't let herself down, or him. She was going to have to stay on her toes.

Gustave Humbert sat relaxed in his favourite armchair in the stuffy morning room of his home. His eyes were trained on his niece, a bundle of nerves, seated opposite him on the edge of the sofa.

Having handed the document to him, she watched him scan its contents. At one point he glanced up at her, before looking down again with no change to his expression, leaving her lost to what he was thinking. If he declared the document to be false, how would she bluff her way out of it? She could see her chances with Frédéric diminishing by the second.

Beside her, Frédéric held her hand comfortingly. On a nearby hard, straight-backed chair sat her Aunt Marie-Emilie, her back ramrod stiff, her narrow face a portrait of disbelief. Thérèse clutched Frédéric's hand tighter as his father leaned towards her.

'Tell me again,' he said in that deep commanding tone that spoke of his position as a senator. 'From the start. As far as you remember it.'

Her voice was small. 'I've told you all I know, or at least what I have been told over the years. I was too young to remember for myself.'

'I would like to hear it again from your own lips, if you don't mind. Don't be worried, my dear, I do understand. It isn't easy for you to remember every last thing you have said and I am not casting doubt on the truth of what you have told me. I merely need to have it clear in my mind. The first time of hearing any tale seldom allows the listener to properly take in every detail. So, please, if you don't mind, my dear?'

It was a command. She took a deep breath and straightened her back a little more. 'Not at all,' she said, this time firming her voice a little more.

She began again, starting from the beginning, remembering to hesitate, repeat a sentence more than once, frowning as if fighting to recall what she had gleaned. It was not word perfect, but no one would be when asked to repeat a story that they hadn't personally experienced.

As well as that, she tended to mix two stories into one: the casting out of her father's mother and her own mother's Portuguese lover.

'It was a long time ago,' she apologized when she'd finished, her voice trembling so pitifully that Frédéric put a consoling arm about her shoulders. 'I only know that whatever the version, my father has documents to prove the property is ours. He says it will come to me, his oldest child, when I am of age.'

There were tears in her eyes now. It hadn't been easy telling. In any other circumstances, or to anyone else, it wouldn't have mattered. If it didn't draw sympathy and subsequently cash from someone, she'd have shrugged and given that listener a wide berth from then on. But here her future with the man she loved depended on how her story was received and she felt every nerve inside her body quivering as if made of jelly.

Oddly it was her very hesitancy, the way her lips persistently trembled, that seemed to add to the truth of the story she'd told. Even the small errors in telling it, as with those natural lapses of memory that occur in trying to remember details of some past event, added credence to all she'd said. As her voice died away, Gustave Humbert leaned back again in his chair.

'Marcotte, you say?'

Thérèse blinked, snapping out of the hypnotic vision she always spun for herself when referring to the property that one day would be hers.

'Pardon?'

'This property you described. The Chateau de Marcotte that will eventually be yours.'

'It *is* ours!' she broke in vehemently. 'It has always been ours. It's just that my father has never had the will or the money to pursue his claim.'

'I understand. Your father has never been known for his purposeful nature. You should have come to me about this inheritance earlier, my child.'

For a moment Thérèse couldn't believe what she was hearing. This man, this astute politician, had believed every word she'd said. But then she too believed every word of it. To her it was real. Somewhere there had to be a Chateau de Marcotte with gleaming marble terraces and vast orange groves overlooking the blue sea – how could she believe otherwise? Only the story and the people in it changed, for she didn't know the full rights of it.

Sometimes her father's tale rang true, at others the tale involving her mother seemed more plausible. The names of the testators were those she had heard in the dim and distant past: there was Crawford, whose name she used when telling that old tale of some long-lost natural millionaire father; while other names she dimly remembered or had invented – Mademoiselle Baylac, Mademoiselle Latremolliere, Demoiselle Lagourdere, spinster aunts as she liked to think of them – often seemed to her more than merely made up.

Crawford she was sure had been an American, though why he should have ended up in Portugal, she didn't know. It didn't matter. So long as people were convinced of her inheritance, she would milk them as much as she could. But this had been a very different situation. She was fighting for the man whom, seeing herself faced with the likelihood of losing him, she knew she couldn't live without.

Finally Gustave re-rolled the document and handed it back to her.

'Tell your father to put these in his strongbox. I suggest he keeps it padlocked. Labelled "Not to be opened". Just in case.'

Even as she and Frédéric came away from his home, she was still unsure if her uncle had been totally convinced by her. And with visions of her aunt's unaltered scepticism, she lifted her face to him. 'You believe me, don't you, Frédéric?'

He looked down at her, smiling, his eyes dark and trusting behind the rimless spectacles. 'Why shouldn't I, my sweet? It's wonderful news. And to think that because of your father's lack of initiative your family has had to remain poor all these years.'

Even so, she couldn't feel satisfied. Frédéric might believe in her, but she was still unsure about her uncle. And her aunt – not for nothing was she her mother's sister, untrusting to the last.

Thérèse decided she must brave it out. 'My inheritance won't come to me yet awhile. I hope your father doesn't have a change of mind about it.'

'Why should he?'

'None of us knows exactly where it is situated. Those deeds indicating its whereabouts are the ones that are missing. And they are vital.'

'The documents you do have are proof enough of your family's right to the property. We shall trace the place eventually. As you say, your father is the only remaining heir. Of course it is his by rights, being that there is none to prove otherwise. So stop worrying your little self, my darling.'

He drew her to him, his lips pressing down on hers. For minutes the two people remained in each other's embrace.

When finally they broke apart, he said with a tremor in his voice, 'I need to speak to my father as soon as possible to request his blessing on my intention to ask you for your hand in marriage, my dearest love. That is if you will have me.'

It came so suddenly she was lost for words. All she could do was utter ecstatic little sounds of joy and throw herself into his arms again, as he went on, 'You shall have the finest engagement ring I can find, my sweet darling. And we'll be married as soon as I leave university, I promise.'

As she clung to him, she pushed away the thought – if his father was not convinced she was heir to a fortune, would he even consider a union between his son, destined for high places, and some practically down and out brat?

But all that was now changed. His father did believe. From abject poverty, she'd be marrying a man of means. No longer would there be the need to extract money from others with fantastic yarns. Yet to give up what had always been so pleasurable? It had become part of her. It would be like parting with a true and beloved friend.

# Ten

Marie-Emilie's pale brown eyes stared at her husband at the other end of the dining table, her voice high and querulous.

'How can you say you actually believe that little hussy's outrageous stories?'

Marie-Emilie's anger had been simmering ever since her son's request for his father's sanction to court Thérèse, but all her complaints had been ignored. This time Gustave, normally a man of firm conviction but studied restraint, looked up sharply to meet her irate gaze.

Sensing disharmony in the air, the sommelier gave an unobtrusive nod to his two female serving staff to leave the room, he himself remaining discreetly in the background with eyes downcast and ears closed. He didn't approve of the Daurignac girl but it wasn't his place to voice or even foster opinions.

Ignoring his presence, Marie-Emilie ranted on. 'She has been telling these stories all her life. I tolerate her because she is my sister's child. And who am I to stop you if you wish to encourage her into our home? But a union between my son and that scheming...'

She broke off to take a quick, irate breath before continuing. 'I would have thought you the last person to believe anything she says. This chateau of hers, what's it called? Marcotte. It doesn't exist. It's something her dreamy fool of a father conjured up years ago. He's always been that way.'

'My dear, she has the deeds.' His deep voice remained calm. 'I am aware of her reputation. And I hope you give me credit for enough sense to differentiate between truth and lie.'

'Then you're more a fool than I took you for.'

Her husband's keen eyes narrowed a fraction. Behind his grey but generous beard his lips thinned. 'So you married a fool, my dear? It says very little for you. And I gather that you think it takes a fool to become a senator.'

'I didn't say that!' She dropped her glare and made a play of cutting a piece from the serving of cooked goose on her plate. 'I merely wish you to see that she is pulling the wool over your eyes, just as she does everyone, just as she has done all her life.'

'Then what do you suggest I do?'

'For a start, forbid our son to have anything to do with her. She's only after the prestige that marriage to him will give her. On top of that, they *are* related. They are cousins.'

'The same is true of Alice and Emile. But you approve of that.'

'That is different.'

'Why different? Because you see Emile as a respectful, quiet and thoughtful young man whereas his sister is an exuberant, excitable young woman. I know you have never liked her.'

'I have cause not to like her.'

'But for her, my dear, that family would have gone under long ago. We expected to have to take them in, being obliged not to have your sister's children cast out on to the street. How would you have liked that, looking down on them as you do? Not visibly, I admit, not as your sister does with all the venom she can muster and not afraid to show it...'

'And why not? I may be able to curb my feelings better than she but we both know Rosa married beneath her, a good-for-nothing scrounger!'

Gustave's lips twisted quizzically. Neither of them had cause to feel elevated over others, sired illegitimately as they'd been by that old devil Duluc who'd had his way with more women than most people could count.

'He who casts the first stone,' he muttered to himself as he turned his attention to his own food.

Marie-Emilie compressed her lips, let out a small puff of agitation and continued eating, but was unable to resist having the final word.

'Well, don't expect me to like her,' she pouted before falling into a sullen silence.

Both ignored the presence of the sommelier who, the small disagreement ended, raised his head and with studied dignity came forward to replenish their wine glasses.

Having made the briefest of investigations, Gustave's mind was in turmoil. He told himself that he was satisfied, while ignoring the voice inside his head that said he should be delving further.

Yet, it was enough to set his blood tingling with controlled excitement. On the face of it, there seemed to be no apparent reason why the property should not exist and his niece's account had been very convincing. Would so young a girl as Thérèse Daurignac ever have the courage to lie about a legacy worth not a few thousand francs, but a few million?

While the location of this vast property remained unknown due to the lack of the essential document which, with luck, might eventually be unearthed, the deeds were there, her father's name on them. He'd named Thérèse as his heir, signing everything over to her on his demise, stating his wish that it be divided as she thought fit between herself and her siblings.

Nothing could have looked more authentic and Gustave couldn't escape his deep need for it to be so. He wasn't a greedy man but he was ambitious and despite all efforts to ignore it, a small demon kept hammering away inside his brain that this marriage could take him to the top.

Another spur to approving this marriage between his son and Thérèse Daurignac was that Frédéric was mooning over her, contemplating his father's possible rejection of her, so much that his studies were being affected. The last thing he wanted was to see his son a failure in his field.

Also, having given his blessing to a union between Emile Daurignac and his daughter Alice, how could he deny his only son his happiness?

It was October when Frédéric finally slipped the

ring on to her finger, on a dull but dry Sunday afternoon as they stood in the beautiful Place Saint-Pierre. There were very few people about, the church of Saint Pierre-des-Cuisines having emptied earlier of worshippers.

They had been wandering across the open space, intent on each other, when he suddenly stopped and reached into his breast pocket. Intrigued, Thérèse saw him take something small from it. Even more intrigued, she allowed him gently to take her left hand and lift it. She thought he was intending to kiss it but instead, with a deft movement, the ring was slipped over her third finger as easily as one would draw on a glove.

She was taken aback as he continued to hold the tips of her fingers between his, and she found herself gazing in awe at the band of five graduated diamonds, the central stone dominating the rest.

'I had no idea you would—' she began, but Frédéric interrupted her with a long and ardent kiss, right there in the centre of the Place St-Pierre.

'Sorry it took me this long to put a ring on your finger, my love,' he said softly as he released her, still breathless, from the kiss. 'I couldn't propose to you properly until I had the ring. But it has taken a while to find the perfect one for the most wonderful girl in all the world.'

Mesmerized as she was by the glints of light continually flashing off each facet even on this dull day, his trite effusion of love passed over her. 'I am now engaged,' she said dreamily.

'Engaged to be married.'

'Do you like it?' he probed uncertainly.

She came to herself. 'Oh, Frédéric, it's wonderful!'

'I wanted to find something really perfect for you. I had to save quite a bit before I had enough to get it.'

Her joy became surprise. As the son of a successful politician, surely money would be his last problem?

'You mean you had to *save*?'

'My father has never believed in spoiling his children. He attained his own position through hard work and sacrifice and I understand when he says it is the only way a man can prove his worth.'

He'd told her some time ago how his father had begun with no money to speak of. His grandfather, a small wine merchant living in Metz before that part of France, Alsace-Lorraine, had been annexed by Prussia, had been a member of a revolutionary society and, according to Frédéric's father, had helped man the barriers during the students' uprising in 1848.

'From a poorly paid law teacher,' he said now, 'my father has risen to become a senator, purely on his own merit, and I shall follow in that vein as he would wish.'

She should have felt deeply proud of him, but all she could see was this gorgeous engagement ring. It far outdid those her mother had left for her and her sisters, fine though they were – one a garnet, another a small pearl set with smaller pearls, the third a sapphire engagement ring that

Thérèse would flash on a finger only when really needing to impress; all three being otherwise kept hidden lest her father be tempted to sell them. There was of course the hoard of paste jewellery that stood her in good stead and which, when wriggled in front of those she was attempting to impress, looked as real as any. But she could hardly believe this ring was hers.

'So will you marry me?' Frédéric was asking, as if he needed to.

She stopped looking at the ring and raised her eyes, then her lips, to his. 'Oh, of course I will,' she whispered. 'With all my heart.'

It had been decided that they would be married the following September after he had graduated.

Her brother Emile had already got there before her, sacrificing some of his savings to buy Alice's engagement ring. Perhaps it was not half as good as the one Frédéric had bought but Alice wore it with as much pride as her future sister-in-law.

It was decided too that theirs would be a double wedding. It would take all year to arrange, for Thérèse had already decided that this would be a wedding such as none had ever seen before, one that all would talk about for years to come. Too long had she been in poverty's tracks. Now she was branching out on to a highway where lay her future.

Suddenly there was money to spend. Frédéric's father was proving generous almost to a fault. For all that he stinted his son – for his own good, it was quite obvious – she had only to mention needing help with some small financial problem and it was granted. Her family were already benefiting from it. Her father had bucked up miraculously. Emile, still with his belief in turning an honest coin, kept at his low-paid job but Romain had given his up, taking advantage of their improved situation. Before long they were moving from their garret into far more prestigious accommodation.

'The lease on our home has expired and I'm so worried,' she'd told Monsieur Humbert as winter came round. 'We've been notified of a rise in rent quite out of keeping with the accommodation, but we haven't the cash to move. And that legacy will not be mine for another two years.'

She could see she had taken him by surprise. *'Two* years!' his deep voice echoed incredulously. 'I understood it to be when you come of age.'

'I too,' she said, nibbling at her lip in a show of uncertainty. 'But it turns out I must be twenty-three. Meantime,' she hurried on before he could dwell on it, 'I must find my family somewhere to live. I do intend to buy them a really lovely home with some of it as soon as I come into my inheritance, but until then...'

She'd let the words die away with a shrug of resignation. 'How can I ask them to go on living where they are, paying higher rent to greedy people, when I know how wealthy we will be two years from now?'

It was a good ploy. The idea of a two years' wait had come to her out of the thin air; her uncle had swallowed every last word so easily that she could hardly believe it.

His answer was to put a deposit on a tidy little property she'd admired here in Beauzelle. He'd never seen the poverty in which they lived. It was an immense relief to her that he never would, now the family were moving to their new home. She thanked him for his generosity demurely yet profusely, saying over and over that she would pay him back as soon as she came into her money.

Of course that vow would go the way of all others, would be submerged by all the preparations for this fabulous double wedding.

Already it promised to be elaborate to a degree that would take everyone's breath away. Even those Toulouse shopkeepers who had earlier let themselves be swindled by her were tempted by her coming wealth. After all, with the backing of a prestigious senator as her prospective father-in-law, they would be paid this time and most handsomely – and not for one wedding but two. Why wouldn't it make the mind boggle and the heart greedy?

Even her two younger sisters' academy fees – Louis, now fourteen, had left his school, though its fees were still owing – had been put aside in lieu of a goodly lump sum when the young heiress came into her fabulous legacy. The sum was said to be several million francs, enough to put a glint in everyone's eye, from Gustave Humbert and young Armand Parayre down to the smallest butcher, baker and chandler.

Their new house was soon filled with furniture

and drapery, all of the finest quality – and why not, with people only too willing to give credit? The place hummed with happy voices, their miserable quarters in Toulouse now behind them.

Louis was the happiest. 'Never to see my school again,' he said.

He'd never been happy there. Strict, insensitive and heavy-handed, as his Trappist tutors were harsh with themselves so were they with their students. The young growing boys were expected to eat as frugally as they, avoiding idleness by spending their leisure time in hard labour as did the monks themselves and, instructed as they were by a mainly silent order, receiving punishment for too much chatter or for being too noisy.

A naturally talkative boy, he'd written to his father and elder sister on several occasions: 'I feel I am caned almost daily.'

It seemed to him that Thérèse feared to complain about his treatment – treatment meted out to other students as well as him, as a matter of course – lest the school come back to her with even firmer requests to settle the previous term's fee. She always replied to every request that she'd be sending payment forthwith. Of course she never did, yet she seemed to get away with it. But that was Thérèse.

Now he'd left for good, and good riddance too, especially as this new house bore no resemblance to that awful garret. He'd had to stay there when he came home on holiday, sharing the bed with Emile and Romain. A night or two

138

and he'd be yearning for the austere but sanitary and orderly conditions of the school, despite its rigidity on conduct.

But this new home his family had moved to couldn't be more removed from the previous one in every way. With open country all round, flat almost to a horizon broken by the few but pleasant patches of woodland, the rear of the house gave a glimpse of a little island around which the Garonne peacefully flowed. From the front they could see the squat tower of the sixteenth-century church of Saint Julien rising above the shallow roofs of the village. Theirs too had a shallow roof of red tiles, and weathered sandstone walls.

The two-storey house had a couple of single-storey outbuildings and had probably once been an old farmhouse. Shaded on two sides by fruit trees, it had a little orchard of cherries and apricots and a small vineyard. Louis was going to be very happy here. Even in November rain it seemed bright and cheerful.

Already Thérèse was making the place a home, imprinting on it her lively and carefree personality. As for his father, the years seemed suddenly to have dropped away from him. He was again telling tales to the people of Beauzelle, who were spellbound by his apparent ability to foretell their future and speak to the deceased as well as laying on hands to heal their aches and pains. Louis was as proud of his father's achievements as he was of his sister's quick and clever mind.

It was a home once more full of people.

Having left his degrading shop assistant job, Romain instead loafed about the house in the guise of protecting his sister. And at last Emile too had given up work; now he was in the service of their Uncle Gustave, as befitted the prospective husband of his only daughter.

Only Marie-Louise and Maria were absent. But soon they too would leave that academy and come home for good, and the family would be complete again. At least until Thérèse and Emile married and found homes of their own. Their wedding would be talked about for years to come, judging by the expensive preparations being made with ten months still to go.

# Eleven

Gustave lifted his eyes from the book he was reading to gaze mildly at the winter rain pounding against his study window, his mind on his son.

He felt immense relief at the way things were going. Frédéric's future had often been a worry to him; he feared the boy was too timid for a career in law with expectations of reaching the heights he himself had attained.

True, Frédéric was still young, maybe too young to marry. But what he needed was a strong-minded woman behind him and Thérèse was exactly that. It didn't matter that her trait for telling little lies came as naturally to her as breathing. It might even stand her in good stead. And, after all, wasn't that precisely what the legal and political field called for all the time? Once she and Frédéric were married, she would take the boy in hand and make a man of him, a confident man. With a woman like Thérèse at his side he would go far.

Gustave allowed himself a satisfied nod. One small thing worried him, however. As the day of the double wedding of his son and daughter to the Daurignac youngsters drew ever nearer, he was growing concerned over the authenticity of Thérèse's claim to this inheritance of hers and to the Chateau de Marcotte.

He'd made extensive enquiries, in secret of course – if it did prove to be fraudulent he couldn't allow himself to be made to look a fool. He knew full well how easily deeds could be forged. As a rule he trusted no one. But his niece had such charm about her. Even so, a man of his standing had to think of his position in society. Gustave lifted a hand to his full beard, fingers toying speculatively with the wiry grey hairs.

He was well aware of her reputation, her ability to convince even the most intelligent with outrageous tales. After having been totally sucked in, too late the victim would see how duped he'd been; needing to avoid ridicule at all costs, he would keep quiet. If this oft-related tale of Marcotte turned out to be pure fabrication, he too needed to prevent himself being seen as having been taken in by a mere slip of a girl with a nimble tongue.

When first he'd suspected something was amiss, he could have denounced her but there'd been his son to consider. Frédéric was in love, and putting a stop to the union would have ruined what zest the lad had for his chosen profession. Besides, Gustave couldn't help liking Thérèse. She had strength of will and an ability to spring up from adversity that matched his own.

Not only that, he could see himself sharing the vast fortune that was to be made from what she did – with the proper guidance of course. She was young. He could teach her poise and self-restraint. He could take her, and himself, into the world of big money. His word stood for something in the community. People believed in him. Even so, his legal brain told him this couldn't be done alone.

So far the girl had thrived on her vivid imagination alone, but if big money was involved, he'd need to make use of someone of like spirit to himself, ambitious and eager to accrue wealth and status. His confidential secretary, Armand Parayre, was a free thinker, a radical, whose wife had a soft spot for Thérèse.

Catherine Parayre was Thérèse's best and most loyal friend. She had known her from a baby; according to what he'd heard, had practically brought her up. If Armand expressed reluctance at coming in on this enterprise then he'd have a careful word with the wife. Without doubt she'd persuade him. Women were good at that.

Had he not been a strong-minded man, his own wife might have convinced him to steer clear of the scheming if endearing Thérèse Daurignac and her somewhat dangerous brother, Romain. But what did she know? Her dislike of her niece sprang purely from a woman's foolish notions of whom she did and did not like.

Yes, he would have a word with Armand Parayre at the earliest available moment.

Gustave remained at ease in his deep, comfortable, brown leather armchair as Parayre was shown into his study. With a friendly sweep of his hand Gustave indicated him to avail himself of the other armchair.

'Thank you Senator,' Armand replied politely as he perched himself on the edge, his tensely curled fingers opening enough to clamp over the thin knees protruding well forward from the seat.

Gustave smiled at the other's awkwardness. The man wasn't afraid of him, merely cautious, as always.

'Come, my friend, this is a purely social invitation. Something on which I need to ask your valued advice, that's all. What will you have to drink?'

Armand blinked at this unexpected courtesy, but gathered his wits in an instant. 'A brandy would be most acceptable.'

His tone was quiet, smooth and unruffled. This was what Gustave liked about the man, this deceptive composure. Deep down Armand was not all he seemed. He was down-to-earth, a perfectionist yet idealistic, and could become quite carried away by acts of injustice. Many a time

Gustave had seen those rimless spectacles topple from his nose to dangle at the end of their cord as his eyebrows shot up, had seen the upturned moustache above the small, dark, neat beard twitch with indignation at some wrongdoing.

Yet oddly enough, for someone who professed not to indulge in fantasy, Parayre believed in the famous inheritance and of Thérèse receiving huge baskets of fruit and flowers purported to come from Marcotte. She had often written about it to Frédéric, who this July would be coming home from university for good, a man soon to be married.

Blind with love, Frédéric accepted her word. 'It's actually her father's inheritance which he has generously passed over to her,' he told his own father.

Gustave wasn't so easily fooled. Who in heaven's name would believe them genuine when in one breath she told of the chateau standing empty and uncared for and in the next was being sent fruit from its extensive orchards? Who in God's name would be there to send them? If truth were known she was sending the gifts to herself, secretly. By now he knew all her ploys, but of course he said nothing to his son. Let him believe whatever he wanted to believe. It was all part of the game. He would quietly finance her. It was worth the deceit. Before long they would all be rich beyond measure.

Already it seemed to be working. The wealthy from miles around, hearing of the millions of francs shortly to come to the fortunate bride, were falling over themselves for her patronage, supplying everything from clothes and food to tablecloths and wine in readiness for the fabulous double wedding, the date of which crept ever nearer. But they must continue to believe. Nothing must go wrong. Not at this late hour.

Armand sipped the brandy Gustave had poured for him. Gustave resumed his seat but leaned towards him.

'Now, about this advice I need from you,' he began. 'It is of some importance to me.'

'Whatever, Senator,' said Armand, putting his brandy down on a small side table at his elbow and looking attentive.

'Cigar, Armand?'

'Thank you.'

The smokes lit, Gustave leaned back and watched as Armand did the same, settling more easily into his chair, puffing at the cigar.

'To begin with,' Gustave began in a deep, easy tone. 'This property that is coming to my future daughter-in-law.'

'Yes,' Armand prompted as he paused.

'I feel it may not be being maintained to the standard it should, without even a caretaker to keep an eye on it. I haven't seen it myself, but I gather it must be in some state of disrepair after all these years unattended, its orchards fallen into decay.'

'What of the fruits and blooms received from time to time by Thérèse Daurignac?'

'Those, I think, come from whatever village lies nearby. An old retainer, I shouldn't wonder, who wishes to keep on the right side of the beneficiary.'

'That has gone through my mind too,' said Armand.

'I have spoken to Thérèse, and she is in agreement with me that what we need is a steward to keep an eye on the place, someone trustworthy such as yourself who could manage and run it, someone to act as its custodian.

'But without the bother of having to be there in person,' he added quickly, having seen the sudden look of reluctance come over his secretary's normally stern face. 'No need to relinquish your position here. I could never manage here without you at my side.'

The face had relaxed. 'But I know you could do the job of managing the estate from afar, large as it is. We'll employ a surveyor we can trust to assess the restoration needed on the place, a local workforce to see it done, a good gardener to employ a team to manage the orchards and vineyards, and I will have drawn up a power of attorney allowing you to take charge of everything for me. Are you content with such an arrangement?'

Armand Parayre almost choked on his cigar. Hastily he put it down in an ashtray, picked up his brandy and took a long swig.

'I am indeed, Senator!' he said, the corners of his lips curling upwards under his moustache, his beard twitching, his spectacles almost ready to slip off his nose.

Gustave thought he'd never seen such eagerness as shone in this man's dark eyes, as he envisaged the rise in prestige that would accompany this exulted appointment. The man would prove a good and utterly loyal ally indeed. And if ever he discovered what Humbert was already sure was the truth, he would be too humiliated ever to disclose it.

Good, the first hurdle had been cleared. Now he would go to Thérèse, let her know that he for one was not fooled by her; he would put his ideas to her and assure her of his one hundred per cent support. What could she say but accept?

Thérèse was living the life she'd always dreamed of. Though Toulouse was a lovely city with large, open squares and wide boulevards, to one brought up in rural surroundings it had felt claustrophobic. Here she could breathe, gaze across open countryside with its heavy scent of cherry and apricot blossom, feel the freshness of the breeze as she and Frédéric wandered among tall poplars beside the River Garonne, and when autumn came she'd have grapes fresh off the vines, perhaps gather walnuts and chestnuts as they fell from the ageing trees.

Autumn. Not too long now to wait. It was nearly summer, her wedding only months away. She and Frédéric were deeply in love. Her standing had risen to new heights as the fiancée of the son of a senator. Who cared if her Aunt Marie-Emilie remained cold towards her, though why she had no idea. Aunt Dupuy had always disapproved of her anyway, so what did it matter? Today she and Alice were on their way to Toulouse to look for their wedding trousseaux and it was going to be an absolute joy.

Sitting beside her in Alice's dainty little chaise

– such a fine morning called for an open vehicle – she felt quite elegant and grand. So different from the last time she'd gone looking for a trousseau. Today there was none of that tension underlying the pretence with which she had set about pulling the wool over the eyes of the shop proprietors with her trumped-up tale of a looming marriage. This time her husband-to-be was truly the son of an eminent, respected figure. After all those years pretending, now it was true. She lifted her head with sheer happiness as she watched Toulouse draw nearer.

'Let's browse for a start,' Alice said, reining up in front of one of the more select dress boutiques. As they alighted a small boy scampered up to take charge of the horse, in exchange for a coin or two when they returned.

'We've the whole day to ourselves,' she added as they entered the shop, an assistant already hurrying forward to greet them. 'We can take all the time we need to find exactly what we're seeking. And there are plenty of other places to choose from.'

She spoke as if Thérèse had never lived here. Thérèse knew all about Toulouse boutiques, though this time there was money with which to make any purchase she wanted. Even so, old habits brought a faint touch of apprehension that she might not be seen as the genuine client they'd first supposed her to be.

Alice of course was quite at ease. She'd probably never had to tell a lie in her whole life, had certainly never had to pretend to be well off when she hardly had two coins to rub together.

With her sweet, engaging smile she moved, relaxed and confident, past the other customers in the shop.

'We would like to view your full range of trousseaux,' she said to the thin assistant who came towards these potential customers. 'They will be made to measure, of course, so we wish to look at what materials you have in stock.'

He regarded her with a calm, experienced eye. 'For Mademoiselle?'

'For both mesdemoiselles. My father is Senator Humbert and this is his future daughter-in-law. I am to be married to her brother and she is to be married to mine.'

She said it with an amused expression as he looked a little taken off guard. The next moment the small eyes gleamed with recognition. With so much being broadcast about this fabulous double wedding, talk already abounded, and here were the very two young ladies in the establishment where he was employed.

'Ah, of course,' he acknowledged in an even tone, refusing to display unseemly excitement.

'We are not concerned about the cost,' Alice said. 'We want to see the very best you have.'

'Of course,' he repeated with a dignity that might have struck a foreigner as haughty. 'We have a costume salon for ladies to view the latest fashions at their leisure. Whatever you wish can be made for you in our very competent workrooms. Naturally our brochures contain all the latest Paris gowns, millinery, lingerie and accessories. If you would care to follow me...'

Conducting his valued charges through the

149

haberdashery department with its scattering of plaster models draped in the latest fashion in gowns, its dark wood shelves and drawers of handkerchiefs, gloves, hosiery, ribbons and trimmings set behind sombre, dark wood counters where several lady customers were being dealt with, he led them to the salon.

With a flourish he held aside the brown plush curtains for them to pass through. An older woman and her husband were already in there, being attended to by another assistant, the woman seated on a small chair with a pink plush seat, the man standing beside her. Thérèse and Alice too were invited to sit while their assistant brought a thick catalogue.

'These, mesdemoiselles, are the absolute latest Parisian creations, which I am certain you will...'

A full-bodied voice interrupted him. 'Thank you, Monsieur Pirot. You are needed in haberdashery. I shall take over here.'

Having held aside the curtains for his assistant, the proprietor approached, his broad features attentive, the smile beneath the generous dark beard not so much ingratiating as full of dignified attention. With a shock Thérèse recognized him as one of those she'd deceived with her story of an approaching but reluctant marriage to the son of a millionaire.

At that time she had been pleased with the way she had fooled so many. And they had included this very same man, the last person she imagined to be so gullible, a man who surely would never forgive the humiliation she had put him through.

Now, as the dark eyes moved towards her, she was sure he could not but recognize her too. Her heart seemed to be gripping her, but the glance moved on to settle upon Alice, leaving Thérèse trying to relax. After all, it had been three years ago.

Holding on to her composure, Thérèse strictly avoided the proprietor's eyes, keeping hers trained on the fashion book she had been handed for the rest of the time they were there. Indeed it seemed that he was concentrating purely on Alice.

She could hardly wait to be out of the shop. She was almost overwhelmingly glad when Alice handed back the catalogue saying: 'They are all so very beautiful. I am so very tempted. But this is the first we have visited this morning. I'm sure you understand. For this very important day in our lives we do need to look further before deciding. And who knows, we may well find your establishment the most suitable after all.'

No sign of disappointment crossed the dignified features. 'Naturally, Mademoiselle needs to chose carefully for that most eventful day in her life.'

'A most eventful day in both our lives,' she reminded innocently.

'Yes,' came the cool reply. 'And may I offer my congratulations on the coming wedding.'

*Wedding*, not weddings. Not once had he referred to her. Thérèse was left in no doubt that she was indeed remembered, even though her coming vast fortune was now seen as genuine.

She could feel his glare almost touching the back of her neck as she followed Alice from the shop into the brilliant sunshine.

'Don't you think we should have ordered something while there?' she asked as they moved off.

'Oh, we will,' assured Alice, full of happy confidence. 'We shall give our patronage to every establishment we visit today. It's only right. But we do need to look around a little before that.'

They had settled on the main part of their trousseaux from a small, select but vastly expensive boutique Thérèse had missed that last time round. The proprietor was a happy man. If he had heard about the scandal three years previously he either had a short memory or hadn't connected this customer with the Daurignac girl. With the proprietor rubbing his hands at the money to be spent in his establishment, Thérèse came away deeply relieved.

All that remained now was the fittings, with the resultant magnificent gowns to be ready a month before the wedding. With nearly every shop in Toulouse supplying something or other towards this twin wedding of all weddings, the sole talk of the whole area was of the coming Grand Event.

Time began to fly by. Before she knew it, there were just weeks to go. The entire cost was being borne by her future father-in-law, as generous to her as he was to his own daughter, in some ways far more generous than she had ever expected.

\* \* \*

Rumours of the Daurignac inheritance had begun to spread far and wide. Gustave found himself hardly needing to put his hand in his purse; people were falling over their feet to accommodate his every need. In fact the very word inheritance was like a magic wand – one he had only to wave for people to part with their cash and goods without question, positively clamouring to secure his patronage.

Never had life been so sweet, now his daughter's happiness was established. Since his future daughter-in-law had all that money and property coming to her, of course people saw profit to be made. All were eager to provide anything that was needed towards the wedding, investing money, gifts for the brides, help towards anything asked of them, each certain of reward for their efforts. And he had Thérèse to thank for it; he now saw the value of those far-fetched stories she had told people in the past.

Reaping only moderate and, more often, meagre rewards, her failing as he saw it was that she had been a mere child and as such had made errors. Now she was a woman, he could guide her in the more subtle art of manipulation, an instinct that came naturally to any successful politician – that ability to look another in the eye and swear what was being said was gospel. And to be believed.

With him behind her, he and she could have anything they wanted. Their families and trusted friends like Armand and Catherine Parayre – along with whoever would become their mouthpiece, innocently or by design – would live off the fat of the land. This inheritance must be made to work for them. But they must go slowly to begin with. The celebrations for the grand wedding would be a test case.

Sitting back in the swivel chair behind his desk, Gustave Humbert smiled knowingly up at the barber from Aussonne.

# Twelve

'That girl still owes me money,' Tulard said to his wife.

Talk of Thérèse Daurignac's coming marriage had reached his ears some time ago. Trust her to land herself in a field of clover. But he wasn't surprised at anything that happened to her.

'It is quite a substantial sum,' Tulard was saying, trying not to appear deferential. He wasn't scared of the man but perhaps a little awed. Senator Humbert had risen to great heights in these last few years. His word counted in these parts. He walked with men of equal respectability, enjoyed a life of comfort and prosperity and was driven each day by his own coachman into Toulouse, to his council chambers.

Tulard, however, prided himself as not being one to be cowed by any man, least of all one who would take in a family like the Daurignacs, related though they were. It was known that for years that side of the family had shunned them, ashamed of their goings-on. Now suddenly they were all over them. Of course it had to be the promise of huge wealth to come, and that brought the well-respected Senator Humbert low in his eyes.

'Now that there is substantial money coming to the young woman,' he said boldly, 'a few francs wouldn't make much of a hole, do you think?'

Gustave leaned forward, hands on the desktop while he concentrated on toying with his well-manicured fingernails. 'May I ask how much is the *few* francs you are owed, Monsieur Tulard?'

'Perhaps not a great deal in your eyes, Monsieur Senator, but a barber, even a successful barber, can easily miss what is owed to him.'

'How much?'

Tulard hesitated. 'Er, near two thousand, monsieur.' It might have been less, but what harm in adding a few francs, rounding it off so to speak? For the inconvenience he'd gone through.

'I see.' Gustave sat back in his chair again. He looked at his fingers, then at Tulard. 'Then I myself will settle what you are owed...'

Relief shone in Tulard's pale brown eyes at not having had to face a humiliating argument. It had been so simple.

'Thank you, Monsieur, that is most generous of you,' he gushed.

He made to rise, a word of farewell ready on his lips, but the senator's gently raised hand stopped him halfway off his chair.

'Provided...' Gustave began, compelling him to sit back down again. 'You do a little favour for me.'

'Whatever,' Tulard said reluctantly. He might have known there'd be a catch.

'I understand your wife is an accomplished seamstress.'

'That was her work before we married,' he replied. 'Indeed, she is very accomplished, I might add. There is nothing she cannot make.'

'Then I should like to engage her to make the wedding gowns of my daughter and future daughter-in-law.'

'But I heard they have already been ordered.'

'I do not trust shops to find exactly the materials they are looking for. I would like your wife to help find the very best silk money can buy – from Paris, obviously – and arrange a small team of the best seamstresses to work under her instructions. Naturally it will include the whole of the trousseaux, lingerie and night attire, tea gowns, morning and afternoon gowns, dinner and evening gowns, costumes for travel, in fact everything a young lady would need for her coming marriage. No expense is to be spared. Corsetry, hosiery and footwear will of course be purchased separately.'

Tulard felt quite faint. His wife commissioned, with a free hand to choose the finest materials, the man willing to spend whatever it cost? Why, their fortune was assured.

'Of course,' he gushed. 'My dear wife will see to it that your daughter and your future daughter-in-law will have the very best there is to be had.'

Gustave rose from his swivel chair and came round the desk to put an arm about the man's chubby shoulders. As he was walked to the door of the senator's study, Tulard was almost beside himself with pride and the trust put in his wife. Just wait until he told her!

'You might as well include what you are owed in your final expenses,' Gustave was saying. 'Then we can settle the whole amount plus your fee in one payment when the work is finished. I assure you it will be the grandest wedding anyone has ever seen. And of course you and your lady wife are invited.'

*Of course!* How those words echoed in Tulard's head as he left. He still glowed from the touch of that respected notary's arm about his shoulders, as though he were an old friend.

Everything had now arrived, on time as promised. Thérèse's excited squeals joined those of Alice as they tried the garments on, items of clothing and accessories spread all across Alice's bed, on her dressing table, on chairs.

Everywhere lay hats and travel wear, lingerie, hosiery and shoes, embroidered gloves to match each outfit. And the bridal gowns themselves – beautiful, one a pale walnut colour, the other slightly lighter, almost cream, but both made in wild silk trimmed everywhere with Brussels lace and sewn here and there with seed pearls in clusters of tiny flowers, duplicated on the tiaras and the long mass of flowing veils.

The gowns were not exactly alike, but each took the breath away. Madame Tulard had excelled herself, showing herself to be wasted as the wife of a mere barber.

'She should set up shop on her own,' Thérèse remarked.

Everything had been sewn with stitches so tiny as to be virtually invisible. The dresses seemed to have been floated together; Madame Tulard, apparently influenced by the recent 1878 Paris Exposition of the Third Republic – the cost of her visit to the capital would go on her bill, of course – had returned with the latest Singer sewing machine. That too was to be included in the bill, no doubt. But the resulting creations were worth it.

'I'm sure,' Alice said, 'the boutique that was going to make them up for us could never have bettered this work, nor the material. Though I must say I do feel a little sorry that we turned the proprietor down.'

'As customers we can spend our money wherever we like and however we please,' Thérèse said, thinking momentarily of the past as she gazed in the mirror at her reflection, clad in the magnificent finished result. 'We did spend quite a lot there on other things, so he shouldn't be too disappointed.'

Alice let it go at that, engaged now in posing for the mirror in her own gown. 'It's so beautiful,' she breathed in delight.

Dispensing with the current fashion, the gowns were classical and exclusive in design, not crinolined or bustled but looped up about the hips in the way of shepherdesses of old. One might have said both were almost alike but for a slightly

158

different design of bodice and a different trim to the skirt, but both were divine, as Alice put it.

'Madame Tulard said she was inspired by what she saw at one of the exhibitions while she was in Paris looking for materials for us. She said it was now such a beautiful city. I'm beginning to wish I were going there on honeymoon instead of Tuscany. They say Tuscany is very quiet.'

'But you like that,' Thérèse said as a maid came to unhook the back of her gown for it to be hung away until their special day a week from today. 'I think I'll enjoy the hustle and bustle, it will be a change from the countryside. Madame Tulard said the buildings are nearly all new, quite different to the way once it was.'

During their previous fittings, Madame Tulard had said, 'I remember once seeing the old city. A long time ago, more than twenty-five years.' She had gone on to describe the higgledy-piggledy houses with their overhanging eaves, the tiny, narrow, tangled streets from which emanated putrid and unhealthy odours.

'We have the Third Republic and Baron Haussmann to thank for redesigning the whole of Paris, making it what it is today,' she said.

Alice hadn't been much interested, but knowing her own honeymoon was to be there, Thérèse lapped up the woman's words. Aware she was creating an impression, Madame Tulard had warmed to relating all she'd learned while there.

'Hardly a brick left to be seen of the old Second Empire. You'd never believe there was a bloody battle in the Rue de Rivoli one single week in May only seven years ago. Bloody

159

Week they called it, buildings on fire, our soldiers shooting down their own people and tearing away the barricades they'd built for their protest. Because, you know, seven years ago Paris was under bombardment from Prussian troops. Everyone was starving, they were reduced even to eating the zoo animals. Then with that ad hoc government, the Commune, upsetting everyone...'

The woman had paused, realizing that she was getting out of her depth and her listener was losing interest, as young people so often do when an older person relates their own history to them.

'Well, that's as it may be, but now there are marvellous green spaces and wide boulevards lined with trees, even new churches. They're even experimenting with electric street lighting. It's really unbelievable, all that light. You'll love it there, my dear.'

'They do say they had fifteen million visitors,' she'd said through the half dozen or so pins gripped in her teeth. 'And I'm sure most of them are still there, judging by the crowds I had to struggle through. The roads are jammed with traffic, it's a wonder more people aren't trampled under hooves in trying to cross those roads. They say there's not a hotel room to be had anywhere.'

That didn't worry Thérèse. Frédéric's father had already arranged for them to stay in one of the best hotels in Paris, overlooking the Champs Elysées.

The thought made her feel so very grand as she

160

watched the maid carefully drape protective cloth over the gowns before hanging them up until the wedding. Only a week away! Thérèse shivered with sudden excitement.

No one had ever seen a wedding like it. In the ancient church of Saint Julien the congregation was so tightly packed that it was hard almost to breathe. The early September sun shone down on the tiny village of Beauzelle as though bestowing its blessings on this day. Both brides ravishingly lovely and glowing with happiness, the two couples stood together before the altar to receive the sacrament of marriage, finally emerging into the brilliant, warm sunshine to be congratulated by, as it seemed, every single soul from every village for miles around.

Gustave had prepared for the gathering. No one would go hungry today, nor cease to marvel for years to come at the sumptuous variety of food, the splendid bowers of ribbons and flowers spanning the single village street, the fabulous wedding gowns and those of the train of the brides' attendants, the gifts thrown to the crowd and the endless litres of wine there to be drunk. Even so, there were some here who were not quite at their ease, among them Tulard, the barber of Aussonne.

He, like those other creditors, felt fidgety and he wasn't enjoying the festivities one bit. So much for the honour of being personally invited. People had come from miles around, whether invited or not, and no one seemed to care – Gustave Humbert was throwing his money around as if it grew on trees, which perhaps after all it did.

Again and again the famous inheritance crossed Tulard's mind. As yet nothing had been said
to him about the bills for the trousseaux and so
far it had been impossible to find Humbert
among the cavorting crowd, much less have a
word with him. Then suddenly he caught sight of
Madame Humbert.

Pushing through the throng he made his way
towards her.

'I do apologize for bothering you, Madame
Humbert,' he began as he came up to her. 'But I
need to ask, do you know when the Senator will
be settling the bill for the work regarding the
bridal gowns? My wife has put so much time
and effort into the making of them. I hope the
brides were happy with the finished garments.'

'More than happy, Monsieur.'

The woman's eyes were surveying the
celebrations, which still continued though night
had fallen. Strings of lanterns lit up the happy
faces. Music filled the street. An aroma of cooked food still hung in the air. Many had definitely
consumed too much wine. She'd very soon have
to call a halt to the revelry or it could go on until
morning, and if Gustave was happy to throw
money around, she wasn't. After all these years
of good living, her frugal nature still came to the
fore.

'And my bill, Madame?' But she was already
moving away.

Tulard followed her, aware he was being rude,
but he was desperate. 'Madame Humbert,' he
called. 'About the settling of my bill?'

She paused, only half her attention on him. 'Oh, yes, your bill – I think our son and his new wife have arranged to settle it.'

'Do you know where I can find your son, Madame?'

'They've already left for Paris,' he heard Madame Humbert say. 'They are taking the midnight train. I think that was where my son's wife said they expected to meet you.'

But no one had informed him of this. Totally confused, Tulard let her go. Then as something like panic set in he turned and shouldered his way through the singing, dancing, drinking, jabbering throng to find his wife.

She was sitting with some other women in the light from a doorway, a plate of food on her lap, a half empty glass of red wine in her hand.

'I have to go,' he panted as she looked up enquiringly. 'I need to talk to you. I don't want everyone to hear,' he gabbled on. 'Thérèse Daurignac – I mean Humbert as she is now – has already left for her honeymoon. It was apparently arranged she'd pay our bill for making the gowns, but I wasn't told. They're catching the night train to Paris and I have to get to the station before they leave.'

Before she could reply he was off. It was easy enough to find a cab. At such a huge, well-advertised event, people would need to get home and there was money to be made.

'Toulouse railway station,' he gasped at the cab driver, 'And as fast as you can go.'

Seeing the man's frantic expression the cab driver whipped his horse almost to a gallop.

He'd charge his fare a bit more for the inconvenience to a horse that wasn't used to such treatment.

Tulard hardly gave himself time to pay the man when they arrived, not interested in what it cost. After all, he was chasing six thousand francs, so what was a couple more for a cab fare?

Running on to the station platform, out of breath and sweating, he found the train had gone. 'Five minutes ago,' a cabby informed him.

'Are you the barber named Tulard?' the cabby asked, and as Tulard nodded vacantly, went on, 'I was told to give you a message. The newly wed young couple I drove here, or at least the young lady, told me she was sorry to have missed you and she'd settle your bill later. Oh, and by the way, she said that neither of them had any change for the cab fare and that if you turned up, you'd be happy to settle it, monsieur.'

Tulard stared blankly at him. 'How much?' he heard himself asking.

'Twenty francs should settle it.'

Twenty francs? What had she been doing? 'All right, and I need to get back to the village of Aussonne,' he said glumly.

'Right then, jump in, monsieur. I'll add it on to your bill, shall I?'

Tulard nodded and climbed in. This time there was no hurry. The cabby's horse took its time, his mind ticking in rhythm with the gentle clop of the beast's hooves. Six thousand francs! Six thousand francs! She had promised to settle up later, had she? Huh! He knew her promises of old. Six thousand francs! He would continue to sue for payment, but he knew in advance that he could virtually kiss that goodbye. And, in addition, to be insulted by being required to pay her cab fare!

# Thirteen

In the quiet carriage – very few journeyed from Toulouse to Paris in the middle of the night, even by train – Thérèse and Frédéric slumbered fitfully and awkwardly on the upright seats. Holding hands with the occasional tentative kiss was all their wedding night would comprise. To go any further under such conditions felt somehow wrong.

She didn't feel married. It wasn't as she'd expected, though she'd no idea what she had expected, having no experience of married people and how they behaved.

Her mother had been cold natured, not given to demonstrations of affection. She had never seen her mother kiss her husband and as for love, there had never been any sign of it, not that such things had occurred to her, being only fourteen when Maman died. As she grew older she had marvelled how they had managed to beget any children at all. She suddenly felt sorry for her father, probably never allowed to give full vent to his natural instincts. With Frédéric's hand warm in hers, her love was already a torment.

She thought of Emile and Alice. They would be off to Tuscany early tomorrow morning and at least they had a comfortable bed in her parents' home to sleep in on their wedding night. Though with people in the house, perhaps they too were circumspect. Yet somehow she didn't think so.

Emile was like his father, tactile, prone to put his hand on another's arm, or an arm around a person's shoulders. Their mother would never have dreamed of being so outgoing. Nor would Romain. He could be a cold fish too sometimes. But Emile – she could imagine him passionate, throwing caution to the wind and making love to his new wife without care for formality.

Several times she had seen him put an arm around Alice's waist in full view of others and even drop a kiss on her cheek. Frédéric had seldom done that. Stiff he was, but she loved him with all her being. And now she felt strangely frustrated that though they'd been married just a few hours, nothing but a kiss and held hands had passed between them.

She hoped she would find Frédéric passionate when the time came. She needed passion. He wasn't exactly cold, but held to certain standards. Perhaps once they were alone in their hotel room he might surprise her. She hoped so because she was passionate in nature herself. Even now she could feel a stirring inside her at the very notion of breaking him down when the time came. She turned her face to him.

'I love you so very, very much, my darling,' she murmured softly. But Frédéric was asleep, his head turned towards her moving slightly to the jerky sway of the carriage.

For a while she watched him. Without his spectacles he looked so very handsome, though he was handsome even when he wore them. Eyelids softly closed, the dark lashes fringed his cheeks. The lips beneath the neat moustache were gentle in repose. They were gentle lips anyway – a modest, moderate man, not given to argument. What sort of solicitor would he make with such a quiet temperament?

She knew at that moment that hers was definitely the stronger nature and that it was she who was going to have to take control and guide him if he were to become successful. And tomorrow she would assert that stronger nature by showing him how to make passionate love. The trouble was that she herself had no idea how to make passionate love. Perhaps her love for him would guide her, and him too.

On impulse she leaned over and placed a light kiss on his cheek. His eyes flicked open instantly, looking straight at her, startling her a little.

'And I love you too,' he muttered and closed his eyes again.

Smiling, Thérèse sank back in her seat and gave herself up to the uneven sway of the carriage. Lulled by the rumble and rattle of the wheels over the rails, she let her mind drift on what Paris would be like and the luxury of their hotel room, the two of them alone together. Frédéric's father had booked the best hotel in Paris, he told them. When Frédéric had queried the cost, he'd said mysteriously, 'No need to concern yourself. It has been settled by others.'

'I'm not sure what he meant,' Frédéric said later, but Thérèse knew, fully aware at that moment that she had a true collaborator in her father-in-law – nothing had been said in so many words but an understanding was developing between them.

There had been no need for her to worry about him. He was as sharp as she was. He knew what she was about and was ready to back her, the wily old rogue! Uncle Gustave was hand in glove with her.

Thérèse smiled, ignoring the sooty taint of train smoke in her nostrils, and let her mind drift, lulled by a profound sense of contentment and trust.

She awoke with a start at the train's piping whistle, declaring their approach to Paris. Her eyelids flying open, she saw Frédéric gazing down at her. It was as if he'd been standing watching her for some time, hand clinging to the strap for support against the violent sway of the carriage.

His lips were smiling with a depth of tenderness; the dark eyes, now behind their rimless spectacles, seemed to be drinking her in.

'Did I startle you, my love?'

'No,' she sighed. 'It was the sound of the train whistle.'

'We're nearly there,' he said. 'Come and look at the scene. I've been watching it getting nearer for the past few minutes.'

Rising and stretching her cramped back,

Thérèse went to the window with him. What she saw took her breath away. A slow-moving horizon of buildings, each beautifully sculpted, here and there an ornate church tower rearing above. She hardly saw the old grubby dwellings of the outer, untouched districts moving past the carriage window at a somewhat faster rate than the wondrous horizon as she gazed in awe at the city she had always dreamed of seeing one day.

'Come on, darling, we must make ready for when the train pulls in,' Frédéric reminded her, and almost reluctantly she turned back to him to be helped into her jacket and handed her hatbox from the overhead rack.

Taking out the small creation, she quickly pinned it to her expertly fashioned coiffure, her dark hair smoothed back from brow and temples into a neat, twisted and coiled chignon.

The train was already pulling slowly to a halt in a series of hesitant jerks. Frédéric steadied her, helping her on to the platform while he signalled for a guard to bring their trunk and other baggage.

The ride to the hotel had her mesmerized, and probably Frédéric too. The only words passing between them were exclamations such as, 'Oh look, darling, do look!' and, 'It's absolutely lovely!' from her, and from him, 'All quite amazing!' and 'Such elegant structures!'

Entering the hotel Thérèse felt she was moving in a dream. Awed, an emotion strange to her, she clung to Frédéric's arm as they moved through the richly furnished and decorated foyer in which beautifully dressed people moved or

169

stood about.

As Frédéric signed the registration book – Monsieur et Madame Frédéric Humbert – they were welcomed with a small, polite bow of the head from the man at the registration desk. Conducted up the curving, grand staircase to their room on the second floor, a *porteur* going ahead of them with their luggage, they were ceremoniously shown into the two spacious rooms that were to be theirs for the rest of their stay.

If the foyer, the fine staircase and their rooms had taken her breath away, the view from the windows took it away yet again, overlooking the length of the wide, newly extended Rue de Rivoli that to the eye seemed to continue to the very edge of the city, disappearing into the distance.

'What shall we do today?' Frédéric asked as, having gratefully got out of their now dusty travelling clothes, they began to unpack.

Thérèse straightened up from sorting out her dresses. Her eyes were bright with eagerness. 'I want to see everything, *everything*!'

Frédéric smiled indulgently. 'All in one day? We've plenty of time, my dear, to see the whole city at our leisure.'

'I don't care,' she shot at him in excitement. 'I don't want to miss a thing.'

'Nor will we, my sweet,' he said.

Thérèse snuggled up to her husband of three weeks.

'It's so lovely to be alone,' she sighed. 'We have hardly ever seemed alone. Even when we stroll together there are so many people around.'

He had his arm under her head as they lay in the huge double bed in the luxury of the quiet room.

'What did you expect, my love?' he murmured into the darkness. 'This is Paris. You wanted to come here. You wanted to experience the excitement of a capital city such as this.'

'Yes, but not so many people as this. You can hardly move down any of the boulevards for the crowds.'

He sighed in sympathy. 'It's all those who are still lingering here after the Exposition, reluctant to leave. It was marvellous though, wasn't it?'

She ignored the question and snuggled further against his shoulder. 'I never realized how crowded Paris could be.'

'But you loved it. You did say you wanted bustle and excitement.'

'Yes.'

'Well, that's what Paris is, my darling, all bustle and excitement.'

He spoke as though he had prior knowledge of the city, but he too had been just as awed by it as she; this was his first visit here too.

'I know,' she conceded. 'It *is* exciting, so wonderfully exciting.' She lifted her face to his. 'I can still hardly believe we're married. My husband, my own darling husband, it's been a wonderful three weeks. I so love—'

Automatically Frédéric drew her closer, putting his lips to hers before she could prattle on. In silence now, she held on to the kiss, her hand going about the nape of his neck so that his lips

171

would remain on hers.

That first night she'd had little idea what love-making was about and perhaps neither had he. After the excitement of exploring their rooms – she'd squealed in delight at a bath with actual piped hot and cold water – they had suddenly grown awkward, gauche and shy.

Undressing, she in one room and he in the other, she had donned her nightclothes, hoping he wouldn't come back into the room before she could clamber into the double bed. He hadn't. In the dark she had pulled up the fine cotton sheets and embroidered covers to her chin, suddenly very self-conscious, something she'd never ever felt before, and waited, feeling oddly cold and alone. He had never seen her lying flat before and she felt vaguely embarrassed. But without looking at her, he'd come back in.

In darkness with the thick, velvet drapes drawn against the gleam of the new experimental electric street lighting, she had felt the bed dip slightly under his slight weight and then the warmth of his body crept into hers.

For a moment he had remained quite still. Then his arm had stolen across her body, gently easing her towards him, and she had melted into his embrace quite naturally, grateful for the positive movement. Even so, she had been taut and rigid as he found her, perhaps making it hurt. At her small cry he had stopped, his whispered concern for her making her want to cry and causing him to fail. But they had slept in each other's arms all night and that had been enough for her then.

172

Now she knew more. Natural instinct had her parting her lips a little as he kissed her now so that she could better feel the softness of

his. She'd first attempted this on their second night, the slight moistness prompting a sense of urgency she had never experienced before, a feeling that strangely alarmed her and made her pull away from him.

He'd gazed at her. 'You feel it too?' he'd queried.

'I – I don't know,' she stammered. 'I'm not sure how I feel.'

At that he had gathered her to him again. 'I love you, my precious darling,' he'd whispered. 'More than I can put into words.'

'I love you too, so very much,' she answered, her tone hardly above a whisper. And if he was awkward she hadn't noticed, for she knew no better.

After three weeks, Frédéric had learned how to take his time, while Thérèse found herself hoping babies would come from it. When it was over and he lay back contentedly weary, she kissed him on the cheek. With love still lingering in her heart and the feel of him still with her, she snuggled up to him. To the distant sound of a great city still awake despite the small hours, she drifted into a deep, contented, fulfilling sleep.

Tomorrow was their last day here. Part of her wanted to get back to the new little home her uncle had bought for them (though she doubted very much it had been purchased with his own money!) and part wanted only to stay in this marvellous city with its open spaces and fine old churches, its gleaming new buildings, the gentle Seine with its bridges and its tree-lined boulevards – especially the boulevards with their wonderful shops.

She had bought and bought, Frédéric needing to send back home for more money. It had been an experience buying with actual money. But if she lived here, she would have to see if her old tricks still worked.

'Frédéric,' she cried next day as they stood one last time in the Place de l'Opéra before leaving. 'This is where I am going to live! Paris!'

Arms flung wide as if to encompass the whole of the city with them, she twirled round and round, to the astonishment and amusement of the throngs of passers-by. Her head thrown back, skirts swishing about her ankles, she gyrated until she was in danger of becoming dizzy and falling over.

Frédéric caught her as she swayed. He was laughing. 'Wouldn't you rather be mistress of Marcotte, live in your very own chateau with servants to look after you?'

She recovered herself to look at him. Somewhat astounded, she said nothing for a moment or two, unsure how to answer him. He really believed the accounts she had told him of Marcotte. All those different stories she had made up.

There were times she believed it too – not those stories she concocted to make it look even better than it was but the Marcotte her father had so often described as he remembered it when she'd been a child. Of course, it had been left

empty for so long that by now it would be nowhere near the great estate it had once been. No
doubt it lay empty and forgotten and unattended.
Those baskets of fruit and flowers with which
she had so beguiled Frédéric, and which purported to have arrived from there, had been her
idea.

Her father firmly believed in his inheritance,
so perhaps it was a real place, if little more than
a ruin now. But it was property. That she convinced herself. And it could be improved. At the
very least it gave credence to her tales that it was
all to come to her; the vastness of the sum could
be concocted to whatever amount she liked.

Besides, her father had solemnly vouched for
the deeds that he kept in his still-locked
strongbox.

From her small height she gazed up at Frédéric
in sudden fear. 'But to live there?'

He was still smiling down at her. 'Wouldn't
you like that, after all you've told me about it?'

Her fear began to increase. It made her angry.
'I don't want to live miles away from civiliza-
tion, because that's where it is. I hate being stuck
in Beauzelle as it is, miles from anywhere where
nothing ever happens.'

'There was the wedding.'

'And that's all over,' she pouted.

'Beauzelle is hardly a stone's throw from
Toulouse,' he reminded her, his smile fading.

'Too far for me!' she spat back.

'We can go there to live. It's a busy little city
and quite beautiful.'

'I don't want to live there. I want to live here,

in the heart of a great city, a newly restored city, a city the whole world comes to visit.'

She leapt away from him and again flung out her arms. 'Look at it! Look at all the people. Could anyone live anywhere else but in Paris?'

'Well said, my dear,' remarked a well-dressed, elderly man, doffing his hat and inclining his grey head in her direction as he passed. Thérèse coloured and laughed out loud, her fear and anger forgotten.

It had been their first quarrel, hardly anything really. By the time they alighted at the Gare Montparnasse to be whisked home they had forgotten it and were again loving towards each other. But Thérèse was determined that one day, and a day not too far off, Paris would become her home.

# Fourteen

Paris had captured her heart. Only two weeks since returning home and already village life was driving her mad.

'I intend to live there,' she told Catherine Parayre firmly. 'You can't believe how beautiful Paris is. There are churches as large as this whole village, markets that would swallow up half of Toulouse, and so many people. Everyone has to walk in one direction because it's such a crush. We swam in the Seine and bathed in the

Roman baths and I bargained so well with shop-keepers they almost *gave* me their goods. I bought so much jewellery, but we mislaid the case I put it all in. We never did find it. But I was able to bring home gifts for everyone.'

Indeed she had, paid for no doubt with the extra funds Frédéric's father had forwarded to the newlyweds. Frédéric had confided in Armand, the two men having become good friends, his embarrassment at having to send to his father for more money.

Catherine said nothing of that to Thérèse of course, but merely listened indulgently to this obviously gross exaggeration of the delights of Paris. She knew her friend well. Thérèse and tall stories went hand in hand. Despite being a married woman now, there was still much of the child in her as she expounded with closed eyes on the sights she'd apparently seen and the things she'd done, some so far-fetched that Catherine couldn't help smiling inwardly.

Thérèse would never change. Even now, after returning home dressed like an empress, she was going about exuberantly giving the most outrageous accounts of her trip, so convincingly that, as always, she had everyone believing every last word of it.

Catherine let it go over her head but told Armand, making him laugh. Later Armand recounted it to Senator Humbert, thinking to make him laugh too as they sat together after a good dinner, their wives having retired. But Gustave did not laugh.

'I need to have a serious talk with that young

woman,' he said, frown lines deepening between his brows. 'This frivolous imagination of hers could do us a good deal of harm.'

Armand also grew serious. 'I know some of her tales can be frivolous, but some of what she says does appear to have a certain credence.'

'And they are the ones that we need to cultivate,' Gustave returned, abruptly changing the conversation, leaving Armand vaguely bewildered by what he'd meant.

After nearly a month of hearing Paris endlessly extolled, Catherine was becoming just a little tired of it. Thérèse had bent Alice's ears too, hardly listening to her sister-in-law's efforts to recount her happy time in Sorrento where she and Emile had spent their honeymoon. Her first alarming sight of a volcano, the strange beauty of the rock formations of the Amalfi coastline with their almost magical aspect, the easy-going people – all of this seemed merely to glance off Thérèse, so intent was she on her own stories. Alice felt hurt, so much so that Emile decided he needed to confront his sister on her behalf.

He found her in a little arbour in her garden having taken shelter from a brief October shower. The rain had stopped, but she was so absorbed in a book that she didn't notice him until he was almost upon her. She looked up amicably but he didn't return her smile as he came to sit next to her.

'Thérèse, I need to tell you that Alice is a little upset with you.'

'Oh? Why?' came her mild response, her book

178

falling idle on her lap.

'How many times have you told her all about Paris? Have you once paused to listen to her account of her time in Italy?'

'She didn't seem to want to say much about it,' Thérèse said, confused.

'Because you never stopped talking long enough to give her a chance. You never listen to anyone but yourself, do you? You talk and talk with your incessant stories, but you never listen to anyone else's.'

Thérèse glowered, instantly angry, her words coming thick and fast. 'Well, thank you, Emile, thank you very much! It was my stories that once kept our family together when times were hard, remember? No one did any complaining then. How would we have fared if it hadn't been for me? We're all now living in comfort and now I'm being criticized for saying too much!'

Emile mellowed immediately. Though he'd felt he needed to stick up for Alice, who was no match for his sister, he wasn't a quarrelsome man.

'I know, but you could have stopped just for a little while to hear what she had to say. She so enjoyed every moment of our time in Italy and needed to talk about it. But you didn't stop to listen for one moment. She's upset.'

But as far as Thérèse was concerned he'd gone about it in all the wrong ways. Still seething, Thérèse spoke about it to Catherine who listened without comment.

In her turn Catherine related her friend's chagrin to Armand, who said evenly, 'Don't allow

179

yourself to get mixed up in family squabbles. The Daurignacs have always squabbled among themselves.'

'I know, though they'll unite against the world when in trouble and I wouldn't want to see Alice ostracized in any way. She's so sweet natured.'

'I wouldn't worry,' he said, tiring of the subject. 'As for Thérèse, you'll never change her.'

'I know. And she's my dearest friend. She can charm a bird out of a bush but sometimes she worries me. One day those stories of hers will land her in real trouble again, as they did when the family was evicted.'

Armand smiled. 'Despite that, it seems they haven't served her too badly. She's married into the Humbert family, her father-in-law dotes on her even if her aunt refuses to approve of her. Her own family are doing well, her father is well settled in. I don't think her tall stories, as you call them, have brought her to any harm. Quite the contrary, I would say.'

Catherine shrugged and kept her own counsel, but hoped she would be proved wrong. Thérèse was her dearest friend. If anything did happen to her it would be almost like bereavement to her.

Thérèse was not content just to tell Catherine of Emile's approach. She told her whole family, relating the episode in full, with a little embroidery here and there. They listened as people always did when she spoke, though at thirteen and twelve Marie-Louise and Maria were not much interested; nor was Louis, coming up to sixteen with his mind on village girls. Their father responded even less. Now a contented man, he had all he wanted – a warm bed, a decent roof over his head, good food, his brother-in-law providing should he need money, which was seldom now. Why should he care about small differences of opinion in the family? Romain, however, meant to stick up for his sister.

'I'll talk to him,' he said, so promptly and harshly that Thérèse was instantly alarmed.

'No you won't!' she warned. 'I know you. You'll start trouble and we don't want to rock the boat. This family sticks together and that includes Emile. There's to be no dissension between our two families. Do what you like outside, but we need to keep in with my in-laws. If you go upsetting them like a raging bull, my hopes for the future could be jeopardized. So leave Emile alone.'

As Romain shrugged his shoulders, she went on, 'I intend to live in Paris as soon as I can.'

'Can you afford to?' he asked with a small sneer. 'Your father's old friend, the barber in Aussonne, is owed something like six thousand francs for your wedding and Alice's.'

'That's not my concern,' she cried, angry again. 'If Frédéric's father chose to arrange our weddings for us, it's up to him. All I want to do is to get away from this boring life and live somewhere jollier and brighter.'

'In Paris,' he quoted, his lips curling. 'And you think you could afford it? What your husband's father still owes that man would just about pay the annual rent of a Paris apartment, did you know that?'

This time he didn't wait for her reply 'He hasn't yet settled one single account owed on that wedding. The amount might come to a bit of a shock.'

'*If* it's ever settled,' she said mysteriously.

Roman gave her a searching look but didn't question the remark. She had a feeling he already knew of the unspoken conspiracy between her and her Uncle Gustave. She didn't care, with him as an ally she could go far. She had a nice home and money coming in. But she was capable of making so much more. She so wanted to live in a great city. Gustave had money, but not that much. She knew by instinct that he too wanted more. And with his help she could provide it.

She tightened her lips and looked straight at Romain. 'I *shall* live in Paris. You can believe that. Have I ever not done what I say I intend to?'

Romain had no need to answer that. He knew his sister well enough.

It was her father who fretted most, remembering when her stories had gone a little too far, to the detriment of the whole family. 'Be careful, Thérèse. We're doing well now. Don't spoil everything.'

'How? How am I spoiling everything?' she demanded.

'With your stories.'

'What stories?'

'About Paris.'

'But they're true,' she persisted. Her husband

was the son of a senator, a renowned and respected member of the Third Republic, one of its earliest members. True, he wasn't as fabulously rich as she had first imagined, but he was far from poor and he'd do anything for his children. Her father had no need to worry, they were all well taken care of. Before long they could all be living in Paris. This she firmly believed, no matter what others thought.

None of them believed her. Even Frédéric was telling her to tone down her account of their stay in Paris.

'Aren't you tending to embroider it a little too much, darling?' he asked. It was his way of mildly telling her she was bending the truth a little, more a warning than a rebuke. Frédéric wasn't a person to rebuke anyone. But it dampened her euphoria.

The following day he dampened it even more by saying that his father needed to have a word with her.

'When?' she asked somewhat irritably. 'Why?'

'He said this afternoon if that is convenient. And I'm not sure why. He just said that he needs to speak to you.'

'Well it isn't convenient! I've other things to do.'

'I would indulge him if I were you, Thérèse my love.' The look on his face and the way he said it took away her irritability.

More and more it seemed everyone was prepared to come down on her – Alice, Emile, her father, Romain, Frédéric too, and now her uncle, who hitherto had smiled kindly on her. So now she found herself in his study.

It was a well-appointed room in his fine house, the walls lined with well-filled bookcases, a large, leather-topped desk and dark leather-bound swivel chair behind it, two upright chairs upholstered in the same shade of leather for visitors. There were two deep-seated, comfortable-looking leather armchairs with a brown rug, deep and thick, between them and a small occasional table beside each.

'You wished to talk to me, Uncle?' she said, unsmiling.

With a wave of his hand he indicated for her to seat herself in one of the two armchairs. He hadn't replied but went to a side bureau, his back to her. She heard the clink of glass. When he turned he was holding two glasses of red wine.

'From my own vineyard,' he remarked sombrely, offering one of them to her. Thérèse took it, wondering at this unexpected preliminary to a strict dressing down for upsetting his daughter. She watched narrowly as he came to sit in the armchair opposite her.

He leaned towards her. 'To begin with, my dear, from now on I wish you to dispense with the word Uncle. I am your father-in-law now, and it might be better forgotten that Frédéric is your cousin and that we are uncle and niece. For the sake of our social standing, you understand.'

So this was what he wanted to talk to her about. And she had feared a harsh telling-off from him, had even steeled herself to face him head on. But it might come yet.

'It is best that people do not know of any blood

184

tie between us,' he continued. 'It would not suit my purpose. So henceforth we are no longer uncle and niece, nor is Frédéric your cousin. I also wish you to forget that I once took lodgings above the shop of your mother and her sisters and where I met and married her sister. So whatever stories you tell, that one is strictly forbidden. Do you understand?'

'Yes,' Thérèse said simply. It suited her too, but what was he getting at? The answer wasn't long in coming.

Gustave straightened up, leaning back in his chair as if he were talking to an old friend. 'Frédéric tells me that you have been fretting, that after the highlights of Paris you find it very dull here.'

So this was it, came the thought. She should have known better. 'You mean Frédéric has been to see you specifically about *my* feelings,' she said bluntly, suddenly too annoyed to consider how discourteous that sounded. But Gustave remained amiable.

'It seems you have been constantly telling everyone that you yearn to live in Paris. He came to say that if I approved he would be willing for you and he to go there to live, if that's what you really want to do.'

This was unexpected. Thérèse felt her eyes brighten with sudden anticipation and wonder. She forgot to be annoyed at Frédéric for not saying all this to her face, for preferring to consult his father rather than her. But her father-in-law was still talking.

'I have advised him that if this is what he

wants, then by all means you both must go.'

Thérèse couldn't help herself. About to leap up in excitement, she almost spilled her wine, but Gustave stopped her with a sharp lift of his hand. He hadn't even smiled.

'I still have more to say, young woman.' He waited for her to calm herself before continuing. 'If you do both decide to go there to live, it will not be like your hotel with weeks of fun and enjoyment. You'll have to find somewhere to live. Frédéric will need to find himself a position in the legal profession. I can provide him with an introduction to an old friend of mine, a lawyer of some good standing, and the rest is up to him. I will not finance you both. We all have to make our own way in this world and should not seek others to make the going smoother. I expect my son to follow in my footsteps and make his own way, or he will never amount to anything as I have.'

Thérèse stiffened. 'But I shall be behind him,' she said resolutely.

For a moment or two Gustave studied those sweet, rounded features, the dark eyes often so innocent but at the moment full of resolve. Yes, she would be the power behind this marriage, not his son. If sometimes, like her over-exuberant accounts of Paris, her stories could still be wayward, the person he had once considered to be a mere silly girl was in truth a strong-minded woman, determined and in full control of her destiny. So would she be regarding her stories in the future – he'd see to that.

He put his wine glass down on the table beside

his chair and leaned towards her.

'I may sound harsh, but I'm confident you will adjust to circumstances lower than those to which you have recently become accustomed. You have known harsher and have overcome them, so you'll have little trouble.'

She was pouting, disillusion and resentment plain on her face. She really had thought he would continue to support them.

Speaking rapidly before she stood up and hurried from the room, he went on, 'Listen to me, my dear. I know how you once played on the naïvety of others to help you survive. And you always will, though henceforth not so much to survive as thrive. Of that I am confident. Living modestly in Paris will afford you time to cast aside childish tales and concentrate on the more serious side of your, one might say, *special* talents. You understand what I mean?'

He saw her nod very slightly, anger dissipating.

'I think Frédéric believes all you tell him. I fear he can be naïve. But you need to have him on your side, always. Do you understand?'

Again she nodded.

'You have always known what you are about,' he went on. 'And if you really put your mind to it, with myself as your advisor I know you will reach such financial and social heights as even you could not dream of.'

Now she was looking at him with such light in her eyes that he knew she could visualize exactly the picture he was painting for her. It had always been her ambition to rise above everyone and those eyes told him that she was suddenly seeing this coming true. He sat back in his chair and retrieved his wine glass.

'Go and tell Frédéric that you and he have my blessing to move to Paris.'

He raised his hand to stop her outburst of gratitude. 'Meantime,' he said quickly, 'there is something that needs to be done. This inheritance of your father's, the Chateau de Marcotte which some have been led to believe is yours, should be made official. There is no sense in it just sitting there. It could easily be used to raise money. I would be able to see to that for you, if you wish. But it will take time.'

He could see by her expression that she quite expected funds to come flooding in there and then. 'These things do not happen overnight and we must be patient. Leave it to me and we will see what happens. Now go and tell Frédéric your good news.'

He remained sitting deep in thought long after she had departed, hurrying away in a flurry of skirts, almost running from the room having surprised him with an exuberant kiss on the forehead.

# Fifteen

'I'm not pleased about your going,' Thérèse's father muttered irascibly, more as though talking to himself. 'Careering off to Paris. It seems you've no care for your old father any more just when he needs care and attention.'

He sat slumped in his chair like the old man he was, making the most of his weight of years. 'Our family has never been apart from each other, not since your poor mother died. But it seems that no longer bothers you.'

Thérèse tightened her lips. 'I'm sorry, Papa, but I'm a married woman now. I've my own life to lead. You've everything here you need – a warm and comfortable house in a nice village, no need to scrimp, tobacco for your pipe, food on your table. There's Marie-Louise and Maria to look after you and you've still got Romain and Louis around you. You're all living off the fat of the land now and my going off to Paris shouldn't make all that much difference.'

'Seems you can't wait to be off. And no love or thanks to your old father who brought you up.'

'That's not true, Papa. I still love you. And I do thank you.' She didn't want to say that it was her mother who'd kept them in funds, not he. 'But I have Frédéric now and I should be with him.

Surely you realize that.'

He didn't reply but, sinking lower into his seat, gazed into the blazing winter fire in the grate of his cosy little home, letting his lips and jowls hang down, emphasizing all of his seventy-eight years.

She turned away from him, exasperated, to catch Marie-Louise's eyes gazing at her.

'Wouldn't it be better to wait until spring?' came her sister's instant response. Marie-Louise at fourteen tended to act older than her years. 'I'm told winters in Paris can be cold and wet. Here it's much milder, even when it rains. You'll be miserable there, without us.'

'I've got my own family now,' she said a little too abruptly, making it sound as though she no longer needed them. But she didn't pause. 'Frédéric is my family now.' She saw Marie-Louise pout.

'Oh, go then!' the girl spat, her feathers ruffled. 'And the sooner the better as far as I can see. But you'll miss us before we miss you!'

Thérèse didn't want to think that she might be right. Parting would turn out to be a wrench, though now she didn't want to give her sister that satisfaction.

She lifted her small chin, vowing to say no more on the subject.

They finally departed in January. Unable to wait any longer, Thérèse had made her poor husband's life a misery with her fretting.

Just as Marie-Louise had said, Paris in January proved to be far from the attractive city it had

190

been in golden September. It seemed to her that it rained nearly every other day, interspersed with sleet, the sun hardly ever coming out.

While Frédéric went off to his office, Thérèse found herself spending her days staring at four walls or gazing down into the narrow street below or at the windows of the dull buildings opposite, wondering what on earth to do with herself. Bored and utterly disillusioned, she found herself thinking of the fine house she'd left behind with lots of rooms to explore. She had so wanted to come to live in Paris but she hadn't expected this.

Thinking of her family, she compensated for her faint sense of guilt by sending them fine wines, bouquets of flowers and little souvenirs from Paris. In a pretence that she and Frédéric were enjoying a fine lifestyle, some were quite expensive, eating into Frédéric's modest salary and causing him worry.

'We haven't the money to throw around on others,' he tried to tell her, but she faced him blithely.

'A few bits and pieces. I can cover the outlay, don't worry.'

He ignored or preferred not to know what she alluded to. 'We just have to be careful, that's all,' he said.

Conditions, of course, were not nearly as bad as they had been when she and her family had been forced to live in Toulouse, and she had to admit that Frédéric's salary was adequate for a young, newly appointed solicitor. That was, if one liked living the simple life. And his salary was promised to increase substantially as he began to settle into his profession. But for now there was little left after settling the rent – Romain had been right when he warned that even the most modest accommodation in Paris was exorbitant. Food and wine too took their toll. There was still a little left to clothe themselves, but what sort of clothes?

She had dreamed of fine gowns, costly jewellery, hair dressed by a maid, socializing with people who mattered, dining at expensive restaurants with good food and good wine and sparkling conversation. Instead they had to settle for the occasional dreary supper with the cheapest of wine in some nearby noisy, grubby little bistro in the Latin quarter, hardly a stone's throw from where they lived. It was colourful, but not the Paris she'd dreamed of, the one she had so enjoyed for three brief weeks on honeymoon.

Frédéric's father had been true to his word. When she wrote that they needed somewhere better to live than this tiny – she termed it sordid – apartment, he referred to his advice to rely on her wits. 'It will be good training for you, and perhaps something for Frédéric to become used to,' he wrote.

Indeed Frédéric was not so much growing used to it as worried by the tall tales she had begun to spin to almost every shop owner in the area. Very soon she was picking up her old ways and, with growing maturity, improving on all she had learned.

In fact he was quite alarmed that first time, a few weeks after settling into their apartment, as she pirouetted before him in a golden-brown velvet dress of the very latest style with the over-skirt looped back over the derriere, bustles having suddenly gone out of fashion.

'Do you like it?' she cried excitedly, after greeting him with a kiss on his return home from his office.

'Where did that come from?' he burst out, his suspicions already aroused.

She smiled prettily and did another twirl. 'I put a small deposit on it. I'm paying the rest later.'

'You can't.'

'I've always done that. It always works.'

'It's still got to be paid for.'

'Why?'

'Because...' he paused, taken aback by her innocent question. 'You mean ... surely you can't mean you don't intend to pay the balance?'

'I shall pay it back bit by bit. Don't worry, darling, I know how.'

Quickly she told how she'd spun a tale of woe to some gullible soul, she in her fine gown that always helped to convince the listener that she was not penniless, only temporarily out of im-mediate funds, waiting for her senator father-in-law to send her this month's allowance.

She saw him frown at this bold-faced lie but hurried on. 'I know what I'm doing, darling. No one comes to any real harm. I merely use part of it to pay the shopkeeper, then borrow more from elsewhere and pay a bit back to the first lender. It's so simple and it can go on for ever. I know just how to do it and in the past it was how we survived. It was a matter of—'

'That was the past,' he'd interrupted harshly. 'You're married to me now, my dear, and it's my task to provide. You don't have to do those things any more.'

She had grown angry, casting her dark eyes around the little room in which they stood. 'You call this providing – the two of us living here like poor church mice? Your father is a respected notary and we should be living up to his standard. But look at us. I was better dressed when I had to provide for my own family.'

'I'm sorry you think that way, my love,' he said quietly, his calm rebuke sending a flood of remorse through her at her sharp words. She slumped a little, chastened for the moment.

'I suppose I can always return it in a few days and tell the man that it isn't quite what I wanted, or that I found a fault with it. In the meantime,' she lifted her chin again, back to her normal self, 'we might go out to supper. I can at least enjoy watching others seeing me nicely dressed for once.'

'That would be dishonest, Thérèse.'

She pouted, angry again. 'I'm not being dishonest, not with you.'

'But it's being dishonest with others.'

'Oh, stop being so pompous, Frédéric,' she had burst out in renewed anger. 'We need to live, have more money, and that's all there is to it.'

Before her anger his temperament remained mild, his nature not given to antagonism. 'We knew when we came to live here that we could not afford to throw our money around,' he said quietly. 'Not until I was able to command larger fees. You did agree to that, Thérèse.'

No one could argue with Frédéric for long. 'All right,' she relented reluctantly. 'I'll return it tomorrow morning if you feel so strongly about it.'

'And promise me you'll be good?'

'Yes, I promise.'

But she had no intention of being good, as he put it. This was how she was. It was part of her, like breathing. How dull life would be without the joy of imagination and the ability to make it do things for her.

'But can we go out for supper tonight?' she begged, in such a small voice that he had to consent.

She was careful now not to let Frédéric know too much. Within days she was telling of an inheritance held up by legal matters. The eyes of the owner of the little restaurant further along the street, whom she'd lately taken into her confidence, had opened wide at her story.

A few days later he was hearing that she had to go to court in Lyon to hurry things along, but had no money for the fare or for expenses once she got there. He understood that his loan would be returned with a little extra for his wonderful generosity.

Frédéric remained in ignorance of the little hoard being put away. Very soon, loans were paying back loans, a little being held back each time as had been done in the past when her family's survival had depended on it. But now with Frédéric's regular income it had become a game once more. The dress hadn't gone back, but only part of the balance had been paid so far, the rest put aside to work for her in some other little plan she had tucked up her sleeve. And so it began to multiply. Her wardrobe too was steadily growing; she could now look the part, while paying out of her own money for the wine, flowers and presents for her family which she proudly sent as a mark of her achievements.

In triumph she wrote about it to her father-in-law. Receiving no reply, she took it as approval. Before long, using her wiles, they'd move to better accommodation. She'd have new clients, as she liked to call them, leaving the previous ones with no idea where she'd moved to. Not unless they turned to legal investigations. And she knew that few cared to do that, thereby making themselves look fools for being taken in so easily. She knew her trade.

But her father-in-law's previous advice was sound. Frédéric needed to learn that he could not alter her and must eventually join her.

'We're soon going to have to move, darling.'

Frédéric glanced up a little sleepily from his evening newspaper. He'd had a good supper. Thérèse could always provide good food, brought up from the restaurant down below. He was now relaxing after a long day. Today he'd been dealing with a difficult case and all he wanted was to sit and read, perhaps doze a little in front of the fire.

They'd been in this accommodation for nearly two years. He was earning better legal fees and had finally come to terms with his wife's activities. Although he still didn't approve, there was no changing her. She seemed adept at what she did but recently he had grown worried. People were beginning to wonder about this inheritance of hers and asking why it hadn't yet materialized. There were also concerns that she wasn't paying back all she borrowed, even though some had been satisfied. How she managed this, he wasn't keen to know. All he knew was that it was impossible to stop a woman like her, one to whom what some might angrily call deception was as natural as breathing.

'We should be living somewhere better than this,' she was saying, interrupting his reading. 'A man of your status. Successful now. Soon we'll need to entertain legal people. We can't do that here. We have to move. And besides...'

She lowered her voice, coming to perch on the arm of his chair.

'Besides,' she repeated, 'I am pregnant. We'll need somewhere larger than this now that we'll be raising a family.'

For a moment he stared up at her. Then, letting go of the newspaper which fell rustling to the wooden floor, he grasped her around the waist and pulled her on to his lap.

'Are you sure? Is it certain?'

'There's been no sign of my flow for three months,' she laughed as she put her arms about his neck. 'And I feel different somehow, here and here.'

She touched each of her breasts, which he noticed were looking much larger these days. In sudden elation he planted a kiss on her lips, then held her away from him in concern. 'Have you visited a doctor?'

'No, not yet,' she said blithely.

'Then tomorrow morning you must.'

Thérèse enjoyed abounding health, had never needed to resort to a doctor. 'There's no hurry,' she laughed.

'I think there is, my dear.' His forcefulness took her by surprise. She had not so far seen this side of him and she fell quiet as he went on, 'There is a doctor living not far from here. You can go there first thing tomorrow. I will accompany you.'

'But your appointments. Won't you be needed?'

'I shall send a telegram to my firm explaining my absence. Then I shall set about finding us larger accommodation in a better part of the city.'

She looked at him. 'Can we afford it?'

'I shall write to my father for his help. He will do that for me.' He seemed so positive and in control, he might almost have been another person. 'Now promise me you will go and see the doctor.'

'I promise,' she said soberly and he kissed her again, this time letting the kiss linger.

Thérèse thought she had never felt so happy. Already she could see the lovely apartment they would have, in a lovely part of the city near one of its many parks – at last there would be greenery to look out on to. They would leave behind the slowly mounting debts she'd accrued this past year and enjoy the luxury of the money she'd saved. No one need know where she and Frédéric had gone to, and she'd have fresh fields to conquer and thus fill in her time.

'That is all!' Thérèse couldn't help the outburst as she gazed at the money Gustave Humbert had sent his son. 'How are we going to find anywhere decent to live on that?'

Frédéric passed over the disappointment in her voice as he read his father's accompanying letter.

'He says he's going through rather a lean time at this moment. He is in the process of entertaining quite a lot and needs to circulate among certain people of influence, which is costing him more than he anticipated.'

'This is his first grandchild. Isn't that as important as anything can be?'

But she knew that it wasn't, Frédéric's loving smile confirming it.

'For now we might have to stay here just a little while longer. Not long,' he hastened to add as her face fell. 'A month or two at the most, until I can sort out my finances. We cannot let ourselves fall into debt.'

Thérèse hid her disappointment along with her growing concern. If he knew how much debt she was in, that she was at this moment striving to keep one wolf from the door by distracting another, so to speak...

So far she had managed to keep her head. Just so long as she stayed in control. She'd experienced this problem many times before, but she hadn't been pregnant then and it was making her panic, where before she had been able to think things out calmly. And she was becoming irritable with poor Frédéric, who was doing his best for them both.

Fortunately he put it down to her condition. And when she burst into tears in his arms, crying that soon she wouldn't be able to cope without help, he innocently assumed she meant help in the home.

'If I'm saving for somewhere better to live, then any hired help is out of the question,' he said miserably.

His words gave her an idea. 'I'll write to my sisters. They'd love to come and live in Paris to look after me.'

His expression held something like astonishment. 'Where would we put them?'

'Where you'd probably have to put hired help,' she came back at him, instantly but excitedly. 'We could make room in the attic. As you say, it will only be for a month or two. When we move somewhere bigger, they can have a proper room. You could make the attic habitable for the short time we're here, surely.'

She had it all cut and dried. Having her sisters here would be glorious company. She was so bored here. Telling her stories was her only enjoyment these days. Now she'd have her family again, or some of them. She hadn't realized how terribly she had missed them until now.

To her relief, Frédéric nodded and in a flurry of ecstasy she flung herself at him, kissing him all over his startled face, his father's letter crumpled between their bodies.

# Sixteen

She hadn't banked on her two sisters bringing their father with them. Five people crammed into the tiny apartment made the need to move all the more urgent.

'What are we going to do?' Thérèse cried, though Frédéric had hastily had a board partition put up in the low-roofed attic so as to separate father from daughters as decently as possible.

Marie-Louise's first words had been: 'We can't possibly stay here. We'll be able to hear Papa coughing and snoring and breaking wind.'

'It's only for a few weeks,' Thérèse told her, having given her the news of their imminent move to somewhere much nicer.

Her sister was not impressed, being almost paranoid about their father's habits of late.

'He is getting terrible, Thérèse. It's bad enough during the day when he does it at the meal table, but at night when we're trying to sleep? No! And to think we've left a perfectly lovely house to come here. We could shut our doors and not hear a sound. But here, with just a flimsy board partition...'

'It won't be for long,' Thérèse told her yet again, but Marie-Louise was not listening as she stood in the dark attic with its tiny window at one end.

'Romain once said that the next time Papa did it whilst we were at supper, he'd throttle him with his own bare hands.' She gazed at the flimsy boarding. 'And without a window, Papa will be in total darkness. We can't have that.'

'There'll be an oil lamp for him,' Thérèse said. 'One for you and Maria too. And an aperture could be cut in the partition to give Papa more light.'

Marie-Louise looked as though she'd been hit. 'Oh, no, Thérèse, that would be impossible! We'd hear him even louder.'

Thérèse's eyes had filled with tears as she again promised it would be only for a few weeks, explaining that she couldn't carry on in her condition with no one here to care for her and saying how much she missed her sisters, reminding them of all the sacrifices she'd made in the past to keep the family together, and all of it almost in one breath.

Marie-Louise's delicate features lost their resolve in the face of her sister's tears. 'All right, we will put up with it if it's only for a few weeks. But any longer and we'll have to return home.'

With that thought in mind, Thérèse redoubled her efforts at extracting funds, desperation giving her the fillip to do rather better than she might otherwise have done – shades of when the family had once upon a time been in dire straits. The money from these extra efforts to defraud, together with that already accrued, she handed to Frédéric.

He gazed at the heavy purse. 'Where has this

come from?'

Thérèse's eyes remained wide and innocent. 'I've been putting a tiny bit away ever since you promised to find us somewhere nicer to live. It's to help towards hurrying things up. My two sisters agreed and put something toward it. But please don't say anything to them. They will be embarrassed. They want somewhere nice to live too. And I shall see them recompensed in time.'

'How will you do that? This is quite a deal of money.'

'I can be thrifty when I want.' The look she gave him made him lift his head, as if in retreat from something he wasn't quite prepared to give tongue to. He said nothing more on the subject. Frédéric was learning.

She stood in the main room of their new apartment. 'It isn't quite what I imagined,' she said, a little subdued by the location Frédéric had found.

'What did you imagine?' Frédéric's sharp tone caught her off guard for a moment. He was behaving this way more and more these days.

She turned to him with a placating smile. 'No, darling, it's fine.'

'At the rents they charge in this city, it has to be.'

'Honestly, Frédéric, this is fine. I do like it.'

But it was hard to hide her disappointment. Pleasant and roomy as this apartment was compared to their previous poky accommodation, and despite being much nearer the city's more fashionable boulevards not far from the Opéra, it was still in a back street.

Nor did it overlook any of those green areas she'd hoped for. There would be nowhere to take gentle exercise in the evenings except along hard pavements, walking on Frédéric's arm for short distances as her waist grew thicker.

She made an effort to enthuse, dropping a kiss on his cheek. 'I do love it, darling, I really do.'

Her sisters appeared happy enough, their sleeping arrangements now out of earshot of their far too audible father. And they were now nearer the centre of Paris and looked forward to making the most of it, shopping, strolling along the wide boulevards, eating at fine restaurants and mixing with a better class of Parisian; they might even find themselves a young man who might eventually become a husband. Surely there was nowhere better to find a really wonderful husband than in Paris?

'We can't stretch to anything more expensive,' Frédéric was saying. 'Even with your sisters' contribution.'

'Ssh!' Thérèse warned as the eager tones of her sisters, off to inspect their quarters yet again, floated past the open door where she and Frédéric stood. 'They'd be upset if they realized you knew about their generosity.'

'Why should they be, Thérèse?' There was a faint light of suspicion in Frédéric's eyes. 'What is so secret about their generosity?'

'Because...' For a second or two she was lost for an answer, taken off guard, something she seldom suffered from. 'Because they would be embarrassed.'

'Why should a person offering to help towards paying for a better place to live be embarrassed?'

Her confusion made her suddenly angry. 'Oh, stop asking stupid questions! They offered to help and that's that! They hated living where we were and they were only too eager for us to leave.'

Having found her voice, her words tumbled out in a torrent. 'If I'd not accepted their money they'd have gone back home and then who would have looked after me in my condition? They left a lovely home to come here. And they did so out of sheer generosity of spirit because they are my sisters. And then to be asked to live in squalor for their pains ... I shall pay them back if that's what's worrying you.'

She stopped short as she noticed her two sisters standing at the door, alerted by her shouting.

'What money are you talking about, Thérèse?' said Maria, the expression on her youthful face one of perplexity. Taller than her sisters despite being the youngest, and far slimmer, she promised to become an attractive young woman in a year or two. 'We've given you no money.'

Thérèse stared at them, then back at her husband in dumb appeal.

His brow was furrowed. 'Thérèse,' was all he said. But it sounded so reproachful that it was enough to spark off her anger again.

'Very well, I had to find money from somewhere,' she burst out, 'or we would never have moved.'

'But you led me to believe it was they who gave you the money. You even asked me to say nothing to them. How did you get it?'

'You must know how I get it!' she shot back at him. 'If I hadn't done so we'd still be living in that awful apartment we've just moved away from. I and my family were reduced to living in a place like that in Toulouse and I don't ever intend to do so again.'

'But to obtain money – that's fraud.'

'It's not fraud! If people want to lend us money, that's up to them.'

'But you had no intention of paying it back, Thérèse.'

'I do pay it back.'

'By borrowing off others – robbing Peter to pay Paul. That's not the way I want us to live.'

'Whether you want it or not, you'll have to get used to it. I'm sorry if you don't approve but sometimes it can be the difference between a decent living and poverty. I know, it happened to my family. And you must have known how things stood. Even your father understands.'

'My father?' Frédéric was looking horrified.

'He has been encouraging me, he's even been in collusion with me. How do you think we had such a magnificent wedding? He didn't have the sort of money to pay for all that. We got the money together the way I have always done. Your apparently impeccable father is no better than I am, if that's how you see me.'

'No, I don't believe that,' Frédéric cried, his expression making her almost want to laugh.

'He's a politician, darling. They thrive by

doing exactly as I do but on a grand scale. Perhaps less noticeably, but they do. And if they can get away with it, so can I. So don't frown at me, Frédéric.'

She stopped, breathing heavily from the argument as she glared up into his face. Her two sisters were looking amused now, knowing her and enjoying the shock she had given him. At least Maria was grinning from ear to ear while her sister looked on with a faint twinkle in her eyes.

Thérèse became a little calmer. 'Your father is only human and so am I. And so are you. We need to look to our future. And with your father's help we will have such a future. But I need you to understand. I need your cooperation. Without it we might as well spend the rest of our lives struggling. I for one have had enough of struggle.'

Frédéric was nodding. Was it in agreement or defeat? Whichever, Thérèse's smile suggested the slow dawning that she might at last have kindled a tiny flame of condonation, however reluctant. Of course he had to support her – he was her husband. She had triumphed. But then didn't she always triumph in the end?

'Aren't we supposed to be going out this morning? It's so lovely and sunny.'

Maria at sixteen could hardly get enough of the Paris shops, keen to be off gazing at the luxuries to be had and very often coming back with something nice, usually at Thérèse's expense, who seemed to her never to be short of money.

Despite being in the late stages of her pregnancy, Thérèse was still managing to bring in extra cash to top up Frédéric's income. There was new prey to be had here: a wealthier class of person, but no less gullible so long as she kept her wits about her. She hadn't lost her touch; as far as she was concerned, she had improved on it.

Much of her money went on clothes, fashionable accessories, hats, gloves, shoes, and dresses in newer, lightweight summer styles with hardly a bustle to be seen. Some were obtained from the small, select shops typical of France, others from stores such as Bon Marché and Lafayette. Even these people could still be induced to supply goods on a small deposit with the usual promise to pay later, their demands for final settlement kept at bay. But that didn't mean she enjoyed doing the same for her youngest sister.

Luckily Marie-Louse had no yen for shopping, having discovered a little local seamstress, and purchasing any material she required from small drapers. Papa too was easily satisfied. So long as he had his tobacco and his regular glass of wine, he was content. Though on the rare occasions he did venture out he still liked to dress like a nobleman, had lately even taken to considering himself as one.

It was only Maria who saw what Thérèse did as easy pickings. If only she knew. It called for talent. It called for patience, imagination, something the others did not possess – apart from Papa, and he was now too old to do what he had once done, although he could still tell a tale or two when he wanted. Thérèse blessed her father for having handed on to her his talent. But for him —

'Are we going out today?' came the interruption. 'You can't sit there all day long. Let me help you up and we can get ready.'

Thérèse remained stubbornly in her deep, comfy armchair with its soft cushions. Maria had no idea how hard it was in this late stage of pregnancy to get about, much less go shopping for the mere pleasure of it.

'I'd sooner not today. I really feel I need to rest.'

By her doctor's reckoning she had three weeks to go, not a time to go browsing around shops. She should have begun her period of lying-in some weeks ago, according to her doctor, but she hadn't. Now she was feeling the strain.

'You were resting all night,' Maria pouted, disappointed. 'You've been sitting in your chair since you got up and it's getting so late.'

Something in Thérèse snapped at such callous disregard for her condition. 'Well, I'm sorry, Maria! I apologize if I'm being a burden to you! Can't you understand, I'm very near my time and I don't feel able to go far any more.'

'I can't go out on my own,' Maria persisted as her sister gazed down at her bloated stomach. 'It's not right. A girl should have someone with her when going into shops in a big city.'

'What is wrong with Marie-Louise going with you?'

Again Maria pouted. 'She's stuffy. She hardly lets me buy a thing.'

She had to admit that Marie-Louise, despite being only eighteen months older than her sister, was staid for her age.

Plainest of the three sisters, she'd soon tired of the excitement of hurrying from shop to shop or exploring the bustling excitement of flea markets. Instead she had started to enjoy wandering around museums and galleries and the many fine Parisian churches, strolling through its parks or beside the Seine. Markets with their wonderful bric-a-brac stalls had her wrinkling her nose. In the same vein she tended to be almost aloof towards others, especially men. At times Thérèse wondered if she might not end her days a spinster.

'Oh, do come, Thérèse,' Maria was begging, the brief exchange of words forgotten. 'I won't bother you again after this once. I know you must be beginning to feel all in. I do understand.'

How easy it was for a young girl like Maria to say she understood. Only those in Thérèse's condition could know how she felt. It was a chore just getting dressed, let alone venturing out, and she never went out of doors unless well dressed. A well-dressed woman was looked up to, her word honoured.

That thought suddenly brought a spark of anticipation to her. She could turn this one last jaunt into a little profit before preparing herself for the birth. Lately she had been making her distended stomach work for her before a sympathetic shop proprietor or two; with small, distressed sighs, one hand pressed feebly to her throat as though she were about to collapse, her expression would become weepy and pale. She could actually make her face turn pale and wan just by thinking about it, quite as easily as she could cause an embarrassed blush by pure force of will.

When asked whether she was in need of assistance as she held on to her sister's hand for support – Maria, acting as her chaperone, would, under her guidance, look worried – her voice would come faint and breathless.

'I am alone but for my sister here,' she would sigh. 'I have been forsaken for another by my husband, I've no money until a settlement is finalized; even my dresses have been taken, my lovely home is in jeopardy. A substantial legacy from a deceased aunt is coming to me in a few weeks. Until then...'

She would sink against Maria, whereupon the proprietor would hurry to assist.

It always worked. Recovered, she'd leave the shop with the dresses she desired, to be paid for with the substantial legacy when it came. It sometimes amazed even her just how easily people could be fooled.

If she worked her spells well today, they might come away with a few nice purchases and not a single franc spent. One or two items could be sold to pay for the goods in part, with a promise to pay the rest in a week or two. Paris was bigger than Toulouse. Here there were enough small shops for her never to be exhausted. There was every chance that she would never be found out.

She made sure never to say too much about it

to Frédéric, although he was now well aware of her transactions. He said nothing, but she had begun to observe a gleam in his eyes as he saw the profit of her triumphs.

'Very well,' she sighed before Maria's pleading gaze. 'I'll go and see what I ought to wear.'

As the piercing shrieks that had ripped almost continuously through the apartment slowly weakened, Frédéric was in terror that his wife would succumb before the babies could ever be brought into the world.

'She is having twins,' the doctor had warned after examining her.

He was one of the best. Frédéric's father had made sure of that. 'I've no wish to lose my first grandchild for lack of money,' ran the letter that had accompanied a sizeable bank cheque. However, no amount of money had a say in whether a woman might or might not die delivering a child – or in this case two – and Frédéric was gripped by fear for her life.

For nigh on forty-eight hours he had listened to her sighs and her cries, along with, for these last few hours, the frantic coaxing of the doctor and attending nurse. What he most wanted to do was to run out and down into the street and not to hear any of it, but love for her kept him here as the cries began to diminish. Then sometime that morning all went suddenly quiet.

Outside in the main room, Frédéric dropped to his knees in desperate, hopeless prayer. His wife was dead, neither she nor her babies had survived. Moments later came a thin wail. He scrambled to his feet as the nurse came into the room, her grave expression making his heart sink inside his breast as he prepared himself to hear the words that would inform him that he was a father but no longer husband to a beloved wife.

# Seventeen

His two young sisters-in-law and their father, who'd been waiting in another room, came to stand in the doorway. Despite their presence, the bleakness of what he was about to hear seemed to wash over him like a dark flow of mud, his world collapsed. He had never felt so alone.

'I am so very sorry, M'sieur Humbert,' began the nurse. 'I regret that one child did not survive. The other, however, is strong and perfect, a fine, healthy girl, and for that we must give thanks.'

'My wife!' he blurted.

There was still that grim look on the woman's face. 'She is resting. She is very weak after her ordeal and has not yet been told of the loss of the other child. It will have to be broken to her gently.'

But all Frédéric heard was that single, blessed word, 'resting'. He dropped to his knees again as if there was no strength left in him, tears of relief misting his eyes.

'Thank God! Oh, thank God!' was all he could

blurt out.

'We must give her a little time to recover, then you may see her,' the nurse said. 'She will need your support when she is told of the loss of her other little one. When it is time I will fetch you, m'sieur.'

Of what happened after that, Frédéric had little idea except that he was being virtually surrounded by Thérèse's two sisters, hugging him and deafening him with their cries of joy, for they too had feared the worst.

'I never, never want to go through that again,' he said with tears in his eyes. And those were the exact words Thérèse used as she lay looking up at him, her child cuddled to her breast.

'Never again,' she said with firm determination, and the look on her strained and exhausted face told him she meant every word.

They named the child Eve. Frédéric was surprised that Thérèse hadn't made more of the loss of the other twin.

'I'm only too glad to have been spared, not only this little one but my own life,' she would say each time the loss was mentioned and commiserations offered. 'All I need to do now is get back my strength and be my old self again.'

But it took longer to recover fully than she had reckoned and by the time she was fully restored to health it was well on the way to Christmas.

Frédéric had hoped that her sisters and father might begin to fret to return to their house in Beauzelle, but Thérèse would have none of it when he suggested they do so and became quite angry.

'And what do you expect me to do when they go? Get out of my bed and go down on my hands and knees to scrub the entire apartment?'

When he protested she continued to rant. 'Then I take it you propose to squander our money hiring help. Doesn't the rent this place demands take more than enough of our hard-earned savings without throwing it away on engaging help? Don't forget that my sisters come cheap.'

She'd made sure to say this when they were out of earshot, of course, accusing him of wanting to be rid of them. He tried to placate her, telling her that wasn't true, that he enjoyed their company; finally she threw herself into his arms in tears, begging his forgiveness for her angry words.

Luckily for her, her sisters had no intention of returning to Beauzelle, Maria having not lost her zest for the capital and Marie-Louise having happily dedicated herself to the care of mother and child.

Their father too was enjoying the comfort and companionship of his daughters. Now their brother Romain, having read Maria's letters to him all about the delights of Paris, was minded to join them. Not wanting to leave young Louis behind, it seemed the whole family were set to descend on this one small apartment.

Unable to prevent them, his wife badgering him too, the only course Frédéric could see was to open up the attic to accommodate them all, as he had done for her sisters and their father in the

215

last place they'd lived.

'If they come, they're going to have to contribute their share of rent and food,' he said tersely.

'They're not spongers!' came Thérèse's sharp reply, which brought a grim smile to his lips. If the Daurignac family were not the biggest spongers he'd ever known, then he was at a loss to say who was.

While he was left worried how to cope with the threatened influx, Thérèse seemed to have no such worries. By the time Christmas arrived, bringing with it the rest of the family, she was practically back to her old self, enjoying the pleasure of having them around her again. Her only concern seemed to be not having regained the trim figure she'd had before her pregnancy; all else apparently went to her head.

'Pull! Hard as you can!'

'I *am* pulling!' Marie-Louise responded, giving another strong tug on the laces of the corsets Thérèse had worn before her waist had begun to expand.

She was determined to retrieve the measurements she'd enjoyed before, but it seemed that her whole figure had changed, threatening to become rounder; her small stature would make it look even worse.

'Well, pull harder.'

'I *am* pulling harder.' Marie-Louise's tone was one of impatience. 'There's not another centimetre I can get out of you. It will have to do.' Despite Thérèse's protests she tied off the laces with a firm resolve.

'You're never going to be the same as you once were. You're a mother now and as far as I'm concerned you are being conceited, as usual.'

Hardly able to breathe, Thérèse turned on her. 'What...?' she puffed. 'What ... what do you mean, conceited as usual?'

Marie-Louise tossed her head, a habit that Thérèse found intensely irritating, along with an accompanying huff. 'You've always been conceited, Thérèse, and childish. Like those stories you spin. I so dislike the lies you tell.'

'They're *not* lies!' Thérèse cried. 'Some are true and don't you dare go about saying otherwise. If you do,' a touch of menace stole into her voice 'if you do, you might have to go back home to Beauzelle.'

Her eyes had narrowed and though she stood clad only in drawers, petticoat and corsets, something about her, those narrowed eyes, made Marie-Louise start back a little. They looked almost snake-like, venomous. She had never seen that look before and her heart cringed.

'And you like being here in Paris with us all, don't you?'

As Marie-Louise nodded silently, the dark eyes widened, became mild and kind. Thérèse was her own loving self again. She even laughed.

'Besides, who would I have to look after me? Maria wants only to enjoy herself. She can be a little minx sometimes, don't you think?'

Again Marie-Louise nodded, but her self-

217

assurance had returned. She lifted her rather plain face, her set lips twitching into a smile. 'And who would look after the baby for you if I went away?' she said primly, as if the boot was now on the other foot.

'No one,' Thérèse said readily. 'I really don't know what I'd do without you. You're a real treasure to me, you know that.'

'I hope so,' Marie-Louise huffed and turning, she walked with stiff-backed dignity from the room.

By February Frédéric's father was writing to say that he was increasingly involved with people of influence; great influence, he added. Thérèse had already guessed as much from the handsome cheque he had sent his son for Christmas.

Reading his father's latest letter aloud to her, Frédéric could hardly disguise how impressed he felt. 'He says his status is growing considerably and he has also become acquainted with the politician Charles-Louis de Saulces de Freycinet.' But Thérèse knew little about politics and cared even less.

'Freycinet,' he explained patiently when she shrugged her ignorance, 'was President of the Council and Minister for Foreign Affairs two years ago, though he resigned last year. But he still has ambitions, as my father has, and he is thinking to take up the office of President of the Council come next year. If he does, there is every chance of my father being nominated as Minister of Justice. It's one of the highest offices in France. It would mean a rise in status for all of us.'

She grew alert now. With all the prestige her father-in-law would gain, of course his family would benefit, especially his only son. Her mind flitted over the lovely clothes she would wear, the fine social circles in which she would move, a beautiful house in one of the best districts in Paris, perhaps a second home on the outskirts.

'What do Ministers of Justice do?' she asked, hardly able to wait for this vast change in their lives to happen. One thing she'd make sure of, that her own family would benefit too. Her sisters would marry well, her brothers too, and her father would live in the luxury he deserved and had never experienced.

Frédéric bent his head again to his father's letter. 'It seems the role would include overseeing administration management of the court system, proposing bills on civil and criminal law and procedure. He'd also oversee the career of most judges and advise on those of prosecutors against any form of corruption within the legal system.'

'My goodness!' Thérèse breathed at these high sounding words even though they meant little to her. She vowed there and then to begin to learn what they all meant. It would serve Frédéric well for her to know.

'When do you think all this will happen?' she asked, filled with excitement at the future her mind was laying out before her.

Frédéric smiled at her keenness. 'It all depends on whether Freycinet ever gets back in office. Oh, come here, darling!'

He broke off to pull her to him and cuddle her closely as her face fell. 'You mustn't let yourself be carried away. I know my father. He'll not let anything stand in his way and I hear that Freycinet is of the same ilk.'

'That's all very well for you to say,' she cried against his breast. 'But first you get my hopes up, and then you just dash them.'

Try as she might, it was all she could think about over the coming months, months that began to stretch into almost a year until she finally discarded all thought of the fabulous wealth she'd at first imagined. It was the story of her life: buoyed up, only to be sucked under again. It was so unfair!

Little Eve was now eighteen months and toddling, taking up all her time despite the ever-present attentions of her strait-laced Aunt Marie-Louise. While Thérèse continued to plot her little games as best she could with a child to think of, Marie-Louise was a godsend, despite her aversion to what her sister did, her constant fear of the consequences.

Thérèse, though, was making sure no creditor came knocking at her door. She'd brought shame on her family once and wasn't prepared to let it happen again, not with her husband a lawyer, her father-in-law with his eye to a brilliant future and her own concern for the well-being of her daughter. Having Eve always in her mind kept her one step ahead of those she beguiled.

As usual, she said little to Frédéric, who preferred to remain ignorant of how money sometimes came into the home. She played her hand skilfully and was always the one to come out on top. But her gains remained small, leaving her still dreaming of that big haul some day.

This Christmas Eve saw the whole family around the festive table. Her brothers Romain and Louis had arrived in Paris a few weeks before. Romain had more or less invited himself though she was glad to see him.

'We're staying in case you may be in need of protection,' he told her. 'I'll stop anyone who tries to come back at you.'

Of that she had no doubt. Romain at twenty-two had grown thick-set. Though not tall he was dark in looks, while the lips behind his beard and moustache held a certain grimness about them; if he chanced to smile, his expression would twist as though he knew more than he admitted. From beneath heavy brows the dark, smouldering eyes could charm a woman, or with equal ease instil fear into an opponent.

'If you do get yourself into trouble,' he said, 'your husband is going to be of little use. He's too damned meek and mild.'

'He is a lawyer,' she reminded him. 'He has a wonderful legal brain. He can outsmart anyone. He can be persuasive in dealing with anyone who'd dare besmirch my name, and all without need of violence.'

A gleam stole into Romain's dark eyes. 'What makes you think I need to use violence?' he asked with an innocence that made her smile.

'I know you,' she said lightly. 'But life in this elegant city calls for subtler methods when handling a crisis.'

'Not everywhere in this city is elegant,' he said in a tone that made her shiver, imagining a person on the wrong end of his temper.

'Frédéric will look out for me,' she said dismissively.

'And so will I,' Romain said.

She didn't need to argue. In fact it was good to know that should anything go wrong, if one way failed to put it right, there was always that other way. Between her mild-tempered, clever husband and her watchful and somewhat intimidating brother, she felt she would be well protected.

Thinking this Thérèse suddenly felt a frisson of premonition, but she ignored the slight shiver and sternly asked of herself, as she smiled at her brother, what on earth could ever go wrong. So far she'd had a charmed life and as far as she was concerned she always would.

'I know you will,' she said lightly, taking his arm and going with him into the small dining room that was already crammed with the rest of her family, ready to enjoy their traditional Christmas Eve feast.

# Eighteen

So much for gloomy premonition, the New Year could hardly have opened to more promise. This time Thérèse really could see a brilliant future stretching ahead of her as, near the end of January, Frédéric excitedly read out his father's letter. The first sound to escape him was a yelp of joy, utterly unlike his usual calm and collected self.

'It's happened! Charles Freycinet has been made President of the Council and Minister of Foreign Affairs. He's asked my father to be Minister of Justice in his cabinet. I knew it! I knew it all along! I knew all my father's efforts would eventually reap benefits. He's worked so hard for this.'

He looked up, his brown eyes shining. 'He's coming to live in Paris and Alice and your brother Emile are coming with him. He wants Armand Parayre and his wife and children to come too. Parayre has always been a close confidant and a good friend.'

Thérèse knew that already. But having Catherine come to live here in Paris! That was wonderful. She had missed her so much since moving away. She no longer needed Catherine's protection as she had when she was a child,

Frédéric was here at her side now, but that old memory still lingered. Now they'd be together again. Excitement gripped her.

'You know what this means, don't you?' Frédéric was saying.

Her mind miles away, he smiled at her as if she were an idiot. 'It means my father will be a wealthy man. His letter says that he intends me to become his principal private secretary and we'll have a house to live in – an entire house to ourselves instead of an apartment.'

'Can we choose where we want to live?' she broke in, hardly able to believe what she was hearing. 'And have servants?'

'You can have anything you like, sweetest.'

'A private carriage?'

'I can't see why not. A carriage and pair.'

In her excitement, she threw herself at Frédéric. Taking him off guard, she pulled his head down to her small height to plant kisses all over his face. The beard he now sported felt soft against her skin, making her tingle all over.

At this moment she felt she loved this man with all her being. As his arms came around her in response to her display of affection, she could have let him make love to her right here. It would have been so wonderfully wicked, here in the odd-shaped living room still lit on this dim early morning. But the window was overlooked by those situated just across the street. Anyone there could see straight in here.

Perhaps he realized too as he gently eased her arms from his neck. Although she knew they would never have behaved in such an abandoned

224

manner, knew he felt as much for her as she did for him, she felt hurt. Pouting, she moved away.

'And I mean to make use of our new prosperity,' she said petulantly

'One thing,' he added with a smile. 'You'll have no need to worry yourself, my darling, contributing to the family income as you've done in the past – in your fashion. I was always somewhat uncomfortable with that.'

Thérèse swung round to face him, her eyes widening with disbelief. What was he trying to say? That all those wonderful stories of hers were untrue? They were *not* untrue – not in the sense he seemed to be making them out to be.

From as far back as she could remember they had been more to her than what the sceptical and unbelievers had passed off as vivid imagination. They did have foundation. She believed it. They had taken her off to another world without which she could never have existed, filled her with a belief that some day it would all come true. From a child she had always believed in them, so how could they be untrue? And if people had been fooled into parting with a little cash, it was up to them. She had never forced money out of anyone, though she had needed their help at times.

These days she was old enough to view her stories with a mature eye. Maybe she herself was no longer carried away by them as she had once been. These days it was more important to persuade others to believe enough in this fabulous inheritance of hers to want to invest in it, while at the same time she gained respect and prestige.

She knew now exactly what she was doing and where she was going. But without Frédéric's support and belief in her, it might all fall apart.

With a sense of having been deeply wronged, she almost yielded to a fierce defence of what to her was second nature. Instead she continued to stare at him without speaking. Then something inside her seemed to give way and very quietly she replied to his question.

'No.'

The word held a double meaning – either she was concurring with him or disagreeing. Frédéric appeared satisfied anyway and put his arms about her, his father's letter dropped on to a small side table.

'I do really love you, my sweet girl,' he whispered. 'You can be so unpredictable. It's what makes you so wonderfully exciting.'

His lips closed upon hers but this time it was she who pulled away from him, still feeling resentful. Her glance went to the lighted window opposite.

'We'll be seen,' she reminded him, using it as an excuse to slip out of his grasp.

Couldn't he see that without giving vent to her imagination she might as well not exist? It was part of her very soul. To give it all up now just because fortune was beginning to smile on them would be like a death knell. She could no more let all those wonderful stories die than cease to breathe.

She loved Frédéric very much but he was a gentle coward, unlike his father. With the help of Frédéric's father she could see them making vast fortunes.

From things Gustave Humbert had said in the past, she felt he still half believed in her stories. And even if he didn't, with his rapidly growing credibility he would make sure others believed in them. Gustave Humbert too needed to make a fortune, she knew that all too well. She could hardly wait for him to arrive.

All was bustle and excitement. For the next few days her feet hardly touched the ground. When the dignified figure of the new Minister of Justice, balding, bespectacled and bearded, arrived in Paris to take up his appointment to the highest legal office in France, Thérèse's entire family went to the railway station to greet him, together with a huge crowd of welcoming supporters that she had drummed up.

'The whole of Paris must remember today,' she said to Frédéric the day before, as if visiting royalty was about to show up.

'I don't see the need for all this display,' he told her. 'It might appear too ostentatious. We don't want to make enemies. I don't like it.'

'We need to cause a stir in people's minds so they will not forget us,' she reminded him with firm resolve.

And a stir she caused, having arranged for a brass band to play when the eminent man alighted from the train, while hired carriages would take the many invited guests back to his new residence where a huge party of welcome awaited him.

Frédéric stayed by his father's side, smiling at

everyone, but Thérèse could see he wasn't happy.

The whole reception had apparently been put on at her own expense and she was making sure everyone in Paris was aware of it, gained the impression that money was no object. And money always comes to money – no one was more aware of that than she.

It didn't matter if Frédéric disapproved so long as it reaped dividends. She had visited several emporiums and small banking firms, suggesting the need to welcome the new Minister of Justice. 'I am of course bearing the whole cost myself since I will be coming into a small inheritance,' she told them. 'I hear it is around one hundred million francs.'

As she enlarged on the fabulous property which was soon to be hers, it was heartening to see their eyes widen with anticipation as the amount fell casually from her full lips. For who would ever lie about such a thing? Certainly not a daughter-in-law of the Minister of Justice.

Hot on the revelation of this large sum, she had casually dropped a word that the slightest delay would jeopardize the planned reception for the new minister.

'It would be a great pity for it to fall through for the lack of sufficient funds by a mere week or two,' she'd sighed to each of them. It was still a wonder to her that no one had questioned the validity of her story, but each had been only too eager to outdo their rivals, whose large contributions she had made sure to quote.

'Think of this as an investment. The moment

my money arrives, the loan will be repaid in full plus interest,' she had told them, quoting a rate far above their expectations, one that had their eyes opening even wider even as they made a great play of waving away the figure she'd quoted.

It never failed to make her smile. Greed always got the better of people.

During the reception party she confided to Gustave how it had been funded. 'I did my best,' she said demurely and received his approving nod.

'Nothing about you surprises me any more,' he beamed at her as the hundreds of guests finally departed. 'You have an amazing wife,' he said to Frédéric afterwards. 'Together you will go far, I can guarantee that.'

As the family said their farewells to him, he took Thérèse aside. 'Come and see me in the morning. Around ten o'clock. I need to speak with you.'

'Frédéric and I will be happy to...'

'No, my dear, come alone,' he urged. 'Come to my office.'

Thérèse sat opposite Gustave Humbert in his luxurious office. She had told Frédéric she was going to visit a lady who was making a gown for her.

'Alone?' he had queried.

'I shall be safe enough in a carriage and I'm not going far, only as far as Madame Martell's.'

'Why don't you ask Catherine to go with you?'

'Perhaps another day,' she'd said quickly. 'I

may be some time. She might become bored. And no doubt she needs to settle into her new home. There must be so much unpacking to do.'

'As do we,' he'd said. 'Our own house will be ready in a week's time.'

'And I need an hour or two to look for beautiful things to fill it with after I leave Madame Martell,' she said gaily, as he smiled after her.

Out of sight she gave the carriage driver the address of Gustave's official quarters. He was dismissed the moment they arrived, for she had no idea how long Gustave was going to keep her.

They spoke now over coffee, he settled in a leather upholstered high-backed chair with curved, leather-padded arms, she in one similar to his.

'So, young lady, you've been busy I gather. I commend you for your skill in funding my reception, and thank you. But this is Paris, Thérèse, not Beauzelle or Aussonne or even Toulouse. People here expect value for money and make no small noise about debts that remain unsettled. They are not easily fooled, like country rustics. If you do not honour these loans they will be at your throat, make no mistake about it.'

Until now she hadn't given the repayment of the loans a thought – she'd always got away with it. But it came to her with a jolt that perhaps he was right. This was Paris, hard-headed Paris, full of hard-headed Parisians who would not be gullible enough to wait overlong for repayment. A seed of doubt crept into her mind as she stared at Gustave.

'Parisians are as concerned about their good name as anyone,' she answered glibly, putting on a brave face. 'Each one of those I spoke to was only too ready to outdo the others. I doubt any of them will be too keen to be seen as having been taken in by a country girl.'

He was smiling at her. 'Clever,' he remarked. 'Even so, it was rather a dangerous game you were playing. It's a good thing you now have the weight of my office behind you.' He grew suddenly serious.

'Having said that, this borrowing from petty shopkeepers must stop. If we are going to make anything like a fortune, we must cast our net wider and safely. I now have extensive and excellent connections, my dear, and from now on you should look to me for guidance before you go dashing off with your wild stories. Everything needs to be carefully planned. No rushing off on a whim to negotiate a little loan here and a little loan there so you can buy a pretty little gown or two, throw some petty little party as the fancy takes you. This must be a serious business venture.'

Thérèse stared. He was colluding with her! She watched him put down the coffee cup and lean towards her. 'Listen to me, my dear,' he said slowly. 'This is important. There must be no foolish mistakes. I cannot afford to see my reputation damaged. And before we go any further I will pay back in full all you have borrowed for this surprise reception of yours, plus whatever interest you quoted.'

She wasn't sure that she wanted all this. She'd

always enjoyed the thrill of telling her stories. Now it threatened to become cold business and she feared the pleasure would go out of it.

He was still talking. 'Now, this anonymous benefactor of yours in Portugal, I think you have given him more than one name in the past.'

That was true. The man had several names, as varied as his history. She tried to remember, but her head was suddenly empty.

He watched her expression. 'I seem to recall your mentioning someone by the name of Crawford some years ago.'

Thérèse brightened. 'He was someone my mother took care of when she found him collapsed in the street – at least I think that was how it went.'

'Something like that,' he said amiably. A crafty look appeared on his face. 'Now I think I can contribute a little more to your Mr Crawford.'

He was speaking as if the man was a real person, so much so that she was ready to believe it too. The tales had become blurred with time but she did recall once telling of how a man named Crawford had collapsed of a heart attack on a train on which she was travelling. She had administered smelling salts and he had been so grateful that when he finally died a few years later he left all his wealth to her.

A childish story, but she had believed there was some truth in it, as she'd so often come to believe in all that she told. But it was best not to mention this version and complicate matters.

'Your mother,' Gustave was saying, his bearded countenance now stern and serious. 'Did she not take care of this man at one time? And as far as I gather, was he not an American who eventually married a Portuguese heiress?' She couldn't quite remember but she nodded nevertheless.

'Didn't his wife die not long after their marriage,' he went on, leaning back in his chair, 'leaving him all her considerable property in Portugal?'

Yes, she did remember something about that as she listened to Gustave droning on as if half asleep.

'Did he not remarry an American? I believe they died in the United States leaving no issue. But he had two nephews. Robert and Henry?'

'If he had nephews,' Thérèse broke in, 'why bequeath his property in Portugal to me?'

'Ah!' Gustave gazed up at the ceiling. 'But of course one is not duty bound to consider one's family. One can bequeath one's property to someone else, in this case you. There are still those so-called title deeds in your father's strongbox attesting to that truth.'

He gave Thérèse a shrewd smile. 'I have been making sure that there has been a good deal of interest in the contents of that strongbox. Some believe it holds money, jewels, gold, others that it contains stocks and bonds and papers proving your right as heiress to that vast estate in Portugal with its olive plantations and vineyards.'

This was the first time she had ever heard of olive plantations, but she remained silent as Gustave continued.

'Now, if your inheritance were to be contested by Crawford's nephews, resulting in delays, then those who have already invested substantial sums in that property – and they will – must likewise wait to see their money. In the meantime our credit will be reaping very handsome profits.'

Explaining it all in simple terms she could understand, he looked pleased by her resultant eager expression, but his own smile had faded.

'This could work very well for us in the long term. Meanwhile your father's strongbox must be guarded at all times with the utmost care, safe from public view, not to be opened until the time is ripe.'

He stood up, their meeting concluded. 'Leave the necessary dealings to me, my dear,' he said as she too got to her feet, smoothing her silk skirt free of creases. 'Concentrate on the house being prepared for you and your husband. I will call on you as and when necessary.'

She was already seeing how enormously this business could grow, but what about Frédéric? He hated the way she had always gone about gaining money. How would he feel if it grew any bigger? She mentioned it to Gustave and saw him smile craftily. 'Leave Frédéric to me,' he said slowly. 'I shall have a quiet word with him.'

Whatever the quiet word was, Frédéric came home a different person.

'I'm taking up my position as principal private secretary to the Justice Minister as from tomorrow,' he announced proudly at the end of January. 'Father has shown me my office and it's really grand. Next week we move into our new home. He assures me that if I work well with him it won't stop there, and that soon we will be living off the fat of the land.'

He didn't enlarge on what working well entailed, but Thérèse guessed what it meant. Where she had been unable to pull him into line, his father had skilfully succeeded. But there was no time to dwell on that in the process of taking up residence in the fine house over-looking the green expanse of the Parc Monceau. To Thérèse's delight, Rue Fortuny was a fashionable area with lovely houses. Immediately she ordered her own carriage and horses while Frédéric set about hiring servants, the first Thérèse had ever had, to wait on them.

'I feel so grand,' she cried as she climbed into her carriage, helped up by Frédéric's man-servant. This was no brief episode that would soon disappear as it had when she was forced to sell Fleur and the chaise. This was for ever.

No longer would she have to pit her wits to borrow a few francs, telling herself it did not matter that the money would probably never be paid back. From now on, under Gustave's guidance her role would be to charm and win over those who mattered in Republican high society.

As the year wore on she began to give grand balls, playing the perfect hostess. She and Frédéric found themselves attending political dinners, house parties and social gatherings. She had grown a little plumper since giving birth to Eva, the loss of the other twin now dulled, yet she could turn heads with a single look from her dark, luminous eyes and her seductive lisp. And despite her small stature, she would claim attention and she revelled in it.

Life had become sweet at last. She was wealthier than she had ever dreamed, and if this family played its cards right she would be richer still. She often wondered how rich, what the years would bring. One thing she was sure of, they could only bring better and better things.

# Nineteen

Thérèse wandered from room to room of her new home, bought and paid for with the exorbitant salary Frédéric's father was paying him. Touching this piece of furniture, that piece of expensive glass was like living a dream, a real chateau all her own.

It was called Chateau Vives-Eaux and it had become their second home. Hardly had they been at Rue Fortuny more than a few months than Frédéric's eyes had fallen upon this place, set amid the beautiful Forêt de Fontainebleau just south of Paris.

'I'm tired of continuously living in a city,' he said. 'I was raised in the country. It's in my blood. I feel more at peace here, our country retreat.'

Situated near Melun, it was just a few kilometres from Paris. No more than a step away by horse and carriage from the hustle and bustle of city life, he could still go to his office and return here in the evenings. The house by Parc Monceau was suitable for hosting political dinners, but here in Melun Thérèse and Catherine enjoyed giving huge weekend parties.

It was good being together again, yet something was missing, something she had begun to put her finger on only this morning. It seemed ungrateful to feel this way, yet she did.

As a young girl she'd had a head full of dreams of one day becoming fabulously rich. It was what had driven her. Now there was nothing to drive her any more. It felt as if she had lost something meaningful to her, something precious.

Now she could have whatever she wanted with no concern about paying anyone back. All her dreams had come true. But the easy life was beginning to pall. She had expected it all to be so different but really it wasn't. Perhaps it hadn't been wealth she'd been striving for after all, but fame. To be known far and wide, her name on everyone's lips. Perhaps that was it, the point of being rich was really to be known, even notoriously, for people to regard her not just with envy but with respect and perhaps a little fear. Suddenly she needed to make this come true.

'I think what I really long for,' she told her brother Romain, who she knew understood her feelings, 'what I really long for is some danger in my life. Like it used to be. I need to take risks again. I feel suffocated like this.'

Romain knew exactly how she felt. He'd felt

so too, ever since he'd come to live here with his father and the rest of the family.

'What d'you propose we do?' he asked as they sat sipping cordial in the garden under the trees, out of the strong summer sunlight.

Thérèse watched her two-year-old daughter toddling around on the grass. 'I wish I knew. But I have to do *something* or I shall go mad!'

Romain thought for a while. 'What's happened to your inheritance?'

'That's all being taken care of by Frédéric's father. He told me not to worry about it, he would see to everything.'

'Taken neatly out of your hands then.'

The way it was said startled her. That was exactly how it was, Gustave Humbert reaping the benefits, using her for his own means. Of course she had everything: money, two homes, beautiful clothes, a brilliant social life, close friends, her family about her. But all of it was being manipulated by someone else, by Gustave. What of her role in all this, apart from being expected to look like a goddess on display? Meanwhile her own skills were dying. There was no thrill of battle any more. It was what she had enjoyed more than anything.

'We need to take the reins,' Romain was saying, sipping thoughtfully at his drink.

'How do we do that?'

'Bring the family in on it more. Our father sits there.' He nodded to the old man in his bath chair; at this moment a rug was being draped around his shoulders and legs, despite the warmth of the day, by the nurse hired to take care of him. He looked listless, shrunken, as if life had passed him by and had already forgotten him.

'He has nothing to do but sit, sleep and eat,' Romain grinned. 'Shit and pee.' Having added the coarse aside, he became grim. 'What he needs is to be given an interest.' It seemed to be leading away from the point.

'What has that to do with us?' she queried.

'Get him thinking about his strongbox again. In the old days it never left his side. Now it sits in that locked room in your Paris house, with Catherine's husband charged to keep an eye on it. He keeps the key to that room on his person night and day.'

'So?' she queried impatiently.

'Arouse Papa's interest in it again, have him talk to people about it and what is in it, arouse their interest. I know Gustave is thinking of your future, but we can do even better if Papa can entice backers to invest even more in this legacy of yours. From the horse's mouth so to speak.'

It was an idea, but she felt uncertain. The Minister of Justice, now securely entrenched, had begun to take over from her altogether. 'It would mean stepping on Uncle Gustave's toes. He won't like it.'

'He'll have to put up with it, won't he?' Romain retorted, glowering. 'This all started with you in the first place,' he reminded her fiercely. 'It's you who should be calling the tune, not that damned old swindler.'

He was right. Thérèse's back went up. Who knew how much he was creaming off for himself in all this? Until they'd gone to live in Paris it was she who had brought in money for her family.

Of course she had dreamed of riches, of becoming someone, but lately it was slowly being taken out of her hands. So slowly she had hardly noticed until Romain spoke. Hothead he might be, but he was nearly always right. She was gradually becoming the puppet, expected to lure, charm, play the hostess and nothing more.

She saw his sly, satisfied smile at her expression of anger, but he had opened her eyes and she was thankful to him. He had always looked out for her, more than anyone else apart from Catherine, and he was her best advisor and protector.

Within two days she was back in Paris, dragging with her Auguste d'Aurignac, as her father now insisted on being known. It was so much grander than Daurignac from some tiny village in the south, a name worthy of the possessor of a mysterious locked chest that apparently concealed a fortune.

'My father has expressed a need to look inside his strongbox,' she told Armand Parayre.

She saw the man frown. She didn't like Armand much these days. He took too much on himself and he wasn't even family. Neither was Catherine of course, but she was a true friend; still instinctively protective. Sweet Catherine, how could she have fallen in love with and married a stuffed shirt like Armand, borne him two daughters?

Catherine was everything he wasn't – vivacious, adventurous, excited by life. He was an idealistic prig who hardly ever smiled, looking down over his pince-nez at people like the schoolmaster he had been before taking up the role Gustave Humbert had given him – steward of the Chateau de Marcotte, her fabulous inheritance.

As far as anyone could see, her vast estates in Portugal were now managed by the respected Minister of Justice, on her behalf of course. As he had said to her at the time, 'Who would dare doubt the word of the Minister of Justice?' But what part in all this was she playing, other than just a name?

He'd lately taken out a mortgage on the place of around eight hundred thousand francs, from which she had profited greatly; in her earlier years she might never have realized such a sum. But he'd started to instruct her in all she did, taking over from her, and it irked. So now *she* was doing something!

The several valuable bonds to her vast fortune were now locked in Papa's strongbox, to be brought out and waved in the faces of any who might doubt the authenticity of the Marcotte estates – if anyone dared, as Gustave had said.

Removing anything from Auguste d'Aurignac's strongbox called for great ceremony. Several men of the Daurignac family would form an armed guard while the key was inserted in the lock, the lid opened as if it were exceedingly heavy. The enquirer, maybe a financier or bank official, was made to stand well back as the mortgage documents together with her father's apparently authentic title deeds were spread on a table just beyond his ability to make out the official-looking writing. And what could he do in front of such people but nod acceptance and apologize for any inconvenience he'd caused.

Armand Parayre's short, neat beard and moustache seemed to bristle as he regarded Thérèse and her father.

'And why should your father need to look in the chest at this time?' he asked loftily, as if the man was a dotard. 'It is locked.'

Despite his years, Auguste still had some of his wits about him.

Before Thérèse could answer, he said in his low throaty voice, 'And why should I, its owner, not be at liberty to request it be unlocked?'

Thérèse felt for her father's hand and squeezed the gnarled fingers in pride. She felt him return the pressure, almost as if they had shared a secret smile, as once they would when he or she brought home some little booty.

'I think you had best give Papa the key to open his own possessions,' she said quietly to Armand. She took pleasure in seeing the thick, upturned moustache twitch with irritation, the dark, narrow eyes widen with surprise.

'If you wish,' he said primly, taking the key off its chain attached to his belt, making to hand it to her.

'Not to me,' she said stepping back. 'To my father. And we prefer to be on our own. You will have the key back as soon as Papa is finished. He has no intention of removing anything, if that's what is worrying you. Just something he wishes

242

to satisfy himself about.'

It could have meant anything – something purely innocent or some suspicion that the box had been tampered with while under guard. She did not think for a minute any such thing had happened, but his face was a picture to see and enjoy as he took his temporary leave without a word, his expression stiff and set.

He would without doubt report it to Gustave. Nothing would be said, but Gustave would know that from now on she intended to take a little more command of her own affairs. Without harsh words or animosity she would establish herself as her own woman, to be consulted before he next took it upon himself. Yet she did need him. Only two weeks ago he had told her of his latest haul, speaking of it as calmly as if it had been just another business deal.

'I have today negotiated a substantial advance of some sixty thousand francs, Thérèse, my dear.'

When she'd asked him how and from whom he had smiled with self-satisfaction; although this irked her, her mind boggled at the amount.

'I spoke to someone, no need for names except that he is a man of importance residing in Narbonne. In the course of our conversation I mentioned that my daughter-in-law was Thérèse Humbert, heiress to property in Portugal worth several millions. He immediately became keen to invest...'

Seeing her bite at her lip, he'd misconstrued the exasperated gesture for one of trepidation. 'No one is going to question the word of one in my position, my dear. He was only too glad to invest sixty thousand at a very attractive rate of interest.'

Perhaps she did need Gustave Humbert's name, his high office, his unquestionable creditability, but she wasn't going to be ruled by him. She ceased biting her lip and instead gave a formal, businesslike nod.

Think what she would, they were climbing the ladder at such a furious rate that it sometimes took people's breath away; she must force herself to put the past behind her and be grateful for his dedication to her welfare. But it was hard.

The whole family revelled in their growing wealth, not least Frédéric. As his father's principal private secretary he was constantly with him these days, leaving her to continue charming people as an aid to their conspiracies. But couldn't he see that he was really Gustave's puppet, just as she was?

'My father thinks we may be in danger of treading water,' Frédéric said to her one evening in summer after her dinner guests had left, with great appreciation on their lips as usual of her wonderful repast and scintillating conversation.

Thérèse turned on him. 'What do you mean, treading water? Didn't you note how full of praise tonight's guests were? They come here because they want to partake of our high status. And they come more and more often. We are mixing more and more with the cream of society. That is not treading water, Frédéric, no matter what your father thinks!'

'Only that he's of the opinion we need to start surging forward again.'

'I'm not interested in his opinions!' she exploded angrily. 'Why does it always have to be your father who makes all the decisions?'

Frédéric's dark eyes widened with surprise at her outburst. 'Who else better than he?'

'I used to make the decisions once,' she flared. 'Why should I not continue to do so?'

'I know, but he has the greater influence and I appreciate what he's doing for us. I thought you felt the same.'

'I do,' she said lamely. There was never any point losing her temper at Frédéric. He always remained calm, but she hated to see that chastened look on his face when she did so. 'Of course I do,' she said again.

Even so, her outburst continued to play on Frédéric's mind.

He'd seen her grow more and more restive as time progressed, despite her two lovely homes, one in Fontainebleau, the other in Paris, and in spite of endlessly entertaining Republican dignitaries and people of high means. She played her part well, as much an influence on them with her sparkling conversation and pleasing ways as was Gustave with his hard-headed dealings. It was she who charmed them into believing all Gustave told them about her. It would be disastrous if the two fell out now.

It came to him that it might be advisable to have a little word with his father. But his duties hardly gave him a moment to embark on personal matters; both men were forever engaged in the overriding requirements of the country.

With Thérèse's unrest mounting as summer passed into autumn, even though Catherine – to whom she could unburden herself more freely than she was able to with him – was at her side at every social function, he began looking for a break in his and Gustave's rounds of office that would enable them to meet socially. The opportunity didn't present itself until well into September and it was Gustave himself who offered it, suggesting one evening that they take the chance to go back to his beautiful Parisian house nearby and relax for once over a social drink and a chat.

'We work side by side, you and I, but seldom have a moment to talk together as father and son,' he sighed as at home he handed Frédéric a brandy. 'So many demands are there on me.'

'But you enjoy it,' Frédéric chuckled, relaxing in an easy chair.

'Yes. I worked so very hard for this position overseeing the country's legal system, second only to Charles Freycinet. It's an honour I had always dreamed of. But I did not expect to have so little time to myself, too little even to attend your dear wife's delightful social functions.

'I've always thrived on hard work, as you know, Frédéric.' He gave a low, almost cynical laugh. 'Now I have my reward. But I have learned to take nothing for granted. So much in life can happen to forestall our every scheme.'

'You are set for life, Papa,' Frédéric assured him, looking up as his mother came into the room with a dish of apricots for them. 'Papa was saying he has achieved all he set out to. I was just asking him what can possibly go wrong now.'

His mother came over to lay a kiss on his forehead. 'It is so good to see you, dear. It seems so long, but I know how busy you both are.'

'And I was saying I have not a moment's time for myself,' Gustave added as she laid the dish on a side table beside the brandy decanter. 'Not even to enjoy one of Thérèse's social dinners. I hear they are quite splendid. She is doing a grand job'

'Speaking of Thérèse,' Frédéric cut in as his mother went out. 'There is something I need to speak to you about.'

'Ah, Thérèse. It's so long since I too have seen her. How is she?'

'A little unsettled,' Frédéric said bluntly.

'Unsettled,' Gustave echoed thoughtfully. 'Still feeling inadequate maybe.'

Frédéric rushed to her defence. 'I don't think that's true, Father! She wants to take a greater part in this venture of ours.' He felt a little nettled. Thérèse was right. His father could be self-centred and certainly thick-skinned at times. 'She feels she should count for more than just a good hostess, Father. You've taken up the reins and she feels belittled.'

There, he had spoken his mind. But his father merely gave a wry smile. 'Then we'll see what we can do,' he said, and changing the subject completely, left Frédéric no option but to go along with him.

Gustave was true to his word. By the New Year

Thérèse was again in the driving seat, at least in part. Playing the celebrated heiress, she, Fréd-éric, their daughter – now two and a half years old – and her father made the journey down to the south to entice from the greedy rich as many bids as possible on her legacy.

Paris was all very well, but it wasn't wise to milk it too much in case people there became suspicious. But, they thought, the wealthy of her old haunt, Toulouse, and of other southern towns would be easy pickings, for a while at least.

They were right. Wooed by every bank, busi-nessman, financier, by those of the legal pro-fession, wealthy landowners and even private speculators, the Humberts found themselves awash with those clamouring to lend money, one credit bank advancing almost a million francs. At the end of spring they returned to Paris having amassed capital of several millions. And she'd done it all herself, just like in the old days, without the assistance or interference of Fréd-éric's father.

The family was in turmoil, even though Thérèse, believing as usual that things would always come right in the end, said there was no need for panic

No one was listening. Frédéric sat morose and silent; her friend Catherine was constantly in tears on her shoulder, scolded by Armand for her weakness in the face of adversity. In this he alone stood with Thérèse, no matter that she didn't like him.

Romain resorted to showing his fury at how

things had gone. 'Bloody Republican traitors!' he kept saying to a subdued Emile and his wife while nineteen-year-old Louis and his younger sisters, Marie-Louise and Maria, moved about the house like mice as Thérèse's Aunt Marie-Emilie and her Uncle Gustave left their grand home to come to live at Chateau Vives-Eaux.

No more house parties; a time to keep their heads down, for a while at any rate, said Thérèse, ever hoping better times would come out of the chaos.

A few days ago Charles de Freycinet had resigned as President of the Council and Minister for Foreign Affairs, his firm refusal to offer support to Britain's bombardment of Alexandria decreasing French influence in Egypt. His compromise, to occupy the Isthmus of Suez, had been voted against in the Chamber by a huge majority; discredited, he'd had no option but to resign. Consequently Gustave Humbert found himself no longer Minister of Justice.

Now, living with his daughter-in-law's large family, he smothered his humiliation by announcing that he intended to sort out her Portuguese legacy once and for all.

Despite it all, Thérèse continued to believe that time would see them back on form. Nothing lasted for ever, even bad things. She'd seen this all before and come out triumphant. Besides, there was money now, though they would have to curb their spending spree for a while.

And there was always Papa's strongbox that would see them through. She made herself believe they would never fall into the situation that had once seen them destitute, no matter how bad things became. She'd come too far to let that happen.

# Twenty

Think what she liked about him, thanks to Gustave's hard work, the rest of 1883 had seen the family back on track, the panic last year over the collapse of Freycinet's cabinet well and truly behind them.

In fact Thérèse felt rather pleased at having kept her head throughout, finally to sail on into calmer waters. Working with her extensive capital, she'd even bought two more properties to add to this present lovely country retreat of Vives-Eaux. She'd even surprised everyone by acquiring the home of the Comtes de Toulouse-Lautrec for two million francs, which she had calmly borrowed with the usual promise to repay at a handsome rate of interest.

'Do you intend to live there?' Frédéric had asked after recovering from the shock. Despite knowing from past experience how she thrived on taking risks, it seemed to him at the time that she might have gone a little too far.

'Of course not!' she had told him, her dark eyes sparkling. 'We'll raise a mortgage on it instead and make more profit from its vineyards. Armand will manage it. He's still steward of

Marcotte – though he's never been there.'

Armand had enough to occupy him without trooping off to those obscure estates in Portugal, busy running the newspaper she and Frédéric had bought last autumn as a new venture.

*L'Avenir de Seine et Marne* was, to say the least, progressive, Armand making sure it laid great emphasis on political socialist reform. He'd also been instrumental in getting Frédéric elected socialist deputy for Melun.

'If he needs help managing my estates as well as his newspaper,' she said, 'he can call on his brother Alexandre or his brother-in-law Jacques.'

Gustave glanced up from poring over the Humbert accounts as she came into the room where he was working this morning.

'Ah, my dear, I've been meaning to talk to you,' he said as she sat herself in one of the easy chairs of the sunny office he had taken over since coming to live at Vives-Eaux. 'I've been thinking it's time we established the hub of our operations in Paris itself. I've a place in mind on the Avenue de la Grande Armée – with your approval, of course.'

Thérèse frowned and didn't reply immediately, recalling Frédéric's words a few weeks ago. 'I'm beginning to feel a little concerned that decision making is tending to go out of the family,' he'd said, but she'd laughed gaily.

'We need every member we can trust, Frédéric. They all know where their bread is buttered and are loyal to me. That new property will boost our credit rating. We'll be able to raise money any time we please on this new property and no bank will deny us any loan we care to ask for.'

She'd proved to Gustave that she was more than capable of managing affairs equally as well as he. But here he was dictating to her yet again. The hub of *our* operations, he'd said. Was he intending to base himself in these Paris head-quarters? If she were to move back to Paris as a base for herself it would be to rule as she pleased, having guests stay there whenever she pleased, by *her* invitation only; it was not for Gustave to assume he would be taking over.

'Where do you intend to live, uncle?' she queried pointedly. He looked a little taken aback by the sharpness of her tone.

'I wish you would not call me by that name,' he reminded her, recovering quickly. 'I hope to use an office there, of course. We can't be running from one residence to another whenever we need to hold a meeting.'

He gave her a disarming smile. 'I shall have my own establishment nearby, of course, for myself and my wife,' he went on, pointedly refraining from alluding to his wife as her aunt. 'I assume your brother Emile and Alice and their two children will remain in their present residence, leaving yourself and Frédéric, your father, your brothers Louis and Romain and their sisters with more than enough room in such a vast mansion. It will keep your family together just as you have always enjoyed – a close-knit family.'

It was uttered with such easy informality that Thérèse instantly regretted her earlier sharp tone. Here was a man who not so long ago had been one of the foremost legal names in the land.

But no longer. Although his name hadn't been forgotten, he must sometimes feel a little inadequate these days and needed to assert his authority, maybe even felt hurt by her attitude. He might as well have added, 'After all I have done for you.'

'Yes,' she said quietly. 'An office in this new residence would be perfect. Please tell me more about what you've found for us.'

Friction fading with the deliberate utterance of the word 'us', she felt excitement begin to rise as he described this mansion on the Avenue de la Grande Armée.

'It can be counted as one of the great avenues in Paris,' he explained. 'Almost an extension to the Champs Elysées, divided only by the Arc de Triomphe. Every visitor to Paris now gravitates to the Champs Elysées to admire the brilliant new electric street lighting when taking in its wonderful cafés or strolling its entire length, a mere step to the other refined, imposing homes of the *nouveaux riches* among whom you will now be residing.'

Going to her he took her hand. 'I think, my dear, this residence will be the culmination of all your dreams,' he said, more kindly now. 'There you will rule like a *comtesse* and before long all Paris will be flocking to your door.'

She was humbled. 'I can't thank you enough for all you've done for me, for myself and

Frédéric over the years. Without your help...'

She let her voice die away and had him smile.

'You are my cherished daughter-in-law,' he said slowly. 'We have had our differences, to be sure ... Oh, yes, my dear,' he went on quickly as she made to protest. 'I have detected them many a time when you yearned to be your own master. But I feel proud to have trained you out of your innocence to see you become what you are now. Eventually I can see you ruling all Paris, my dear.'

With that he bent forward and, taking her hand, brushed it with his lips almost reverently; she might have said melodramatically.

'Only look to me now and again for guidance, if you will.'

'Yes, of course I will, father,' she breathed and, getting to her feet before he could straighten up, dropped a kiss on his high brow from which the hairline had continued to recede.

'One thing more, Thérèse,' he said gently. 'Don't try to change yourself. Remain as you are, the innocent rustic heir to a fortune. Continue to beguile and draw people to your side.'

She could have told him that this was what she had always done, without need of his guidance, but she said nothing.

'Tomorrow we will go all together to view your new home. But there is just one more piece of pleasing news,' he added as she prepared to leave, hardly able to conceal her excitement. 'I am soon to be made Vice-President of the Senate. What do you think of that?'

His renewed self-esteem was unmistakable

and as she came rushing back to him to fling her arms about his neck he stepped back a little. She had always been demonstrative and could sometimes overwhelm people. It was part of her secret and usually endeared them to her. He took her hands to interrupt the demonstration, merely nodding his appreciation of her joy for him.

'We shall have all of Paris at our feet, your family and mine, my dear, so long as we keep a cool head.'

Soberly, Thérèse nodded, her intention to plant another kiss on his balding pate dissipating, her mind going back to when she had merely dreamed of this day.

Her house-warming party had been a roaring success, naturally. People still talked about it six months later, despite all the other social gatherings she had held since.

Her gift for entertaining now drew those in all walks of ministerial and political life, as well as businessmen looking to increase their investments. The house had quickly grown into a focal point for the enjoyment of excellent food and scintillating conversation, where everyone who mattered regularly converged to socialize and enjoy the wonderful hospitality of Madame Thérèse Humbert.

After one such gathering she now lay beside her softly snoring husband in the great, sumptuous feather bed in their huge, sumptuous, silk-lined bedroom and listened to the silence in the house. It was two o'clock in the morning. Even the servants had gone to bed, but she still lay awake thinking and comparing then and now.

She thought of all the parties she had thrown these last six months, but that first one in this grand house had been the best. It had cost several thousands but hadn't made so much as a dent in the fifty million francs that her fabulous legacy was now understood to be worth, rich plantations of cork oaks having now been added to it along with the best vineyards in Portugal, as well as her various properties here in France.

Thérèse smiled into the darkness. Why should it have made any dent at all? None of it had come out of her pocket. There was no need to spend a single franc on her entertaining; the entire outlay was provided by willing lenders in the sure knowledge of being repaid twofold. It didn't matter that some had to wait for months, maybe years to realize their returns, always of course provided at the expense of some other private investor or credit bank. That aspect had never changed, except in the size of the loans.

The most wonderful part was that people no longer queried it. It had become big business, based if they did but know it on the fact that any who might see through it all wouldn't have the courage to speak up, first from fear of ridicule – a hard-nosed man of business showing himself to have been so gullible – and secondly fear of Thérèse's wrath, or rather that of her brother Romain. Though no one said as much, he was lately becoming a stumbling block to those who might wish to complain about an overdue settlement.

Thérèse's smile faded. Whatever methods

Romain adopted to silence a recalcitrant didn't worry her. She was more concerned that Gustave was slowly beginning to take over again. Only yesterday he had tackled her about her love of telling romantic tales about her legacy.

'No more wild tales of deceased relatives, foreign aunts or ancient godmothers bequeathing their millions to you,' he told her in an effort to curb her natural enthusiasm for storytelling. 'We must have one source and one source only – this deceased Robert Henry Crawford, the American whom your mother nursed when you were young, who consequently bequeathed his estates in Portugal to you in gratitude of her kindness; and it is our good management of those estates that has caused our investments to multiply to the sum they stand at today.'

Thérèse didn't care for the word 'our', as usual placing himself at the head of this enterprise. But she tightened her lips. This wasn't the time to start a war. Patiently she endured yet another reminder that her benefactor, who had inherited his fortune from his first wife, had died childless, leaving no one in any doubt of Thérèse Humbert's rightful claim to that fortune.

'But we do need an airtight story that will satisfy any disbelievers,' Gustave had added. 'We must be ready for them. To continue leaping from one far-fetched figment of the imagination to another is asking for trouble.'

His tone had darkened as he had outlined his plan to thwart the sceptics. 'Everyone believes your father's strongbox holds the documents to your inheritance. But if any should one day demand they be produced, they might very likely resort to legal means to back their requests.'

She knew only too well about that, having once lost her entire home to bailiffs.

'We must not be caught out,' he'd continued. 'I have thought it out very carefully – the original will was signed by your Crawford millionaire, naming you sole beneficiary. However, to guard against awkward customers, we need to confuse the issue a little. So the strongbox will contain a second document dividing Crawford's fortune between your sister Maria and his nephews, the brothers Robert and Henry. In this way proceedings can be held up indefinitely. Meanwhile we continue to enjoy the cream.'

Thérèse's interest had been pricked, leaving her to admire Gustave's cunning. No wonder he was being made Vice-President of the Senate. But his plans had gone even further.

'And then there will come to light an even more recent document,' he went on. 'One in which the two brothers agree that the inheritance itself is to be left in your safekeeping on condition it remains untouched until the dispute over the earlier wills is settled. It means your family will only be in receipt of the annual interest deriving from their uncle's estate, which in itself is a fortune.'

He sat back in his chair, well satisfied with his plans. 'This will work well for us, my dear. As you cannot avail yourself as yet of your inheritance, you need to rely on the smaller income for the time being. But once all is settled...'

Breaking off had added significance to his

words as he relaxed even further in his chair. 'All will continue to be eager to invest their own savings in this great fortune once it is realized. They will be willing to wait virtually years for their returns. We cannot lose, my dear.'

Suddenly he'd leaned towards her, his hands linked together in his enthusiasm. She had never seen him so animated.

'And here's another slant, my dear. Since then there will have been found among your father's papers an even more recent document, only a year or two old, stating that the two Crawford brothers would be happy to waive their claim entirely in exchange for six million francs and the hand of your sister Maria to whichever brother she chooses, thinking she too is an heiress to their uncle's estates and thereby getting their hands on her share.'

His beard and moustache twitched suddenly to a small grin. 'It seems they have both fallen in love with your sister. Our creditors will have to wait while the case goes to court. It will be long and drawn out, Maria not being in love with them and suspecting she is being used, a pawn in their game. She will refuse first one offer of marriage then the other, yet she will keep them dangling for as long as she chooses. It could well roll on indefinitely.'

In her big comfortable bed, Thérèse turned her head towards Frédéric. His gentle snoring had ceased. She felt him fidget.

'Are you not asleep, my dearest?' she whispered.

His voice came softly. 'I can't sleep. I keep

thinking about what you told me after seeing my father.'

'And what conclusion have you come to about it?' she asked.

He turned to her and kissed her lightly on the cheek. 'I think it's a wonderful plan, dearest. He's a wise old bird, is my father, and I think we should go along with it.'

She had to agree. She could always depend on the decision of her even-tempered, shy and reserved husband with confidence these days. He'd proved himself a perfect ally, melting into the background as she lavishly entertained, but he was the one on whose word she could always rely.

# Twenty-One

With relief Thérèse sank into one of the large easy chairs in the withdrawing room. The mourners had all left. The members of her family had retired to their own separate private rooms to grieve and remember in their own way, or not. Emile and Alice would no doubt console each other in their usual loving manner; Alice was a demonstratively loving girl, she gathered, so different from her brother. Frédéric had never been one to openly show affection. But she was happy enough with that.

Even he had gone off to bed only after being told that she preferred to be on her own for a while and didn't really need comforting. Nor did she. She had no regrets. Papa had enjoyed a long life, eighty-five, and had realized his dearest wish – to be someone, to be rich, to live in comfort and be buried with great pomp having given himself a noble title, his name remembered.

Thérèse smiled – the Comte d'Aurignac. Many would have given their soul to achieve such an illustrious end. She'd done him proud today, just as she had promised him long ago she would. Little had anyone dreamed that promise would be kept, though she had never doubted.

Sipping a glass of wine, she let her gaze wander about the darkened room. Half past two in the morning, she didn't feel a bit tired. If anything she was excited, pleased at the way everything had gone so smoothly. But she'd always made a success of everything she did, even as a child, even when their home had been taken by the bailiffs.

The house lay quiet, soothingly quiet. The staff too had gone to bed. No sound came from the Avenue de la Grande Armée, stretching away below in a straight line into the distance.

Catherine had lingered for a while after Frédéric had departed, but she too had finally followed, having asked if she was all right.

Dearest Catherine, her truest and most loyal friend. 'I shan't be far away if you want me,' she'd said as she left.

She and Armand had their quarters on the topmost floor, three beautiful large rooms situated at the rear overlooking extensive greenery. Emile and Alice had those facing the avenue with equally fine views. There was also a small room, bare but for a wooden table and Papa's strongbox; the room was securely locked, the key kept by Armand, never leaving his person. Below that were hers and Frédéric's private apartments and those of his father Gustave and his wife, her aunt Marie-Emilie.

The second floor of this great house was given over to banqueting and drawing rooms like the one in which she now sat; the adjoining rooms, smaller but all as finely decorated, were where she'd entertain more privately.

From the wide balcony the marble grand staircase curved down to the ground floor and an entrance hall that gave every guest who entered a lasting impression of splendour and luxury. There a huge and ornate tall clock that had cost her thousands ticked slowly and sonorously. But nothing in this house cost less than a small fortune. She'd made sure of that, first to impress, secondly merely to indulge herself, remembering her years of poverty.

Further along the hall stood a green marble-topped table supported by four white marble winged lions on a white marble plinth, the whole heavy enough to need a crane to move it. The highly polished wood floor gleamed like deep bronze and its paler, wood-panelled walls held costly paintings; these had taken Frédéric ages to search for and were admired and envied by all who entered this beautiful place. And above it all hung a huge chandelier of pure crystal.

To one side was the vast library with enough books to take several lifetimes to read – Frédéric's idea. Here he had his gun room as well. To the other side the anteroom where her guests waited before being received.

There were other doors at the rear of the hall, but one stood virtually unnoticed beneath the rise of the grand staircase. It led to Romain's quarters at the rear of the house, just above the servants' quarters in the basement, with private stairs, like those from the kitchen that led up to the banqueting areas without intrusion upon those in the house.

His was a warren of small rooms and passages with a door at the rear through which he could come and go without being seen. Here he carried out his work on her behalf, though she felt it better not to query its exact nature. That she trusted him to look after her welfare and safety was all she needed.

Thérèse put down her empty glass, sighed and stretched her arms. She was tired now. It was time for bed. She would probably sleep like a top, secure in the knowledge that her family was around her looking out for her. Life was good. This autumn of 1886, she'd been here just over a year, yet it seemed as if she had lived here all her life.

She rose languidly, her hands absently smoothing the ample folds of the ruched and ruffled skirt and bodice of her high-necked, black mourning dress, and adjusted the ample bustle as she went slowly from the room, closing the door softly behind her. Yes, life was good.

'Are you ready yet?' Thérèse called a little impatiently. 'Maria is here and the carriage has been waiting ten minutes already.'

This morning she, her sister Maria and Catherine were off out, she for one final fitting and to warn her dressmaker that the gown must be delivered in time for the opera tomorrow night. Jacques Ducet, who made most of her gowns, would not dare to delay, not even if his best friend were to die.

Tomorrow evening she and Frédéric would be there in their own opera box. As always it would be packed with guests; there was virtually a waiting list of the most important people in Paris.

There would be the usual queue of carriages waiting for a glimpse of her and whichever great names she had invited, waiting maybe to gasp at her latest ensemble.

'I have to check everything before we leave,' Catherine called down. 'I'm nearly ready. A few more minutes.'

Since they had all taken up residence in this almost palatial establishment on the Avenue de la Grande Armée, Catherine had taken it upon herself to oversee the whole place, in fact had made herself unofficial chatelaine, running the staff with a rod of iron and allowing no one through the portals who didn't have prior invitation. She'd always had that managing streak in her and with her here to manage and advise, Thérèse felt safe. She had no quarrel with the somewhat domineering, straight-backed attitude that could prove so formidable to any trying to seek an audience without a precious personal invitation. In fact Thérèse welcomed it.

'She won't be long now,' she assured Maria, who smiled sweetly and shrugged.

Maria was so easy to manage, so amiable, unlike Marie-Louise always ready to argue at the least provocation, wanting always to be right. Thankfully Marie-Louise hated shopping, preferring her own company.

Today Maria too was having a fitting. Thérèse smiled at her as they waited. They had much in common, not so much in looks – Maria was tall and willowy where she was small and round – but in the ability to tell a good story. These Maria would relate in a shy and retiring manner which was enough to attract no end of possible suitors, though she'd not yet seen anyone handsome enough to marry.

The latest story that had them queuing up to woo Maria, seeing the prospect of an excellent dowry, was that she had been left a more than substantial sum in her grandfather Duluc's will, he having been a wealthy farmer in his time. Thérèse had to admire her ingenuity.

Catherine appeared at the door to the kitchen area. 'I had to leave a few instructions with the staff,' she said breathlessly. 'But I'm ready now.'

'I find myself being thwarted by them at every turn,' Thérèse stormed, pacing Gustave's office while he sat calmly watching her. 'They exasperate me, the pair of them. They're driving me mad. They're like thorns on a tree I'm trying to climb. I don't need any of this. I can't take much more of it. But what can I do?'

'Get rid of them,' came the quiet reply.

Thérèse stopped pacing, her small body shaking with rage. 'But they're family.'

'If they're driving you to such a state of rage, then you should.'

Thérèse turned on him angrily. 'How? What do you suggest?'

She saw his tight-lipped smile. 'You've always had a talent for subterfuge, my dear. You'll find a way in time.'

But she wanted a way now, not in time. If she had to take any more of her younger brother Louis's holier-than-thou attitude, she'd throttle him. He'd always hated the way she had gone about keeping her family together and lately had made no bones about saying so. It was so unfair.

'I had to do what I did,' she told him time and time again. 'It's thanks to me you're where you are now.' But he refused to see her side of it.

'All well and good, but it's now become sheer greed on your part and I want no part in it.'

'You don't have to,' she'd rage at him. 'All I ask is that you stop treating me as if I'm some sort of criminal. Needs must, Louis.'

'I agree, but our needs are no longer what they were. It has become cruel. Some are enticed into investing all they have in your fantasies without realizing that they stand to lose their life's savings. Others become bankrupt. Because of you.'

'Then they deserve to. It's they who are greedy, not me. And it's not fantasy. Every bit of the property I've bought is real. You know that full well.'

'But it's all bought with money you've swindled out of others.'

'How dare you! You're my younger brother and I won't have you speak to me like that.'

'It's the truth.'

'Get out!' she had stormed. 'Get out of my sight, you unmitigated prig!'

It was always like this, and he was sending her insane.

The same went for his sister Marie-Louise, always criticizing her methods. None of the others complained, neither were those two averse to taking what she gave despite what they said. She was sick of it.

'What can I do?' she appealed to Gustave, coming to sit down as she saw that thoughtful look steal over his face. 'Quick, tell me!' she demanded.

He lifted a calming hand. 'Give me a moment to think, my dear. All in good time.'

She sat watching him. Then at last he began to speak. 'Louis needs to be given something to do,' he said. 'Something that will take him out of France. And keep him there.' He frowned, ruminating. 'Tunisia.'

'Tunisia?' she queried.

He looked up at her, his blue eyes glistening. 'You could buy some property, a new project, a sideline, an estate bringing in money from date palms or something similar. And put him in charge. He may carp at our methods of making money, but if I know your younger brother he wouldn't say no to an apparently legitimate

267

venture that will bring him status, even if it is bought with what he calls ill-gotten gains. You see if I'm not right. He is a Daurignac, for all his high ideals.'

Gustave was right. Within weeks she had bought the property and said goodbye to an excited Louis. Marie-Louise was another matter. A prim body cramping her style, she was destined to remain a spinster; sending her away was certainly out of the question. Thérèse was at a loss what to do with her.

Seven months later, after one particularly nasty brush with her, she'd reached the end of her tether.

It had been a most enjoyable day at the milliner's with Catherine and Maria. She'd bought them a beautiful hat each, and for herself two of the most marvellous creations: narrow brimmed, tall crowned, to add height to her small stature, and decorated with bird's wings and artificial flowers.

Madame Pinon's bill had come to around one thousand five hundred francs, but money was no object these days and she returned home happy, hardly able to wait to wear them and have half of Paris gasp with envy. She needed to be at the pinnacle of current fashion, no matter what the cost.

The boxes having been borne in by a couple of servants, she was met by Marie-Louise standing in the hall. The short, dumpy figure, hands folded over her stomach, oozed displeasure.

'More of other people's money spent on fripperies, I see,' she began maliciously. 'You disgust me, Thérèse!'

Thérèse came to a halt, while the other two carried on up the staircase. The shy Maria hurried; Catherine followed at a more measured pace, not at all intimidated but preferring not to become involved in another of the many noisy arguments that took place in this house when Thérèse let fly.

And let fly she did, the servants keeping out of the way until finally, after almost half an hour, the battle was won and Marie-Louise fled in tears. But Thérèse felt no triumph, only frustration and simmering anger. Her whole day had been ruined, her determination to cling to the joy of spending money felt more like a Pyrrhic victory.

'I've had enough,' she burst out next morning when Frédéric said he thought she was looking tired. 'I had such an awful row with Marie-Louise yesterday afternoon. I don't think I can stand much more of it.'

'I was told,' he returned quietly as they made their way to breakfast, but little more could be said as others of the family, including a pale-faced Marie-Louise, came to join them.

Indeed, nothing more was said about it until he and Thérèse were making their way that evening to the opera. As they settled back in their gently swaying carriage, he took her gloved hand in his and held it firmly in a gesture of sympathy.

'You still look wan, my dear. Have you not recovered from yesterday's bother with your sister?'

When she shook her head, he went on carefully, 'Something will have to be done about her, dearest. I can't have you being continually upset. She lives under your roof only by your generosity. You are generous to all your family and it's not fair to be treated with the contempt she shows you.'

'But what can I do?' Thérèse sighed. 'How can I turn her out? What would everyone think of me, my own sister? I can't send her off to look after some estate of ours as I did with Louis.'

'That's true.' Frédéric turned his face to gaze out of the window at the passing scenery of the Rue de Rivoli. They would soon arrive to be met by their guests for the evening, a gathering of Republican notables and the usual socialites.

While he continued to gaze from the coach window, Thérèse heard him murmur, 'It's time Marie-Louise was married.'

There was no chance to ask what he meant as the coach drew up outside the imposing new opera house in the Place de l'Opéra, the wide hub of several radial roads – Boulevard Houssman, Rue Auber and Rue du Quatre-Septembre.

The evening went well, the reception afterwards as always a success. She wasn't able to bring up his remark until they were finally preparing themselves ready for bed. Then she reminded him.

'What did you mean it's time my sister was married? You said it in such a strange way.'

'Ah, yes,' he replied, as he clambered into his nightshirt while she sat, already in her nightdress and lace cap, her back propped against three soft feather pillows. 'Just something that went through my mind,' he muttered.

He said no more until he was in bed beside her. Then, before settling himself to sleep, he sat upright to gaze down at her. His lips behind the dark, trim beard stretched into a crafty smile.

'My cousin Lucien. When he was last here, you remember, dearest, at your birthday party, he had eyes for no one else but Marie-Louise. I recall watching them through the crowd and noticing that they'd become deep in conversation for a while and each of them seemed most interested in what the other was saying. I recalled thinking it had been ages since I saw her smile so openly.'

'Lucien?' Thérèse queried. 'He's the stuffiest bore I've ever met.'

'Two of a kind, I think,' laughed Frédéric. 'I've always thought he was destined to remain a bachelor all his life, and your sister a spinster. Both of the same ilk, prim, aloof, very proper, a well-matched pair I would say.'

Thérèse remained sceptical. 'What makes you think she'd want to marry, disliking as she does to be ruled by anyone, much less a husband? Or that he'd want to marry her once he knows what she is like?'

'There's one thing your sister rebels against more than anything else – being dependent on you. If she were to marry well...'

'Your cousin isn't much of a catch then,' she broke in with a laugh.

He didn't even smile. 'But what if my father could arrange for him to be given an important post? I could speak to him. He'd do anything for you, my dearest.'

'Would he?' she echoed sarcastically, but Frédéric was in earnest.

'Yes, he would. You're the source of all he has achieved.'

'He'd have achieved what he has without my help,' she said with a touch of resentment.

'Perhaps, but you are both of a kind. You both enjoy a challenge. I think he saw you as a challenge, and needed to strive that bit harder not to have his daughter-in-law and niece put him to shame.'

Resentment dwindled away. She was intrigued. Without realizing it, Frédéric had restored her good nature towards his father in one innocent swoop. She relaxed back on her pillow, thoroughly at ease with herself for the first time in a long while.

Over the next few months she watched Frédéric's quiet manoeuvres; his cousin and her sister were thrown together at every opportunity, though she remained concerned that Marie-Louise was still proving difficult to woo.

Two months later, Frédéric was telling her that his father had spoken with Lucien who had agreed to go as the French consul to Baku, situated on the Black Sea in Russia. One stipulation was that it would be preferable if the French consul were married.

Within weeks, having wed in a quiet ceremony, Lucien and Marie-Louise moved off to the sunnier climes of the Black Sea and a new life, hopefully to stay there. She was at last rid of her sister.

'Now all I have around me are loyal friends and family,' she told Frédéric as she kissed him fondly.

# Twenty-Two

It was good to get away. Paris, as exciting and adored as she was, had begun to stifle her citizens as the summer heat grew in intensity. Here near Melun the woods and the gently flowing Seine cooled the air and lifted the spirit.

'It's so good to be here!' Thérèse cried as she and Frédéric roamed from room to room of her cherished Chateau Vives-Eaux. 'I can feel my nerves unwinding by the minute.'

Though she seldom suffered from nerves, it was always a business leaving the city for her summer vacation, everyone rushing about packing, people coming to wish them a pleasant journey. 'All looking for an invitation to one of our house parties here,' she'd laughed.

Before leaving had come the annual opening of the famous strongbox, in which a bank official was allowed from a safe distance to watch it being ceremoniously unlocked with the key still attached to Armand's person by its chain. The lid lifted revealed bound and sealed packages of precious bearer bonds – investors' guarantees of payment – put there temporarily for the man's benefit. The coupons were solemnly clipped and put into a large, black valise ready for the journey to Thérèse's summer residence. Brought down to the hall, it had been padlocked to Armand's wrist in front of the usual crowd of onlookers.

Now the valuable bonds lay fiercely guarded by Armand and Romain in a locked room in an inner sanctum of the chateau, leaving her to relax. But two days later she was again on edge as she read the note from her solicitors – a query regarding a serious cash problem that might cause a few raised eyebrows, or worse.

Refolding the letter she went in search of Maria. This needed to be dealt with.

Slowly she'd been cultivating public sympathy over the question of the Crawford brothers' outrageous claim to her Portuguese inheritance. But this letter was saying that with a slight cooling of that sympathy being detected of late, it was imperative that public belief in her inheritance be reinvigorated.

Another small drama was needed. Perhaps Maria could be persuaded to play a leading role. But she'd have to brief her carefully. Nothing must go wrong.

This time it would be Maria, not she, who would convince everyone of the authenticity of her inheritance. Her sister had become almost as good as she for playing a good story to its full potential. She found Maria with Catherine in the cool, vine-covered conservatory.

'We have problems with the Crawfords again,' Thérèse began as she sat herself down beside them in a wicker, cushion-strewn lounger.

Quickly she explained the contents of the letter. 'We need something spectacular that will have the whole of Paris talking for months to come. But if we don't act soon, we could lose our whole fortune.'

They grew instantly attentive. This had become as real to them as it was to her since Gustave had voiced the suggestion that, to the advantage of the entire scheme, one or both of the Crawford brothers may have cast their eyes upon Maria and begun vying for her hand in marriage.

It was quite plausible that both brothers should be attracted to the one girl. It was not unknown. Maria might not be pretty in the dainty sense but her tall, willowy stature and the way she held her head, high and noble, drew men's eyes.

Where Thérèse could charm with her coquettish smile, Maria did it with her serious, almost haughty expression. Between them they'd reawaken the sympathy of all Paris, Maria with her reluctance to be used as a pawn in the game and Thérèse as her loving supporter.

'My solicitor says that the issue of one of the brothers becoming your suitor has again been raised,' Thérèse said as she held the letter aloft. 'This is becoming serious. This claim of being the rightful heirs to the whole of our property in Portugal is keeping us from making use of it. Things are becoming far too fraught. But to give in to them will mean we'll have nothing to bargain with when trying to raise money on our property. Something must be done.'

Maria was already well acquainted with the tentative suggestion of a deal whereby, in exchange for promising to drop their claim to the whole of Thérèse's vast inheritance, the Crawfords would receive a substantial sum of money and Maria would become engaged to marry one of them.

Thérèse recalled her sister's drawn expression when the idea was put to her. She had wanted to laugh: how easy it was to deceive one's mind into believing one's own lies.

She remained gazing at her sister. 'You don't have to consent to anything,' she said. 'We'll fight them through the courts if need be. And we will win.'

'I do hope so,' murmured Catherine in all seriousness. Thérèse folded the letter and put it away, not quite sure if her friend meant it or was just going along with her.

The solicitor's letter had been expressed in dour terms, enough to alarm anyone. Though Thérèse knew the truth, even she felt uneasy as to the moves they would have to make once they were back in Paris.

As summer waned and the time to return to Paris drew nearer, her edginess grew to the extent that she was constantly rowing with someone or another, even Frédéric. Of course her solicitors knew what they were about. She paid them well to know. It was put about that Madame Humbert had been made extremely unwell by the trauma of this unsavoury business and would need time before she was well

276

enough to consider the Crawfords' offer.

For the last month she had ceased receiving; no one had been invited to the chateau, which in itself was worrying. Finally in September a pale and weak Madame Humbert was seen being gently assisted down from her coach and into her Paris mansion. Parisian society, creditors and well-wishers hung on to news of her health as well as news of what these false claimants intended.

'My solicitor thinks he may shortly have some good news for me concerning the claim,' she revealed when she finally began to accept visitors again, fully recovered by mid-autumn and back to giving sumptuous dinners.

'I've been informed that these Crawford people will be willing to waive their claim to my inheritance,' she told her thirty guests – eminent politicians, businessmen and ecclesiastical dignitaries and their wives – over a particularly fine dinner, 'if my dear sister Maria will agree to be affianced to wed the brother Henry Crawford.'

There came gasps of horror from around the banqueting room's long table with its pure white damask cloth and beautiful decoration, its fine bone china, gold-handled cutlery and crystal glassware glinting and gleaming under the two huge chandeliers.

Thérèse smiled beseechingly at her guests from her end of the table. 'It seems he is besotted by her, but what are we to do?'

'But that's preposterous!' Gustave, sitting nearby, burst out in his deep, carrying voice.

Along both sides of the table, every one of her guests nodded in agreement. 'What does your sister say to all this?'

'What can she say?' Thérèse answered pathetically. 'It is either that or people will see those rogues contesting my right to my inheritance and claiming the whole property for themselves. What am I to do? People know that should they win, I shall be bankrupted and all those who have invested their money will stand to lose everything. *Everything!*'

This last cry almost shivered the chandeliers. The concerted gasp from all around the table was almost like a receding sea wave. Tears began to brim in Thérèse's eyes and Frédéric threw down his napkin, leaping to his feet to come and comfort her.

'I am sorry, everyone,' she said after a moment, dabbing her eyes. 'It was rude of me to upset my guests this way. Please, forgive me.'

'Madame, no need to apologize,' came cries from those around her and she smiled bravely once more as Frédéric resumed his seat.

'Your dear sister must not give in to them,' a female voice protested from further down the table. 'It's virtual blackmail.' She was quickly hushed by her husband.

'My sister is of marriageable age,' Thérèse returned in a sad tone. 'I believe Henry Crawford is very handsome and well set up. I saw him once and believe that he would make her a good husband.'

There came sad nods. No one asked if Maria was in love with Henry Crawford. It was accepted in society that many a marriage was more or less a business settlement between families, whether the woman was in love or not. Even so, it was sad.

Thérèse looked down the table at them all. 'I have such wonderful friends,' she said tremulously. 'I know that with kind people behind me such as my present company here, we will win.'

A week later, with Maria apparently half consenting to accept the offer of marriage, Thérèse let it be known that the contestants had announced that in return for some ten million francs they would be willing to drop their claim to the inheritance.

'I'm in such a dilemma,' she told everyone. 'It's so cruel. For years they have dogged me at every turn. I am heiress to a vast fortune, yet until the business of my inheritance is settled I do not have that sort of money at my disposal. If I had, all would be settled once and for all and those who have invested could breathe again.'

It was a heartrending appeal for the support of her friends in banking and finance, yet couched in the form of a mild threat that they might lose money they had already invested. It instantly brought offers to help her settle the Crawfords' outrageous demand – offers she graciously accepted with tears of relief.

'You are so generous and good to me,' she told them as she signed each promissory note. 'You will be paid back every franc at ten per cent above the normal rate of interest. I cannot tell you how grateful I am for your kindness. Between us we will defeat these wicked upstarts.'

'Don't you think we're going a bit too far?' Maria queried as Thérèse instantly applied to bring the brothers before the Civil Tribunal of the Seine.

'It will stall our creditors,' Thérèse told her happily, far from the gentle victim her creditors had seen. 'A tribunal could take a year or more to reach its findings. Meanwhile we invest the money, and when our creditors come clamouring for repayment of their loan we will be able to settle in part as we've always done.'

'And what about my promise to wed Henry Crawford?' asked Maria, making her sister smile.

'A young woman put in your situation would naturally be disinclined to marry a man she didn't love. There can be all sorts of ways to stall their advances.'

'And this business of a tribunal? You can't pretend to take it to a tribunal. Hundreds of people owed money will be attending the proceedings.'

Thérèse laughed. 'Oh, the proceedings will be genuine enough, with genuine advocates and proper lawyers.'

'And what happens when the plaintiffs do not present themselves?'

'A plaintiff doesn't necessarily have to appear. It's sufficient and quite permissible to have a representative in court. I know what I'm doing, Maria.'

As she had predicted, there were crowds inside and outside the court for the outcome of this litigation. They heard the court rule that the plaintiffs had been found to have gone back on their apparent 1883 agreement with Madame Humbert, their so-called representative adeptly managing to bungle his job. Left with no option, the tribunal directed that proceedings be put off to another, unspecified date.

'It could drag on indefinitely,' Thérèse told her delighted family as they sat down to enjoy a private celebratory dinner together in the smaller banqueting room. 'And until it is settled, we need not pay back one franc of what we owe. We can borrow on the money until Kingdom come.'

'They will appeal,' Gustave said in all seriousness, making everyone laugh.

'And we'll counter-appeal,' Romain put in fiercely as he cut savagely into an entrecote that, being so tender, needed no such application. 'We'll employ the finest lawyers in France and take it through every court in the land.'

It was uttered so vehemently, as if the case were genuine, that it sent peals of laughter around the table. Romain scowled, having made a fool of himself. 'You know what I mean!' he countered, seething. Nothing angered him more than having his nose put out of joint, and as soon as dinner was over he took himself off into the bowels of his basement lair to recover his dignity.

'It has been going on so long, I do sometimes wonder who these Crawford people are, or if they exist at all.'

'How do you mean?'

The two ladies sat together over morning

281

coffee, the first stirring the dark liquid so energetically that a few drops slopped over the rim of the cup.

'I mean that we've never laid eyes on either one of them. My husband and I have attended every hearing, yet not once have they appeared. Who are they?'

'I don't really know, except that they appear to be the bane of Thérèse Humbert's life. I hear she is sometimes beside herself with worry.'

'Well, she has enough money to worry in exceedingly good comfort,' retorted the first woman, who herself was more than comfortably off; her husband, a banker, had lent quite a deal of money to Thérèse Humbert.

'Something strikes me as being not quite as it should,' she went on. 'I've spoken my thoughts to my husband several times, but he will not hear a word against her. I said he should begin to ask for some repayment of his loans but he will not hear of it. That loan of his has been going on for three years. He should at least have received some return on his investment. But he calls me a silly, chattering female with no notion of the financial world who doesn't know what she is talking about. Either she has bewitched him or else he does not want to be seen as having possibly been swindled.'

'How do you mean?'

'Your husband feels the same way, I gather.' She fixed her companion with a steely glare. 'So you must know what I mean.'

As the other wilted before her gaze, she went on. 'To my mind it is all part of the power she

282

has over her creditors. No one wants to be the first to speak out against her, lest he be held up to ridicule by those who still trust her with the huge sums of money on which she lives like a duchess!'

'My husband refuses to discuss it with me, so I don't know.'

'Then there are these elusive claimants of this Portuguese inheritance of hers. Where are they? Why does no one ever see them?'

'I do know of someone who has,' her companion offered tentatively. 'Or at least she knows of someone who has.' She leaned forward. 'One of the staff of the Humbert mansion knows one of my friend's staff and said she saw one of the Crawford brothers pass the open door of a room where she was making the bed. She said he glanced in and nodded to her. She said he was in his twenties and very handsome. She saw him again later when she was with another servant and was told his name was Henry Crawford, and he was visiting the Mademoiselle Maria d'Aurignac in an effort to persuade her to accept his offer of marriage. So there is such a person.'

'Huh!' muttered her companion, and fell to sipping her coffee.

'Time is going on. We can't postpone this marriage any longer,' Thérèse was saying, pacing the drawing room while the rest of the family watched.

Her small round figure seemed dwarfed by the dress she wore, in the newest style with wide puffed sleeves and enormous adjustable improver, as the support for the modern curved bustle – briefly resurrected after having disappeared for several years – was termed. In blue silk, the gown, like all her clothes, was glaringly costly; over her shoulders a fine sealskin cape held out against the winter cold despite the roaring fire in the room.

She paused suddenly from pacing to regard each member in turn.

'Something will have to be done soon or people will begin to question the Crawfords' existence. People will become restless and that could lead to rumours and disbelief. The last thing we want is to be accused as liars!'

Romain's dark gaze met hers as it settled on him. His handsome face was grim, his lips thin under the moustache that followed his side whiskers. 'We'll have to see that any rumours are picked in the bud,' he said darkly.

'We shouldn't resort to violence,' Thérèse reminded him quickly, aware of the way her brother's mind worked.

Only three weeks ago Romain had been a little too active. He and Armand had waylaid someone who'd spoken too openly his thought that few seemed to be seeing any return on their honest investment in the fabulous Humbert property in Portugal.

The man, a friend of the Humberts and a well-known financier, had been discovered in hospital with head and body injuries, saying he'd been accosted by ruffians and robbed of cash, a gold ring, gold tiepin and gold fob watch while

284

passing a back street in the city's suburbs. Subsequently a letter arrived to say he was more than happy to enjoy the fruits of his investments in all good time.

Nothing more was said, but later Thérèse noticed Romain wearing a gold tiepin suspiciously like the one the man had worn while being wined and dined in her home.

Since she had come to live in the Avenue de la Grande Armée there had been other, similar incidents involving those who crossed her, especially if the matter was to do with finance. Romain's dark eyes would follow the miscreant while he was in the house; as he left, Romain too would disappear. He'd return later, entering his warren of basement rooms to appear upstairs immaculate as if nothing had happened. But his expression always told Thérèse exactly what had transpired.

Armand was a different kettle of fish. For a man whose normal mien was a calm and thoughtful one, he could suddenly explode and let fly with his fists. He'd been in many a scrap, after which Catherine would soothe and bathe his cuts and bruises. Romain had never been known to fly off the handle. His was the slow, silent stalk and cold, well-planned revenge from which he usually emerged virtually unscathed, though Thérèse had seen the odd bruised eye and scraped knuckle. She assumed that where Armand was wont to use his fists, Romain went in for harder implements. Lately he had resorted to carrying a pistol and that worried her.

Thérèse turned her eyes from him to Maria,

who immediately glanced down knowing what she was about to say.

'We have to revive your association with Henry Crawford, Maria. It does us no harm for things to drag on. That is what we want. But it has gone too quiet. People will grow suspicious. If Henry Crawford doesn't reappear very soon, they are going to wonder, are we merely faking my inability to gain my inheritance? Before long it will begin to be asked, is there in fact an inheritance? That must not happen. It must never happen. We are going to have to dig up your Henry Crawford, and quickly.'

'I hoped the matter would be dropped,' Maria said tentatively.

'Haven't you been listening to a word I've said? The matter cannot be dropped! True, for the last eighteen months all has been well, but it cannot last. We must think up a plan, some small drama. I will talk to Frédéric's father. Between us we will think of something.'

She turned away. 'Our guests will be arriving in an hour and we must get ourselves ready,' she concluded, and hurried from the room leaving them all to disperse.

# Twenty-Three

As her contribution to this year's Paris Exposition, Thérèse had invited fifty dinner guests, each a pillar of Parisian society. Later there would be music in the music room, and dancing, and on leaving, costly gifts handed to them by nine-year-old Eve, who as a charming touch had been allowed to stay up.

They would finally depart around midnight, well fed and entertained and with a feeling that they'd been honoured to have been invited to one of Madame Thérèse Humbert's more elaborate banquets. Of course all her dinners were elaborate; Thérèse Humbert was known for her generosity and the gifts she gave would be well appreciated, not just for their value but because the recipients appreciated having been singled out as special.

Dinner over, liqueurs were being sipped. Very soon the ladies would withdraw, leaving the men to talk over their brandy. Thérèse glanced around at her guests before returning her attention to the man seated on her right. Monsieur Gustave Eiffel was expounding on the success of the 1889 Exposition and particularly of his construction, the wrought-iron tower which now soared eight hundred and ninety-four feet above Paris. 'It is

287

proving most awe-inspiring, I'm told.'

She was about to say that she wondered how anyone could be brave enough to climb so high, when a disturbance below made everyone look up.

There came shouts from staff, and the sound of many feet pounding up the grand staircase reached the ears of the gathering. Before anyone could say a word a young man burst into the room, followed by half a dozen male staff.

As he evaded their efforts to grab him, Frédéric leapt to his feet. 'For God's sake, monsieur! You cannot come bursting in here. We are at dinner.'

'I cannot wait any longer,' cried the man, his eyes on Frédéric's sister-in-law seated further along the table. 'I crave an answer to my pleas from your dear wife's sister, that most charming lady Maria d'Aurignac, or I shall go mad!'

'Get him out!' roared Frédéric, but the young man pushed away the hands that clutched at him.

'I've written time and time again,' he cried, almost in tears. 'I have sent her flowers and jewellery, but not a single reply have I received.' The tone was strongly American.

'Monsieur!'

Thérèse too was on her feet, Monsieur Eiffel trying to persuade her to stay calm. But the man was staring at her.

'Madame Humbert, hear me out! I'm mad with love for your sister and have now come in person for her answer.'

'Henry Crawford!' Thérèse cried. 'How dare you interrupt my guests?'

288

At the sound of the name, every guest gasped. Ignoring her, he turned to Maria who was now blushing deep red. 'My beloved! How long must I wait? I am a patient man, but you constantly spurn me. I adore you, Maria. I know you love me. I crave your attention.'

Two of the staff had him by the shoulders. He flung them off, going down on his knees in front of the furiously blushing girl whose eyes glanced from him to the people around the table, at once alarmed and embarrassed.

'My sweet darling, I beg you to accept this gift,' he cried, trying to thrust a badly folded package into her hands. As she frantically tried to push it away, it fell open spilling its contents on to the tablecloth. Those nearby gasped as they caught sight of a magnificent diamond and ruby necklace, a pair of matching earrings and a huge diamond and ruby ring.

Before anyone could blink, Crawford had snatched the ring up and, grabbing her left hand before she could withdraw it, made to fit it on to her third finger.

Maria gave a shrill cry of alarm and leapt up. With a tremendous pull she snatched her hand back from his grasp and turning, ran from the room in a flood of tears. Those at the table sat on, silent and dumbstruck.

Moments later the young man was being dragged from the room by footmen. His shouts of protest – 'I love her, let me go, I love her. She loves me' – echoed all the way down the grand marble staircase, ceasing only as he was flung out into the street.

So it was true then. Guests exchanged glances. Maria d'Aurignac *was* being courted, if reluctantly, by the fabled Henry Crawford. For twenty-four months or more rumour had flown: who was he, who had ever seen him, was there an affair or not, was it on or off? Now here was the evidence.

What was mystifying was why she continued to spurn such a fine young man, for they had seen how handsome he was – his face smoothly rounded, his fair moustache luxuriant, his head of thick, wavy, fair hair now dishevelled by his struggle with those trying to restrain him.

Who could resist such a suitor? But Mademoiselle d'Aurignac was known to be something of a prude, despite her arresting appearance. Perhaps his advances in the past had been a little too explicit for her. Around the table eyebrows were raised in free speculation.

Madame Humbert was addressing her company. 'May I beg everyone's pardon for this unseemly business – it's embarrassing and upsetting for my sister so to be taken by surprise in company by Mr Crawford. Unforgivable. He has no finesse. It is partly that which makes her reluctant to accept him. If you will excuse me, I must go to my sister and comfort her.'

'Of course,' came the concerted, sympathetic consent. As she hurried away, a low murmur broke out as the diners resumed the enjoyment of their after-dinner liqueur, prior to the ladies' withdrawal to further discuss and speculate on this evening's little drama.

\* \* \*

'It's the worst thing you've ever asked me to do. My heart was in my mouth the entire time. Please don't ask me to do anything like that again.'

Emile, his false moustache and wig resting on his lap, glared at his two sisters as they sat in his and Alice's room. The guests had gone, leaving the family to relax. Maria, quite recovered from the ordeal of Henry Crawford's invasion – recovered, indeed, the instant she'd left the banqueting room – now broke into laughter.

'I think you did a splendid job, my dearest! I hope I performed my role well.'

Thérèse smiled with satisfaction. 'None could have bettered you.'

'I don't wish to be asked to take on such a part ever again,' Emile continued to grumble, refusing to smile at the joke.

'You complain too much, my dear Emile,' Thérèse said lightly. 'I think it all went off rather well.'

'You take it far too lightly for my liking,' Maria said, sipping her nightcap. 'I do admit I'm becoming a little concerned where it's leading us.'

'But you do enjoy the benefits it brings,' Thérèse said slyly, and Maria went quiet.

Frédéric was gazing out of the window into the dark avenue below. He turned to look directly at his wife.

'Benefits, yes, and I think this little charade went off very well. But I agree with Maria, we are beginning to make a few enemies and I don't like it.'

'I've had *enemies* all my life,' Thérèse returned sharply. 'I'm still here and doing better than ever.'

'I keep remembering that woman who burst into the house a few weeks ago brandishing a knife almost in your face, saying her husband was facing bankruptcy because of you, Thérèse. She threatened to kill you!'

'Romain was able to deal with her. She was arrested and taken away with no harm done.'

'But there could have been. You could have been seriously injured.'

'I wasn't,' she reminded her husband airily.

'One can be too brave,' he said slowly.

Thérèse laughed and put down her champagne glass. 'It wasn't bravery. I knew she wouldn't carry out her threat. I've faced so many threats in my life that I can deal with them.'

'One day, someone will mean it,' Frédéric said darkly and turned back to the window.

'Anyway, I'm glad this evening's over,' Emile sighed. 'I've never been so scared, so sure that someone would recognize and denounce me.'

'In that wig?' Thérèse laughed. 'They were all too taken aback by our performance to see your features. I have to say that you made a wonderfully handsome, distraught suitor. You almost had me believing it and I'm sure Maria was carried away by it.'

She smiled towards her sister who was sipping her champagne far too quickly. With allies like this family around her, how could she ever lose?

She was right. Talk of the incident at her banquet

during the last Paris Exposition, with Gustave Eiffel himself a witness, continued for the rest of the year and well into the next. The Crawfords' existence was established.

Yet another year gone and the case of Humbert versus Crawford was still being dragged through the courts, crowds flocking to see the outcome of the most recent appeal. If Thérèse's name hadn't been known before it was known now, far and wide, even beyond Paris. Everywhere newspapers carried various snippets about sightings of the Crawford brothers – some people had actually heard them speaking in French with a distinct American accent.

Thérèse and her family went on with their lives; she divided her time between her Paris mansion and her retreat in the quiet countryside of the Forêt de Fontainebleau, though the chateau seldom remained serene with hordes of guests constantly arriving to avail themselves of her generous hospitality.

But occasionally she and Frédéric, and their charming twelve-year-old daughter Eve, would escape to some foreign part. No one knew where. Some said she might be revisiting her old haunts in Toulouse or could be at her beautiful Chateau de Marcotte in Portugal, others that she'd bought property in Italy or Spain and was spending time there or even that she was visiting her other sister. Marie-Emilie was supposed to still be residing abroad, a widow, her husband having died of cholera some time ago.

Whatever, her absences were mysterious, and there was much speculation that she and Maria d'Aurignac were holding talks with Henry Crawford on a possible marriage settlement. But so far nothing had come of it, the case was still ongoing. And with people still willing to invest in the success of the eventual outcome, the Humbert family fortune grew to proportions large enough to rock all of Paris.

At fourteen Eve Humbert couldn't remember a time when she hadn't lived here on the Avenue de la Grande Armée, hadn't all her life been given everything she asked for. Then, after she'd been rude to a servant, Papa had taken her aside and reminded her that she'd come into the world, the sole survivor of twin babies, in a humble top floor apartment that was more like an attic, in Rue Monge, one of the city's back streets.

It had been a shock. She had refused to believe it until Papa, who was usually so quiet, had raised his voice, saying every bit of it was true and she had no cause to put on airs and graces. But Maman put on airs and graces all the time. No one would have dreamed she'd once known poverty as Papa said. But it seemed that she preferred not to remember it. When Eve had gone to her about it, she had turned her back and said, 'Nothing to do with me!'

Maman was always so charming and amusing. But sometimes she could be quite sharp, as she had been with her that day. Papa was so different. He was studious and intelligent. He was also an excellent artist and would spend hours painting. He had painted a wonderful portrait of Grandfather Gustave that now hung in some important place and was called a state portrait or something like that. But being a shy man, Papa always kept in the background. It was Maman who shone, though he was her constant support and she went to him whenever she was troubled.

Eve loved him, of course, but it was her mother who bought all these lovely clothes for her and showed her off to everyone and made her feel special. She knew she was special; at fourteen she was tall and willowy, taller than Maman who was small and dumpy though she held everyone's attention with her wit and humour, her laughter filling a room, even a crowded one.

But today there was no laughter in Maman. At this moment she and Papa were holding each other's hands in the drawing room as they sat with their family doctor. She'd not been allowed to be present, had been told to get on with her studies under the care of her governess. But something was definitely very wrong.

Doctor Charles Sauval regarded the two with sympathy. The rest of the family had been banished for now. They would be told later, after these two had come to terms with what he had to tell them.

He leaned towards Frédéric Humbert. 'I am afraid you have to face the fact that your father's life is drawing to a close,' he said softly.

'How long does he have?' Frédéric asked, while Thérèse remained staring at the floor.

'A week, maybe a couple of weeks at the most.'

'But seventy-two is no great age. My wife's father lived well into his eighties.'

'Your father has been tired out by pressure of work,' Doctor Sauval said quietly.

'Your father is a great man and has borne a great deal of responsibility on his shoulders,' he reminded Frédéric.

Frédéric nodded sombrely. He should have recognized the signs. This past year Gustave had begun to look old and worn. The zest he'd once had for work had fallen away quite alarmingly, although honours continued to be heaped upon him. Now his father was dying. What would happen now?

Thérèse was thinking the same thing, but for more personal reasons. This was like losing her right hand. Before ever meeting Gustave, she had survived on her own wits and would no doubt have continued to do so, after a fashion. But he had boosted her ability to make real money. Between them – with him behind her, his titles and judicial standing – they'd amassed a huge fortune; she would never have achieved as much with only Frédéric behind her, a brilliant mind but a retiring personality. Now Gustave was leaving her and she'd be lost without him.

He died a week later, having got up from his bed saying he felt much better, giving his wife and children renewed hope that Doctor Sauval had been quite wrong. But half an hour later, as he was having his lunch, his heart suddenly stopped.

'Your dear husband's heart was weary of this world and merely ceased to beat,' Doctor Sauval said to Thérèse's weeping aunt Marie-Emilie as kindly as he could. 'A just and fair man, he is in the hands of God now.'

And so am I, Thérèse thought when the doctor's words were conveyed to her by Frédéric. She was alone. All she had to rely on now was the old spirit that had brought her this far. At least she still had all that Gustave had taught her. What she didn't expect were the repercussions the death of Gustave Humbert would bring.

Hardly was the funeral over, a huge and ostentatious affair with followers and spectators numbering thousands, when creditors, fearing his death might be detrimental to their prospects, came flocking to Thérèse's door. She even found herself having to summon police protection, a duty carried out rigorously in honour of Gustave.

'I don't know what we are going to do,' Thérèse lamented, unable to sleep for worry. 'I'm almost relieved my father and yours aren't here to see it all.'

Sometimes her once fabulous world seemed to be falling to pieces, while she was helpless to do anything about it. During the day she coped, but at night the pressure of it all was magnified almost out of all proportion.

'It can't go on like this indefinitely, can it?' She sought Frédéric's reassurance, inadequate as it was these days. 'It has to die down eventually.'

'It will do,' he soothed, putting his arm about

her, drawing close as they lay together in the quiet of the night. 'You've come through worse in the past, but you've the support of the whole family now. There were times when some of them were against whatever you tried to do, but not now.'

He gave a small, sad chuckle. 'Each of them fears the Humbert millions will begin to melt away if they don't support you. And you still have Catherine and Armand. They'll never see you go down.'

She found herself blessing her loyal friend Catherine for her sturdy support. Catherine had taken it upon herself personally to repel the many who sought to gain entry to the house with petitions for repayment of some loan or other. And should things get rough, Armand and Romain were ready to defend her.

Armand's fists had lately stalled a few would-be intruders, her brother Romain shadowing a miscreant into some dark corner to press home the lesson. They'd always made her feel safe until now. But the new year of 1895 heralded a series of events of mounting seriousness, following on the death of her father-in-law.

# Twenty-Four

It was unbelievable how quickly things could change within one year of Frédéric losing his father. So gilt-edged had Gustave Humbert's name been that investors would sink hundreds of millions into the so-called Humbert fortune. Now he was gone, they had begun to see financial ruin staring them in the face.

'How can we repay them?' Frédéric asked. 'I feel sorry for the little people who've invested their whole life savings. I hate the guilty feeling it gives me.'

Thérèse remained angry with it all. 'If they could invest their money then they aren't exactly poor,' she told him, brushing aside his concern.

But within the year threats had begun to be directed at the family. 'Many companies are said to be going bankrupt,' he reported. 'Shouldn't we make some show by paying interest on at least a few investments?'

'How?' she shot at him. 'The interest quoted is too high for that.'

'You did it in Toulouse, using loans to repay others.'

'They were small then. Now it is more than we can deal with. No one is going to be satisfied with trifling sums. Where do I find millions of francs to pay off some of them without others calling in their own investments? And it will get into every newspaper in the country. There'll be a run on us and before long creditors will be at my door as they were in the old days. We'd never survive, Frédéric.'

These days, everything she did was widely publicized. Reports of their apparent reluctance to pay dividends on their extensive borrowing were even now spreading unrest; newspapers were reporting suicides, companies fallen into bankruptcy, even some banks being forced into liquidation.

'It's all lies!' she complained loudly, trying vainly to convince herself, she who could so easily convince others. To repay what had been borrowed all these years would put her back where she had started. Had she never known the wealth that was now hers, she'd have been none the wiser, other than dreaming of what might have been. But having known money only to lose it would be unbearable. To repay one single franc now would start an avalanche.

Even Catherine, her closest friend, was distancing herself from her, no doubt influenced by her husband. Thérèse had never liked Armand and now he was making his wife as discontented as he.

Between the two of them they had looked after her interests as well as Gustave's. Running their newspaper, *L'Avenir de Seine et Marne*, Armand had admittedly worked for a ludicrously tiny wage, but a very substantial house had more than adequately made up for it. Now, the newspaper had been wound up, and as 1895 came in he was no longer seeing any profit in keeping the financial wolves from the Humberts' door.

Just after New Year, he surprised Thérèse with a formal visit.

'I feel I should be receiving some financial recognition for my work,' he stated bluntly, taking her aback. With Gustave, her mainstay, gone and the extra worry of bankruptcies and demands on her shoulders, he was demanding a wage – for what? For protecting her? Romain could do that.

The moment she voiced her thoughts, his lips thinned behind the upcurled moustache and well-trimmed beard and his pince-nez almost fell off his nose. 'Do you expect my family to exist on fresh air alone?' he shot at her, the suddenness of his anger alarming her. 'Both my daughters are now forced out to work while your family is awash with money.'

She knew that but chose to ignore it, furious with him. 'My family is none of your business, Monsieur Parayre. What I have, I have worked for, long and hard.'

Armand's lips tightened even more. His jaw muscles bulged into hard knots. 'I see our loyalty counts for nothing, the loyalty and friendship of your closest friend, my wife, who stood by you when you needed her most, who has never let you down, betrayed you, or turned her back on you during your harder times.'

Leaping up from the chair he'd been offered, he loomed over her, seated on her couch in her private drawing room. 'I came only to ask for some meagre compensation for my efforts in keeping your reputation safe. Instead I receive abuse! I can only say that you have grown mean and miserly and I am left with no course but to withdraw my protection.'

She was still furious. 'You dare accuse me of meanness when I spare no expense entertaining the many who come to my home!'

Her rage had mounted to such a pitch that she no longer considered what she was saying. 'If you intend withdrawing your protection, such as it is, then perhaps the fine house that, incidentally, you enjoy at my expense is not good enough for you either. Perhaps you would prefer to live elsewhere or go back to being a schoolmaster. If so, then you're not welcome here.'

'Nor your closest friend Catherine?' he queried, his voice rising even higher with fury.

'Nor her,' Thérèse cried without thinking what she was saying. 'If she chooses to support you, Monsieur.'

'She is my wife, Madame Humbert. She will of course support her husband over her friend.'

The raised voices had brought Romain to the door. 'What's going on?' he roared, his eyes on Armand. 'Why are you shouting at my sister?

Armand turned on him. 'This is between myself and her,' he grated. 'My business has nothing to do with you.'

'It has everything to do with me.' Romain advanced into the room, his tone gritty and dangerous. 'I find you, Armand, insulting my sister and I will not have it. I must ask you to leave.'

'Not until I have the satisfaction of my request.'

Romain glowered. He spoke slowly. 'I'm asking you, politely, to leave.'

'I will not! Not until—'

He broke off as Romain sprang, finding his arm being jerked painfully up his back, his body twisted round. Flailing and struggling, Armand found himself hustled from the room and down the marble staircase while servants stood mesmerized by the scene. 'Open the door,' Romain bellowed to them.

As they hurried to obey Armand yelled, 'I shall kill you for this!'

'You can try!' Romain growled. But at the door he let go his hold.

Humiliated and rubbing his arm, Armand turned balefully on him.

'You will not get away with manhandling me,' he rasped. 'We've been friends for a long time, so I shall not challenge you to a duel to the death. But settle this affair we shall. I challenge you, Romain d'Aurignac, to a fair fight with fists according to the strict rules of boxing. After which I and my wife, who, I remind you, has been your sister's lifelong friend, no longer intend to remain in her service – I shall not say pay, for pay we have not received – if this is how you return our loyalty to your family.'

His face was working. Romain's remained impassive, though he was breathing hard from his exertions.

'Tomorrow I demand satisfaction with a fair

303

contest. I take it you know how to fight fairly?'

Romain smiled tightly. 'Tomorrow,' was all he said.

The police, summoned by Romain himself to be on hand in case the outcome grew more savage than a contest between two men standing toe to toe in an early-morning flurry of winter snow, had orders to keep well out of sight until called upon to press charges on Armand, no matter what the outcome. That was Romain's way of getting revenge, and the police would find themselves amply rewarded into the bargain. Most public organizations were in his pay these days.

It was a fair fight, but Armand drew enough blood to put his opponent on the ground. At which point the police appeared, ready to charge the man with intent to cause grievous injury. Romain, however, felt he himself had drawn enough of the other's blood to satisfy himself as to the outcome of the duel and sent them on their way. After all, their association had been a long one. For once Romain had decided to be fair – so long as Armand left the country.

The following week Armand and Catherine left for Madagascar where he had secured an educational post. Almost immediately Thérèse found herself missing her friend's company. But developments soon overrode her sense of loss.

Reports were still flooding in of investors in dire trouble. One of her most loyal friends, Paul Girard, president of the Girard Bank, was no exception. He'd often be at her table or sharing her box at the opera with other worthy guests.

His bank had been more than generous in the loans it had continued to grant her. Girard was possibly the family's biggest creditor.

'But isn't that what banks are for?' she said airily.

Then came reports that the Girard Bank itself was in serious trouble. There were even rumours that it might go into liquidation if its debts could not be called in. The first intimation Thérèse had was the arrival of several official letters, each following hot on the last, requesting settlement of her extensive loans.

Ignoring them, she sought Frédéric's advice. 'How can such a large concern get itself in such a state?'

His reply wasn't heartening. With the departure of Armand Parayre it had been left to him alone to protect her. He'd lately taken it upon himself to delve into the affairs of those lending substantial sums. 'It might be advisable to appoint an investigator as a matter of urgency to look into the bank's affairs,' he said, leaving her in no doubt of their potential predicament. She understood.

Seeing a sudden loss of her main and huge source of income looming, she said with complete trust in him, 'Do as you think fit, my dear.'

'My fears have been proved right,' he told her a week or two later. 'It seems Girard Bank means to start proceedings against us for repayment of all loans, together with interest. We're going to have to move fast and send in an investigator immediately. We might be able to force them into liquidation before they can make a move against us.'

Thérèse was stunned. Paul Girard was a long-standing friend as well as a trusted banker. 'Can we do that?' she queried.

'Yes we can,' he said firmly. 'If we don't, it'll set a precedent and we could be done for.' Gone was the Frédéric who'd once been so critical of her tactics, who had preferred to stay in the shadows even after finally supporting her.

'I think I've found someone who could look into it for us,' he said the very next day. 'I have invited him to dine with us here tonight. He purports to be an honest man but I am confident we can bend him to our bidding and assure him that by working in our favour he could do very well for himself financially. I gather he is not a very wealthy man.'

Thérèse instantly understood the significance of that remark. She'd played this game all her life, but now she had others to do it for her.

'What would I do without you, my dearest?' she murmured.

'More wine, monsieur?' Frédéric asked as Jean Duret leaned back from the table, replete after a magnificent meal.

Thérèse Humbert and her husband had been wonderful hosts and exceptionally kind to him. But also at the table was Madame Humbert's brother, Romain d'Aurignac. Duret felt very slightly nervous, knowing the man's reputation, though he seemed amiable enough at this moment.

'Thank you kindly, but I must not,' he said,

feeling the need to keep a clear head.

There were just the four of them in a secluded dining room off the large banqueting room. A private business meal, he'd been told, to discuss a bank which was in trouble and was thereby causing Madame Humbert, one of its most important clients, some concern. It had been explained that he was being engaged as a private investigator and, if suspecting some underhand dealing, was to take on the role of receiver, which was after all his job. It would have appeared straightforward enough but for a broad hint a moment ago that he would benefit greatly from it. Smiling amicably, he'd nevertheless grown wary.

It was hard to keep his gaze from wandering to the brother. Each time their eyes met, Duret let his drop away, aware the man was sizing him up.

Romain seemed to have sensed Duret's wariness, and Duret knew he was seeing the darker side of the man. Hastily he turned his attention to Frédéric Humbert, who seemed far less formidable.

During dinner his role of investigator had merely been touched upon, but he was no fool. Not for nothing was he in the business of dissolving and winding up companies that had foolishly allowed themselves to let their resources get ahead of them, though he'd always tried to remain unbiased, even helpful. But what his host had been hinting at smelled strongly of bribery. If this was so, he wanted none of it. Stupidly, though, he'd let himself be drawn in a little too deeply. Now, as he voiced his concern with a glance at the brother, he saw the man shoot him a black look.

The previous hints at 'co-operation' were suddenly bordering on threats if he declined to conform. He had to seize this moment to escape. Taking out his fob watch, he glanced at it, then turned to Madame Humbert with a look of urgency.

'May I beg your pardon, Madame,' he began as politely as he could. 'I had no idea of the time. I promised my wife to be home by now. She is a little poorly, you know.'

'Of course,' she said gently, as carefully he rose from the table, the others too coming to their feet. He was getting away with it. No harm done after all.

'Please forgive my rude haste,' he said politely. 'And I do thank you so very much for your kind hospitality.'

Frédéric smiled. 'One small goodnight brandy before you go, Duret. It is a cold night. Then I will have our carriage take you back to your home.'

Churlish to refuse! As he nodded, Thérèse Humbert made her excuses to withdraw. It was after she'd left that, as the three cordially sipped their brandy, the veiled threat made itself more apparent.

'Of course,' murmured Frédéric, looking into his brandy glass, 'we shall be most displeased if, after so readily accepting our hospitality, you've decided against helping us out of the predicament we have been discussing all this time. Most displeased, Duret, if you take my meaning.'

The tone brought anger welling up from his very toes. 'I am sorry, Monsieur Humbert,' he burst out, laying his glass down on the sideboard. 'Are you threatening me?'

'Threatening?' Frédéric queried mildly.

'I sensed that discussion at dinner rang faintly of ... dare I say it – bribery. And now you issue—'

He got no further as Romain's deep voice cut in harshly. 'Bribery, monsieur? Are you averse to making a little deal or two? Are the rewards we mentioned not good enough for you?'

'Indeed not,' Duret replied, confused.

'Then what are you saying? Are you accusing us of dishonesty and underhand dealings?'

Of course they were guilty of both. The sum mentioned for his services was far above the usual. He was prepared to stick to his guns.

'Yes, Monsieur d'Aurignac, I am.'

He had no time to think why he'd been so outright as with a roar of rage, Romain's fist caught him full in the face.

Blood spurted from his flattened nose, oozed into his mouth, he found later from a smashed front tooth. He hadn't realized how powerful Romain was until he was bundled into the Humbert coach, having received another pummelling as he was conducted towards it. To add to his injuries, he later found himself confronted by the police, on Romain d'Aurignac's orders, as being the one to have started the fight.

But he had more than one resource on his side. A week later, Thérèse found herself visited by Paul Girard.

It began amicably enough, but his pleas quickly grew into demands so strong that she was temporarily alarmed.

'You *demand*, monsieur?' she challenged as he stood before her in the library off the hall where she had received him. They were alone, the maid who had opened the door to him having gone about her other duties.

'Madame, I request,' he said in a more controlled tone. 'I am here to request that you repay this bank every last franc you owe it, together with the interest quoted on every loan.'

In spite of the cool exterior she presented, Thérèse's heart had begun to thump heavily. She was in this house alone. No Armand and Catherine Parayre to support her. Catherine with her forceful presence would have had this creature off the premises in minutes. Frédéric was in his studio at the top of the house, lost in his painting. Romain as usual was off somewhere. There were only the servants – two of them, who often acted as temporary bodyguards – but at this minute none were about. The house was quiet.

'Your request is preposterous, Monsieur Girard, coming as it does out of the blue,' she stalled in as terse a tone as she could muster.

Her mind was racing. 'I wonder that you have the effrontery to enter my home personally on such an errand. No, monsieur, you shall *not* be paid until the appropriate time and I must request you leave my house. My staff will show you out.'

As she turned to call someone she glimpsed him reach into his coat. Before she could do a thing, a shot rang out, the bullet missing her by centimetres to embed itself in the panelling of the hall.

Whatever he had shouted at her became mingled with her terrified scream. As her legs gave way under her, he turned and fled.

At the sound of the shot and her scream, Frédéric came racing down the stairs to find her crumpled on the hall tiles in a state of collapse.

'My God! What happened? Are you hurt? Who was here?' Questions bombarded her ears as servants came running from all directions.

'I'm not hurt,' she said shakily. Helped to her feet, she gave her assailant's name.

Leaving her in the hands of the staff, Frédéric rushed to the door. But Girard had gone, leaving him to come back to comfort his trembling wife and hear the facts of the hideous incident.

The next day newspapers reported that the president of the Girard Bank had shot himself. Duret, it seemed, was busying himself officiating the possible winding up of the bank's business and blatantly lamenting its president's suicide. Not long after, a reporter for the newspaper *Libre Parole* openly denounced the Humberts as crooks.

Duret said nothing when Romain d'Aurignac ominously let him know that those in his pay, hired to silence troublemakers, had dealt with the matter, resulting in the mysterious disappearance of the reporter.

'Perhaps he fell ill suddenly and died, who knows?' Romain remarked with a shrug, leaving Duret in no doubt as to his own fate should he get in Romain's way again.

Though he knew Romain was not a man to be trifled with, Duret had been bruised and humiliated and he intended to take his revenge, one way or another. With the help of a brilliant young barrister whom he knew well, he was soon instigating proceedings against Thérèse Humbert on behalf of the beleaguered Girard Bank itself, knowing the case might drag on and on as one appeal after another was brought. It would, he hoped, be a small thorn in the side of that family for years to come.

# Twenty-Five

It was so good to have Catherine back. Armand's career in education on the island of Madagascar had been short lived indeed. Ever a radical, his opinion of the French colonial army's recent cruel treatment of the local population hadn't gone down too well and he'd been sent home. Thérèse couldn't care less about his disappointment. She had Catherine back, a staunch ally ready to repel uninvited boarders.

'Just like old times,' she said, although it had been only a matter of months since her friend had left.

'Sometimes I've not known where to turn,' she told her, pouring out all her woes of recent months: the shooting in her own home, her attempt at bribery thrown back at her, her targeting by scandal sheets, and other incidents.

'I cannot understand it. It's for an investor to decide what to do with his money. We put no pressure on anyone. They know they stand to make handsome profits from their investments in time and the interest we quote cannot be bettered anywhere in France. Yet more and more people come complaining of being swindled of their piffling outlays, causing no end of unrest among those who believe in us.'

Piffling! The word made Catherine smile. Thérèse had virtually the whole of France believing in her: respected lawyers, industrialists, finance houses were still sinking millions into the contents of her strongbox – twelve million had come from the fabulously wealthy Marquis de Cazeaux alone. Even the Humberts' savings bank, Rente Viagère, run by Romain, attracted thousands of smaller savers, increasing her vast fortune by even more millions of francs.

But Thérèse was right, voices of discontent were beginning to echo. Maybe she did have cause to worry. She was playing with fire, and wildfire at that. She was rapidly losing control and Catherine in turn found herself concerned for her friend.

Thérèse had an army of lawyers to act for her if the occasion arose. But there was also an army of them acting for others against her.

'Thank God I have Romain to settle things for me,' Thérèse whispered as they sat in her private opera box with their husbands and several friends. Like her female guests she was bejewelled and grandly dressed in the very latest fashion. The bustle long gone, skirts now hugged the hips, falling in wide flowing sweeps; the gowns were cut with low necklines, full sleeves and tightly corseted waists.

'If someone tries to bring legal proceedings against me, he will sort it out for me, quietly, if you know what I mean,' Thérèse hissed in Catherine's ear as the orchestra filled the opera house with the strident minor chords of the strange and still controversial overture to Bizet's *Carmen*.

'I prefer not to ask how,' she went on, the unsettling notes falling silent in readiness for the curtain to open. 'But it does stop the press making a huge scandal of some inconsequential legal wrangle.'

Catherine was well aware of Romain's methods – of his shady dealings, blackmail and extortion supported by threats of violence, often by violence itself. Reports would reach her ears of an occasional eminent personage gone missing, while later a body would be found dead under suspicious circumstances with never a clue as to the culprit. To her such disappearances bore Romain's trademark. He knew what he was about, was clever enough not to be caught; his ring of thugs and spies was wide, its members too well paid to betray him.

'The press would love to discredit me,' Thérèse told her as they and their husbands climbed into their coach to take them back to the house on Avenue de la Grande Armée for their guests to enjoy a huge supper.

'It's sheer jealousy. I'm very well respected, Catherine, but there are some...'

Her words trailed off, then brightened as their coach rattled on over the Paris cobbles.

'Thank goodness for Romain, and my dear Frédéric in the background to advise me. And now you, Catherine, you and Armand. I'm so glad the both of you are back.'

Thérèse faced her brother in the library where she had cornered him, having locked the door against intruders.

Now she confronted him angrily. She had no fear of his temper though others had, even some in the family.

'It really has to stop, Romain,' she said, her tone unusually harsh. 'I know you do these things to safeguard me from those who threaten me but your methods these last two years or so have begun to wear on me. What I do used to be fun but it isn't any more. If you get caught I will be challenged and all I've built will crumble. I could even go to prison.'

This thought had never occurred to her before. Now it hit her and made her shiver. Could that possibly happen?

Romain was glowering at her. 'I'm always careful.'

'I know, but it's happening far too frequently. I've never enquired into your methods. I don't want to know, but it can't go on. I'm becoming afraid.'

She was seldom afraid, but saying so served to make her brother more aware of the situation.

'What I've done has always been an enjoyment to me,' she told him crossly. 'But what you're doing is slowly destroying all the pleasure I ever had in it. It's no longer fun.'

'Fun! I never saw it as fun,' he retaliated. 'I've always seen it as a means to get rich and stay rich.'

'That was never my aim!' She shot back at him then gave a small shrug. 'Well, it was, I suppose, when we were struggling. But I enjoyed pitting my wits against those of others. These last two or three years it's changed. I'm becoming fraught with anxiety and it's all your doing.'

Romain's hands bunched. His eyebrows met in an angry frown as he advanced on her. 'If it wasn't for me, Thérèse, you'd have gone down long ago. We aren't talking about your childish little games any more.'

Her small frame stood its ground, her round face thrust towards him. 'At least my way keeps this family wealthy and famous ... yes, famous, with no need to resort to the tactics you use, even though I know you do it for my good. I can play these people with a mere look of hurt surprise and they melt immediately, no one dares to question me. But what you do could land us all in jail one day if you're caught.'

'I won't be caught!' he grated.

'I just hope not!' she warned. Turning her back on him she unlocked the library door, hurrying away before he could say any more.

For all her anger she was not going to change Romain. But what had prompted her attempt to curb his tactics was the report in the newspaper

316

she still held crumpled in her hand as she left the library. A body found on a train going to Lille had been identified as that of one Paul Schotmann, and he had been murdered. Alerted the moment she read the report, she knew it as the handiwork of her brother, or at least of those acting on his orders.

It stood out so vividly because recently Schotmann had loudly refused to lend the Humbert enterprise a further seven million francs on top of the two million his company, one of the foremost distillers in France, had loaned some three years back. He'd made no secret of his discontent and was soon stirring up discontent in others.

'Something has to be done,' she had remarked to Romain. 'He'll bring the whole of our business down on our heads if we don't do something.'

She should have known then, but she'd been so wrapped up in her own exciting pursuits that it hadn't occurred to her he'd take matters into his own hands. Then, hardly a week later, came another shock, much closer to home and far more chilling.

Thérèse was in her boudoir when Catherine came bursting in, near to tears.

'I've just been told that the police raided the home of your sister Marie-Louise last night. She's here and she's distraught and furious. She blames you. She says she has never approved of what you do yet the police come to her. It's a mystery why.'

Composing herself a little, Catherine came

further into the room. 'She's downstairs talking to Frédéric. He's trying to calm her but I thought to come and tell you before your sister came barging up here.'

Still the stiff and starched, law-abiding nuisance she'd always been, Marie-Louise had moved back to Paris with her two children, Paul and Emilie, several years ago after the death of her husband. But she had steadfastly refused to have anything to do with the rest of the Humbert family, calling them unfeeling and evil.

She never came near the house. Thérèse hadn't set eyes on her for nearly a year. But the incident reported to Thérèse by Catherine had brought her sister here in person, no doubt raging and indignant.

'I'll dress and come down as soon as I can,' Thérèse said, calling for her personal maid, while Catherine hurried back downstairs to help pacify the distraught woman.

It seemed that one trauma followed another. Last year she'd only just survived the final court appeal – in a case that had been going, on and off, for two years or more – brought by that Duret person on behalf of the Girard Bank. She'd finally been called upon to pay a mere two million francs in settlement, money she had successfully raised with loans from trusting investors. But since then she'd found herself being methodically targeted by legal bodies acting for several industrialists from north to south of the country to whom she owed money.

It was becoming a nightmare. Now this. Next the police might well call on her own home.

What if they demanded to see the contents of her father's strongbox, now in its locked room away from public gaze?

Quickly she hurried downstairs to sort out this recent problem.

She found Marie-Louise in a terrible state. Frédéric and her other sister Maria were trying vainly to calm her, though it was Eve, now eighteen, who seemed nearest to succeeding; as she approached, Eve had her arms about her aunt. Thérèse glanced at her daughter with pride.

No doubt, to Marie-Louise, Eve as a niece was neutral and inoffensive. As Thérèse came towards them, she turned away to bury her face in the girl's comforting shoulder. 'I feel so humiliated,' came her muffled voice. 'I have no idea why I've been picked on, singled out.'

'It had to be a mistake,' Thérèse offered lamely, but she was ignored.

'I've done no wrong. I've never been involved in the evil this family may be guilty of. I am guiltless. Yet, out of the blue, the law appears at my door, demanding entry. What have I done? Who could have invoked them to such action?'

Yes, who? And why? The thought flashed through Thérèse's mind.

'They questioned my son,' Marie-Louise went on, still clinging to her niece for support. 'A boy only just thirteen. They asked him what he knew of Romain's movements.'

She broke away from her niece to glare at Thérèse. 'I've always known what Romain can be like. But lately Paul has developed an unsavoury fascination with him, even said he wanted to be as dashing as him. I found he has been seeing Romain in his living quarters and I forbade him to go there ever again. But I told the police Paul had no dealings whatsoever with him. They left, but he was in a terrible state of turmoil.'

Thérèse had no idea that her nephew had been visiting Romain. How involved was the lad in Romain's business? A lad of thirteen – had he been acting as Romain's runner? She would question her brother and demand to be told the rights of it. If it were true, Romain would find himself out of a job, so to speak. She'd finish with him despite his seeking to protect her from her enemies.

It was a sad and solemn funeral cortège that left the home of Madame Marie-Louise. Who would have ever dreamed that such a lovely young boy could wish to end his life before it had hardly begun.

No one spoke of the suicide. It was too raw to put into words. Words of condolence were issued, rather as if the lad had been plucked from life by some sudden illness – though whether he was with God after such a deed, no one dare speculate. But in everyone's mind was the silent thought: what drove him to do such a terrible, wicked thing?

Thérèse found herself burdened by a different thought. True, the lad had been shaken by last week's events, a thirteen-year-old questioned by police as if he were a criminal. But would that have led him, a previously vital and happy child, from the rare occasions she'd seen him ... would it have led him to hang himself from a beam in the cellar of his mother's home?

It seemed so improbable to her, as she and Frédéric sat in one of the last funeral carriages – her unforgiving sister preferred not to see them as family – that it was hard to keep her mind from straying to Romain.

The boy had visited his uncle in secret more than once. If Romain had made use of him to run errands, perhaps even carry messages, young Paul might have become a threat to him once the police began making enquiries. Could he be trusted to keep his mouth shut as a man would?

Had Romain then taken the only course he favoured? It didn't bear thinking about. But she knew it was also in the minds of other members of her family: Frédéric who refused to talk about it, Maria who wept copious tears, saying she never wanted to speak to her brother ever again.

Catherine's face had grown stiff and cold this past week rather than sad, and Armand kept away from all contact with the family as if they might draw out of him whatever lay in his mind.

All speculation, but the thought was there. Had Romain had a hand in it? An awful notion, but borne out all the more by the fact that Romain alone of the entire family was seen to be absent, no doubt raising questions in everyone's mind.

'I've other business,' he'd said brutally when she had spoken to him about attending. He had abruptly walked away, leaving her standing.

Why had he refused to attend? Surely the answer was clear enough. But it was only speculation, Thérèse kept telling herself.

If Marie-Louise had any opinion on the matter she was keeping silent. In fact she spoke hardly a word to anyone as the cortège left the house, nor during the journey to the church and cemetery where her father lay, nor at the graveside, nor even when the mourners returned home to offer their condolences. She merely nodded and turned away, dry-eyed, her gaunt face gaunter than ever, mourning within herself, with no one able to draw the grief out of her and give her relief from her terrible, tragic loss.

It was as the guests were thinking of leaving that she spoke almost for the first time. Without warning her grating voice carried across the heads of the gathering to where Thérèse stood talking to Frédéric and a few others.

'I accuse you, Thérèse Daurignac! Thérèse Humbert! I accuse you and all your family, and especially your vile brother, for the death of my son!'

On those words she turned and fled from the room. No one spoke, but all eyes had turned to Thérèse.

At a loss for a response for once, Thérèse stretched her small, plump frame to its full one hundred and sixty centimetres' height and gave a little laugh that must have sounded quite arid to those around her.

She felt Frédéric touch her arm briefly before he stepped forward to address the assembly. 'On my sister-in-law's behalf I wish to thank everyone most sincerely for coming today to express your condolences to her on this sad occasion.'

He gazed around the room, fixing this one and that with his dark eyes.

'Perhaps this would be an opportune moment for her to be left alone with her grief. Thank you once again for coming. It was most kind.'

There were murmurs of consent. He moved back to place his hand gently on Thérèse's arm, as people began to drift away.

With the house fallen quiet, she, Frédéric and Maria stood for a moment watching the staff clear away the funeral feast.

'Should I go to see if my sister needs anything?' Thérèse asked him quietly. 'She was terribly upset.'

'I shouldn't wonder,' Maria murmured.

'I ought to try to make things right between us,' Thérèse went on, but Frédéric shook his head slowly and thoughtfully.

'I think it best she be left alone. She has her daughter with her, and after what was said I would not imagine she would exactly welcome your presence.'

Thérèse nodded glumly, but as a maidservant fetched their outdoor clothing and a manservant saw them to their carriage, her sister's words continued to ring in her head: 'I accuse! I accuse!'

And whether her own supposition was correct or not, she could hear her own voice thumping in her head like a hammer, directed at Romain, 'I accuse! I accuse!'

# Twenty-Six

What she'd said to Romain must have hit home. These last eighteen months he seemed to have considerably curbed his more violent activities. At her many parties he was suave, well mannered and charming, and though tending to put on a little weight still retained that brooding air so attractive to the opposite sex. Thérèse noted how women's eyes were drawn to him.

She also noted with relief that his glances, rather than meeting theirs, still darted this way and that, covering the room in a single sweep, missing nothing, ready for any sign of trouble. Trouble there still was, but these days he dealt with it as usual without fuss but in a less brutal way. She knew though that could change at a moment's notice.

Just lately there had been more discontent than she would have liked. But her loyal backers were still in the majority; those who trusted her were happy to sit back and to watch the interest mount on their generous loans, confident that the longer their money remained in her safe keeping the more it would accrue.

To them she seemed above the law. She had heard it said that her vast fortune kept her virtually safe from it, that the law might even be in her pay.

She knew what they were thinking, though no one dare give tongue to it. She smiled quietly to herself and let them go on believing the rumours as she continued to entertain, give her fabulous parties and her sumptuous dinners, her table graced by some of the country's top dignitaries and their wives.

Thérèse mentally counted off a few of them as she sat at her dressing table this morning. Of those who gladly accepted her many invitations were some of the country's foremost names – the Defence Minister Pelletan, Bulot the attorney general, Etienne Jacquin the Secretary of State, Chief Justice Périer, Lepine the Chief of Police; even President Felix Fauré had been here. It seemed to her that the whole of Parisian society wanted to be a guest at her table.

Sometimes she had to pinch herself to recall that humble country girl who'd woven fairy tales of rich benefactors, fine chateaux and wealthy aunts who had left their fortunes to her in their wills. She'd come a long way from that child capable of convincing even the most cynical members of the towns that surrounded her village. Thinking of it, she would break into laughter at the height of dinner, startling her guests. If only they knew.

Tonight she was giving a grand dinner party to celebrate the first wedding anniversary of Catherine's daughter Amélie and her husband Henri. Amélie had first met the bearded, red-headed Henri Matisse at his friend's wedding. They had instantly fallen in love and married three months later.

Thérèse had generously paid for everything, including a Maison Worth bridal gown and jewellery worth thousands. Catherine, not a wealthy woman despite their lifelong friendship, had thanked her with unusual enthusiasm. Armand on the other hand had shown no gratitude at all, despite one of his daughter's witnesses having been the State Councillor himself.

As for the young couple, they'd said they were looking forward to meeting the many celebrities who'd be here tonight. She too looked forward to it, but this morning she must set her mind to the complainers downstairs in the anteroom, waiting impatiently to see her.

'Are there many?' she queried as Catherine came in to help dress her hair. She preferred Catherine to do it when she was here, rather than her own personal maid. Catherine had a finer touch, and they could continue to discuss matters such as tonight's dinner party.

'Just two,' Catherine said as she piled the dark hair into the slightly fuller, wider and softer Pompadour style, inserting hairpins where necessary.

'Two. Thank goodness,' Thérèse murmured.

Sometimes there could be a host of them all clamouring for attention, usually with complaints of the non-payment of some loan or other. They might be kept waiting for hours in the big anteroom, its impressive collection of guns and musical instruments designed to awe them, before being summoned to her downstairs office. More welcome callers were shown to the comfortable library before being conducted upstairs to her private rooms.

'I've shown Monsieur Bulot into the library,' Catherine informed her as she patted the finished coiffure.

'Good,' Thérèse said, gazing at the finished masterpiece in the ornate mirror of the dressing table.

She looked efficient in a house frock of grey watered silk ornamented with lace, equally suitable to greet her attorney general, Monsieur Bulot, or intimidate the complaining creditor in the waiting room, who'd given his name as Quelquejay and who seemed to have been making a good deal of trouble of late.

She received Monsieur Bulot first, spending an hour or so listening to his advice and any news he had of threats to sue for repayment of loans. The other man, having been kept waiting for some two hours or more, would be in no frame of mind to be amiable.

This was her ploy. The man wanted his money and would make a fuss the moment she appeared. By then she would have sent for funds enough to satisfy him for a time. He would go away feeling he'd at least accomplished something.

This man, however, did not sit quietly, content with what she was offering. Before she knew it he had refused to wait for his payment to arrive.

'Why am I expected to wait for what's rightly mine?' he challenged, his attitude decidedly aggressive as he got to his feet. 'I've been sitting here on my own for half the morning. I'm a busy man. I haven't the time to hang around waiting on your pleasure. I want these honoured this minute!'

Producing a wad of papers and cheques he flourished them in her face, and as she made to walk away from such rudeness he followed her. Next minute she found herself being pursued up the grand staircase. Not daring to turn her back on him, she found herself having to retreat, step by step, while he waved his papers in her face and yelled fraud.

Hearing the noise Catherine had come to the top of the stairs. She was hurrying down them to deal with the intruder in her usual tried and true manner when the main door opened and Armand, whom she had sent to gather up sufficient funds to appease the gentleman, came hurrying in. By that time Thérèse was practically fighting with the man.

Armand rushed forward, grabbed him and hauled him bodily back down the stairs, in danger of thumping him on the jaw. Instead he thrust an envelope of several hundred large banknotes into his hand.

'Now go!' he thundered. 'You're lucky we did not send for the police!'

As the man slunk away, cowed, Thérèse was led back to her private rooms to recover.

Despite her battle that evening's dinner party went well. Amélie and Henri Matisse enjoyed every moment, laughing and chatting with the other guests, who included two important bankers and their wives and a church dignitary, as well as the priest of her local church, St

Honoré d'Eylau, where the two had been married. There were also several important men of business and their wives, including her current favourite, Monsieur Armand Peugeot.

Some three years ago Frédéric had bought her one of Monsieur Peugeot's first motor vehicles, a Vis-à-Vis, a wonderful contraption in silver and grey, ornately decorated, in which they'd taken frequent spins, rolling along the boulevards at some sixteen kilometres an hour, turning heads as they passed. Since then they had changed it for another of Peugeot's vehicles, this time green with black button leather seats and gleaming brass headlights and horn, its red spokes fitted with substantial rubber tyres, its passengers shielded from bad weather by red and white striped curtains and a fringed canopy. No more did she travel by horse-drawn coach, and she said as much to Monsieur Peugeot as the guests enjoyed their delicious pear and honey tart with cream and brandy.

'Before long,' he replied, pleased, as he dug his spoon into the crispy, caramelized topping of his dessert. 'Before long there'll be no horses to be seen anywhere on the roads. Their day is coming to an end, I'm glad to say.'

Thérèse gave her famous husky laugh. All her guests looked in her direction, eager to share the joke. 'Oh dear, whatever shall we do with all those spare horses?' she quipped, making Peugeot smile.

'Nothing can stop the coming of the motorized age,' he announced for all to hear. 'We have entered a new era. It is a new age.'

At which everyone around the table nodded knowledgeably before carrying on talking.

The dinner had been a huge success, helping her to forget the upset of that morning. But two days later she found herself facing yet another incident. The huge crowd that gathered in front of her home, attracted by the goings-on, found it hilarious, but it gave her an insight into what the future threatened. This time the police had been summoned, leaving her in no doubt that she'd soon be in need of Romain's more severe protection once more.

She'd spent the morning as usual dealing with several small investors, all anxious about their loans. Their numbers seemed to be growing week by week. She relied on Catherine to dissuade any undesirables from gaining entry but it had taken up most of the morning to get through those allowed in. The last man had still to be dealt with come midday, by which time he'd had enough.

He was asking for something like three hundred thousand francs after interest, a business loan to the Humberts. 'Two years! *Two years!*' he had yelled aggressively. 'And so far not one single, solitary sou has been repaid!'

Told abruptly that he'd get his money plus the interest very shortly but that he must be patient, he had fumed that she must have that amount and more in this famous strongbox of hers.

'I'll not leave these premises until I am paid in full,' he screamed back at her. 'I'm staying here till I'm paid, if it takes a week or more!'

'Then stay here!' she retorted, refusing to let

330

Frédéric or Armand, or even Romain deal with it.

'He'll calm down if left alone,' she told them with a light laugh. 'He'll finally get hungry and slink away unpaid. And speaking of hunger,' she said to Frédéric, 'It's well past my lunchtime. I must eat before we deal with him.'

'Is it fair to let him wait so long?' Frédéric queried as they went upstairs.

Thérèse turned on him in pique, her voice raised. 'I'm heartily sick of these troublemakers. They pound on my door night and day! And now you take their side against me!'

'I was only pointing out—'

'I don't need you to point anything out, Frédéric!' she cried, all of a sudden distressed. 'I'm tired, worn out by all these worries. And if you insist on taking sides against me, then I'll eat on my own!'

With a sob catching at her breath she left him standing, disappearing into the small dining room where they always ate together when he was home. The door shut behind her with a tremendous crash.

A maidservant passing by didn't even pause, her young face beneath its cap impassive as her master moved off. She was used to raised voices and slamming doors, prolonged quarrels, even stand-up fights. Her mistress was an impassion-ed creature who insisted on getting her own way. Few could ever stand up to her when she was at her height. The maid would quietly serve her mistress's lunch and then serve the master his. By the afternoon they'd probably be talking again, each begging the other's forgiveness. There was never a dull moment in this great, exciting mansion of a house.

But something was going on downstairs that made her young face frown as she came down the servants' stairs from serving the master. Faintly she could hear the noise of things being broken. Quickly she ran through the servants' door to the hall. The noise was coming from the waiting room where Madame Humbert had left her last caller.

Hurrying to the door, she opened it to a terrifying scene. The man her mistress had left to wait had wrenched one of the larger guns off the wall where they were displayed and was using the butt end to smash the ivory keys of the grand piano that stood in a far corner. Keys already littered the floor.

As she stood shocked into silence, she saw him round the edge of the piano and yank up the huge lid with a strength she wouldn't have thought possible. Next thing she knew he had ripped a violin off the wall that held several expensive musical instruments and with the thin end was hooking up hammers and wires from the inside of the piano.

It was then she came to her senses and let out a scream. The man turned and, seeing her, made towards her, bearded face contorted as he brandished the now ruined violin.

With a shriek she backed away and pulled the door to. Servants were hurrying from all directions. But the vandal had already locked the heavy door. They could hear him crashing and bashing, a cacophony of distorted harp strings being torn away from their fixtures reaching the ears of the distraught listeners.

Thérèse and Frédéric came hurrying down the stairs, followed by Madame Parayre, but the locked, heavy door was impregnable.

Frédéric was beside himself, his precious collection of rare firearms and fine musical instruments being ruined beyond repair. 'Get him the money!' he cried in panic at Catherine, who stood behind him dumbstruck.

'No!' Thérèse cried.

'Bring the money! Now!' Frédéric shouted, ignoring her.

Catherine gave him a startled look and made off to find Armand who was working on the top floor in his own office, no doubt too far away to have heard the hubbub.

'You can't give in to a man like that?' Thérèse cried.

'What he's doing is worth more than a couple of hundred thousand francs. That collection is priceless!'

It seemed ages before Catherine returned with Armand. By that time Frédéric was weeping, hearing the horrific sound of his beautiful collection of musical and military trophies being rendered into twisted metal and splintered wood.

'It is all we could get together in so short a while,' Catherine puffed breathlessly. 'But we have managed to find a few thousand to appease him.'

'Ten thousand,' supplied Armand, none too calmly. 'We must play for time. I will telephone for the police to get this door unlocked.'

'No!' Thérèse shot at him. The rumour that the police were in her pay did have substance, but questions could still be asked.

Frédéric was on his knees, his mouth close to the door as he shouted the offer of cash to the man on the other side.

The demolition ceased abruptly. 'Not nearly enough!' came the harsh voice. 'You offer me such a trifle?'

'We will get more but it takes time. If you'll just be patient, this can be settled amicably.'

'Be quick,' came the reply. 'No cheques. I want cash, and quick or I'll start calling out of your windows how I am being treated!'

Seconds later came the noise of breaking glass. Armand and his wife raced back up the stairs to look for more cash as ordered.

Thérèse found herself praying for Romain but he was away on business. Otherwise he'd have crowbarred his way inside that room by now, she was sure, maybe even bursting in through the very windows the man had smashed; the trouble-maker himself would end up broken and blood-ied, only too willing to leave without a single banknote.

It was an hour before enough cash could be found. All the while the room was being system-atically demolished, the creditor pausing from time to time to yell through the broken windows, 'Fire! Theft! My name is Eugène Papon. I'm being robbed!' to the gathering crowd of spec-tators.

With the sound of cheering coming to her ears,

334

Thérèse hurried to the door to curb them and found, to her dismay, almost the whole length of the Avenue de la Grande Armée clogged by something like a thousand people, all thoroughly enjoying the spectacle. Some had responded to Papon's cries and called the fire brigade as well as the police.

It was the arrival of the police, not the money that induced Papon to come out.

Hoping to pacify him, she and Frédéric had been easing notes under the door in amounts of five and ten thousand, a few at a time as would fit under the narrow aperture; he'd collected a hundred thousand francs, only a third of what he had been demanding. She felt worn out.

Then, as officials hammered on the front door, Papon threw open his door and rushing past her, made for the kitchens and out into the Rue Pergolese which ran behind her house.

Her brother's quarters also opened on to that street. Had he been there, Monsieur Papon wouldn't have stood a chance. As it was, she was left to deal with the police, concocting the tale of an intruder whom Frédéric had apprehended and locked in the waiting room, whereupon he had smashed up the place and finally tried to escape via the window.

The police inspector fortunately had been a guest in her home from time to time, partaking of many a fine lunch, and he failed to ask the obvious question: why the police hadn't been called at the outset. He knew better; his purse like those of many others had fattened quietly and considerably since the magnificent Madame

Humbert had come here. To ask such a question would have been to be denied social contact for ever, to bring to a stop the generous handouts. Police Inspector Dangereux was no fool.

But Thérèse was considerably shaken up. It took days for her to recover, and she knew that from now on she was going to have to take more care.

# Twenty-Seven

Armand was feeling rather pleased. He had made great progress since taking over the family savings bank, the Rente Viagère. When Romain had control of it, it had been run on purely fraudulent lines; the small savers, totally un-aware of its true driving force and lulled by the promise of high interest, had been content to wait for it to accrue, never knowing that the day would never come.

Romain had grown tired of it, like his sister looking for bigger fish to fry. Several years ago control had passed to himself and Armand was at last beginning to turn the tide towards respectability.

He only hoped that Thérèse would finally see sense, abandon her dishonest practices and go along with his efforts to legitimize her business. If she did, then within a few short years the family would be genuine millionaires, their wealth undisputed.

Armand intended to call a meeting and put it to her. There had been arguments in the past about the matter. Her main contention had been his insistence on paying interest to its patrons at the due date rather than defrauding them. He couldn't make her see that it attracted more savers, more money and greater prestige, and that it was paying its way despite all.

'I don't know why we need to have a meeting over some piffling little savings bank,' she told him. 'It was Romain's idea in the first place, only because he felt he had to have something to do with his time. I went along with it to humour him, nothing more. Now you want to build it up? It's hardly worth the bother other than coming in handy for small change.'

Thérèse went in a lot for small change. When a punter began to make trouble, calling in some trifling loan, she would often placate him by sending Catherine out to pawn a highly expensive piece of jewellery – of which she always kept a stock by her should such a need arise – and paying him off with the proceeds.

The pieces came from some of the largest jewellers in the country, as ever on credit, most of them only too keen to have the patronage of the great Madame Humbert. As with loans, when any one of them became impatient for settlement, she only had to pawn a piece gained by similar means from another establishment.

Catherine, her true and loyal friend, was hand in glove with her and there was nothing Armand could do to talk her out of supporting her. 'One of these days, she will cast you aside, like all the others,' he warned her.

But she would never listen. 'We've been friends since she was a little girl. She relied on me then and she relies on me still. We are like sisters.'

He refrained from commenting that in fact one of her very own sisters and a brother had been carelessly cast aside in the past.

Now he sat with Thérèse and Frédéric, putting his point across about Rente Viagère. Frédéric was intrigued but Thérèse seemed indifferent to his suggestions, leaving him feeling irked and let down. He'd done so much for this family and here she was, shrugging her shoulders at him, refusing to see the danger some of her ever riskier escapades were leading her into.

She was one of those people who thrived on danger. She'd lived her whole life taking risks and wanted to go on doing so. Armand felt sure that without it she would fade away like a fine cloud in a summer sky.

'I have to get away! It's all getting too much for me!'

How many times over the years Frédéric had heard that cry as he put a comforting arm about his wife's heaving shoulders – one minute up, the next minute down, breaking down in tears, a frail creature in need of his comfort and support. She could be a raging volcano when angry, yet moments later she might be full of the joys of spring. She could be as calculating as any lawyer, while at other times she behaved with utter lack of regard over the most risky and dangerous projects.

But it was these tantrums that bothered him. She had always been volatile by nature, but over the last couple of years her outbursts were becoming more frequent.

True, this first year of the new century hadn't gone well; it had been enough to alarm her into holding secret meetings with creditors, most of which usually ended in disarray. But as they moved into 1902, very little had appeared to improve. Publicly she was facing up to it with her usual marvellous aplomb, still the remarkable Madame Thérèse, but when they were alone he saw the other side of her, the edginess, the tendency to jump at the least thing said.

And over the last month or two even her public face had begun to slip. After she openly accused the Anglo-Egyptian Bank of usury when its president sued for repayment of a long-standing loan at the sixty-four per cent interest that she had agreed upon at the time, a flood of demands had come for repayment from others. Even the national newspapers had picked up on it, joyfully launching a vicious campaign of accusations against her. It seemed to Frédéric as he held her weeping body close that the whole country was baying for her blood.

She needed to get away from it all. She needed a holiday. She needed to escape until things died down a little.

'Very well,' he murmured. 'We'll go away somewhere for a while, right away from everyone and everything.'

He smiled as she looked up at him, her tear-glistening eyes full of sudden expectation. 'What do you say to our estates in Portugal? You can wander around our vineyards, walk through our cork oak plantations and spend long hours gazing at the sea.'

For a moment she looked at him as if he'd gone mad, then they both burst out laughing, her depression blown away like paper in a high wind.

'But seriously,' he said as their laughter died away, 'What about a few weeks in Carcassonne, just south of where you grew up? It's far enough not to meet anyone who knew you. We could buy some property there. January in Paris is so dreary. We'd enjoy the warmer climate. Come back in spring when Paris is in full bloom. Forget about creditors and court appeals. Put the Crawford business behind us for a while.'

He saw her flinch at his mention of the name. What had begun as a boost to their need for an authentic benefactor now weighed heavily on her. Demands were being made in court for these two elusive characters to be produced.

'We'll say nothing to anyone,' he went on hastily. 'We'll just go as we are, buy all we need when we get there.'

'Yes,' she breathed, cuddling close. 'Just for a few weeks. Then I will feel ready to face people again.'

It was the worst move they could have made. The sudden and unexpected disappearance of

Madame Humbert and her husband caused her creditors to panic. They could see their investments going up in smoke, and now believed the wild rumours that the Humberts were nothing but a gang of crooks.

As an angry Armand said to his wife on a request from the appeal court judge to know the whereabouts of the Crawford brothers: 'How could Frédéric and Thérèse behave so irresponsibly? And especially Frédéric? He's always been so level headed. Surely he must have known that people would wonder and become alarmed.'

It was the last straw. A week of demands, threats of law suits against Thérèse, bailiffs hammering on the door, and only he and Catherine left to deal with it all.

'How can she treat you this way?' he stormed. 'You, who have been so loyal to her for as long as you can remember, and I almost as long. No word, no address we can contact to say what is happening.'

'It can only be for a little while,' Catherine said hopefully. 'Thérèse talked several times about taking a short holiday. She has been so stressed lately. I suppose this is what she needed. They'll soon be home.'

'We hope,' Armand murmured darkly.

He had no need to fear. Within a week, Thérèse had tired of the quiet life, already missing the buzz and excitement of Paris. But she hadn't reckoned on the storm that had sprung up in the short while she'd been away.

Catherine's stark face confronted her immediately she was helped down from the motor car. 'What did you think you were doing?' she demanded, as if Thérèse was still a child in Toulouse and she the young girl who had first befriended and protected her. 'Everyone is in uproar, they thought you'd run off.'

'A week away, a mere week, only to rest my jangled nerves,' Thérèse retorted sharply, but that was ignored as Catherine waved the request from the appeal court judge at her.

'And there's this! You are going to have to respond.'

Thérèse did, but with her usual impulsive first thoughts, giving the Crawfords' address as 1302 Broadway, New York.

'That should satisfy the court. No one has ever really checked up on them.'

'What if they do this time?' came the dour response. 'And what if they discover no trace of them? What then?'

'It'll be all right,' Thérèse soothed, unruffled. 'I know these people. What creditor would want to lose out if the worst came to the worst?'

It seemed she was right. Over the next couple of months things fell quiet. 'I told you so,' she laughed, fully recovered and again the charming hostess, the celebrated Thérèse whom all of Paris clamoured to meet. The Humberts were back on track, their relieved creditors believing in them again. Once more life was sweet.

Frédéric's face was grave as he returned from receiving a note brought by one of his solicitor's junior office staff, delivered by hand well before business had started, to rouse Thérèse from her night's sleep.

He'd left her in bed to attend the summons. Now she wasn't there. He found her instead draped sleepily in an armchair in their salon, surrounded by all its claustrophobic wealth of silk drapery, ornate furniture, soft sofas and expensive antique ornaments.

She was alone, no maid attending her, and looked up with a smile as he entered. 'I had a muzzy headache,' she explained. 'Getting up seems to have cleared it. I'll ring for some breakfast.'

'Not yet,' he said, holding out the opened letter. 'This has just arrived from my solicitor, by special delivery. He says that investigators in New York have reported no sign of the two they were instructed to trace and one of our biggest creditors intends to begin proceedings against us. Apparently the appeal judge signed an order late yesterday afternoon for your father's strongbox to be opened.'

'What?' Thérèse was up on her feet surprisingly quickly for one so small and these days rather well fleshed. 'That's utter nonsense! I gave the address of those two rascals willingly.'

'They could have moved for all I know,' she cried angrily, as if it were true. 'I am being persecuted!' Snatching the letter from his hand, she began furiously to scan it.

'I'll call for Armand and Catherine,' Frédéric said helpfully. Thérèse looked up in sudden panic.

'No, don't! This is a family matter and it must

343

stay that way. Go and call Romain. He'll know what to do. The rest of the family must be told too. But do it quietly. No one must know. We must hide my father's strongbox. The authorities mustn't be allowed even to peep into it. It must be got out of the house – somehow, without anyone seeing. Tonight!'

Her heart had begun to thump with sickening beats against her ribs. For a moment she was back in Toulouse, she and the family struggling to get everything of value out of her father's house before the bailiffs arrived. Her eyes were wide with anxiety as she stared at her husband. 'We need to act quickly, starting now!'

Frédéric returned her stare with forced calmness. He too was aware of the very present threat.

'We mustn't let ourselves be panicked into making rash decisions, my dearest. Legal wheels turn slowly. Nothing is going to happen straight away. They are giving us three days before carrying out an inventory. But if the chest suddenly disappears, that will incriminate us as surely as if—'

Whatever he was about to say was stopped as she threw herself into his arms, giving way to a moment of weakness. 'Then what can we do?'

Gently he eased her back into her deep armchair. 'First I will quietly go and summon the family. I'll tell them one by one what's happened so as to avoid any alarm among the servants.'

'But not Catherine and her husband,' Thérèse pleaded. 'Armand will only give me wrong advice, and Catherine will want to defend me from our enemies and perhaps make matters worse.'

'You don't mean to leave them behind?'

'We can't all run off together! I'll leave a note for Catherine to say I returned too soon from my last holiday and need to have just a few more days' rest away from Paris.' She was relieved to see Frédéric nod before hurrying off.

It seemed ages before the family was finally assembled in her salon. Emile and Alice had been staying overnight, Monday evenings being nearly always reserved for a tranquil family dinner. Maria was still in a blue silk morning robe, while Alice wore a rose-coloured one and Emile was in his dark dressing gown.

Thérèse's daughter Eve, now twenty-two, had been similarly aroused from her morning toilet, a voluminous cream wrap over her night attire; all of them, summoned here so hurriedly, were now thoroughly shaken by what they had been told. Only Romain was fully dressed, having been already at work in the warren of his quarters. Quickly she went over the situation facing them as they stood stunned with growing alarm.

Romain seemed to be the only one to fully comprehend what was expected, the only one who seemed calm and collected, his dark, hooded eyes growing even darker, his lips tight and grim beneath his moustache. It was to him that she appealed.

'We could all be arrested, Romain, when they find what's in that strongbox. We can't prevent them opening it. And when they find what is there, they'll prosecute us all.'

She looked with dismay towards her daughter Eve. 'Her too. And she is the only innocent among us. We have to leave, all of us, immediately.'

'We can't possibly go in daylight,' Romain replied slowly. 'For the rest of today we have to behave calmly as if nothing had happened. Then tonight we'll pack and be away from here before first light tomorrow. We'll take what's in the strongbox – anything that might incriminate us.'

Well before first light the whole family was ready, quietly vanishing at the first glimmer of the dawn with only a few sleepy-eyed night workers cleaning the streets to see their departure. Even Armand and Catherine were unaware of their going.

The next day newspapers were reporting the disappearance, apparently into thin air, of the entire Humbert family; only the staff were left behind, with no idea that their employers had left until the maids went to rouse them.

Armand was awakened to full sunlight by a frantic servant telling him the press were hammering on the main door of the mansion, demanding to see a representative of the Humbert family, having already got wind of an imminent prosecution.

Finding the whole family gone, the Parayres were beside themselves with rage, feeling themselves betrayed despite the explanatory note Thérèse had left for Catherine.

'The word has already gone around,' Armand said when he returned to tell Catherine what was going on. 'I'm being told that there is a court order against Thérèse. No one told me.'

'But you are usually made aware of everything to do with Thérèse,' she said.

'Until now,' he replied grimly. 'I was aware of the Anglo-Egyptian Bank's summons for repayment of a loan, but had not a word that Thérèse is about to be charged with fraud. She must have known but I was kept in the dark. This is how she serves my loyalty to her. Accusations are flying everywhere. Now I find myself being told by the press that there is an order for her strongbox to be formally opened.'

He was more furious at being kept in the dark, at finding those he called friends secretly fleeing with no word to him of their destination, than concerned by the proposed opening of the strongbox tomorrow. He was also surprised by the family's flight.

It was a restless night they spent, following a fraught Thursday during which they'd had to fend off eager reporters and later a small crowd of spectators who had gathered outside the house to gape after reading the rash suppositions in the newspapers. To his mind, the press seemed to excel at such false reports, ready to jump to conclusions before the truth was known.

Now he awoke to find the street packed tight with people jostling to watch what would apparently be the ceremonious opening of the fabled strongbox to reveal the huge treasure it contained.

'There must be at least seven or eight thousand out there,' he told a tight-lipped Catherine. 'The

347

whole length of the avenue is packed. Fortunately there's a police squad outside the door to prevent any break-in or chance of it turning into a riot.'

But it was no comfort. Throughout the morning the unrelenting murmur of the crowd penetrated into the house, with no way to escape it. Trapped, they were forced to endure it. It was almost a relief to hear it change to a cheer as the state prosecutor and his entourage arrived to preside over the eventual opening of the treasure chest.

Armand welcomed his arrival. He was a friend of the family, as were many in the legal profession, and it was good too to have someone here who could support him and Catherine, sympathize that they had been left to deal with this unfortunate situation.

He still couldn't understand why the family had chosen to be absent. What had they to be afraid of? Certainly if the Anglo-Egyptian Bank was successful in its suit against them, it would considerably diminish their millions, but the contents of Thérèse's strongbox would surely provide her with more than enough means to meet their demands.

Perhaps she was loath to see her secret treasure being opened before the prying eyes of the world. 'It seems to me,' he remarked stiffly to the state prosecutor, 'a violation of Madame Humbert's privacy.'

'I'm afraid that cannot be helped,' the man said with all sympathy. 'It is out of my hands. I am only following orders.'

'I understand,' Armand said. 'But it is a pity she happens to be out of Paris with all this going on.' Even now he felt a compulsion to defend her.

'She had fair warning,' came the reply. 'There was no need for her and her family to leave for what you tell me is a few days' rest.'

It was a pointed remark, leaving Armand to fall silent.

In the hallowed room on the third floor, the state prosecutor regarded the locked box. 'It's larger than I imagined,' he said, then after a pause for thought, added, 'I suggest this be opened in full view of the public. Having the business conducted in private may invite suspicion of underhandedness, if you see what I mean.'

Armand nodded silently. Soon arrangements were being made for the box to be brought out of the house.

Considering it too risky to bring the box to the front door, the crowds likely to break through the police cordon and storm the workmen before it could get out to the street, it was decided to lower it from an upper floor window, protected by scaffolding, thus creating a greater impression before the opening ceremony. With two workmen sitting on it, the strongbox was inched down slowly and delicately, each wobble bringing a concerted sigh of anxiety from the hordes of onlookers. Finally reaching the ground, locksmiths had to attack the lock of the lid with hammers, no key having been found. Armand was sure Thérèse had made off with it and allowed himself a grim smile.

All this time a hush had descended over the waiting crowds, but as the lock was finally smashed, a huge cheer went up. Slowly the heavy lid was lifted. Together with the state prosecutor and several others, he stepped forward to peer at the treasures it held. He almost felt his face turn white as he found himself staring into its empty depths, the bottom lined with yellowing newspaper on which lay a single coin and an old trouser button. His first thought was that she'd escaped with the entire contents.

# Twenty-Eight

Thérèse sat enthralled as one of the hotel staff translated into French for her from the Spanish newspaper.

'It's really quite exciting, isn't it?' she said to Frédéric as the young man finished.

'I'm glad you think so,' Frédéric said sombrely.

Thérèse laughed. 'Don't be such an old misery, my dear. No one is going to trace us here.'

The young man was looking a little too interested. She waved for him to go. 'Thank you. You can leave the newspaper,' she said as he turned to leave, still holding the paper. She watched him drop it on to the chair.

As the door closed behind him, she turned to gaze from the window of her hotel suite at the sunlit city of Madrid spread out before her, the wide, tree-lined Calle de Alcala with its triumphal arch and beyond that a skyline of tall churches. The scorching heat of June had still to come, but in early May it was perfect. Below her all seemed so peaceful. She was going to love it here.

'By the time we return to Paris, the uproar will have died down. It always does,' she said confidently. 'Meantime we're here to enjoy ourselves and forget Paris for a while.'

Frédéric didn't reply. The rest of the family seemed set on making the most of this holiday, as they were calling it, deluding themselves that they were safe. But what that young man had read out in his halting French was disturbing. Frédéric couldn't put it behind him even if Thérèse, as usual, could.

The report in the Spanish newspaper was sketchy, just a couple of paragraphs telling of the discovery of a chest believed to contain a vast treasure belonging to a certain Madame Thérèse Humbert, but which on being opened was revealed to be just an empty box. It was thought the owner, who had apparently defrauded many eminent people, had made off with the wealth it had contained. Her whereabouts was at this moment being sought.

Frédéric thought suddenly of the young man's eager face as he read the report to Thérèse. What if he'd realized the identity of the woman to whom he'd been reading and seen in it a huge reward for information as to her whereabouts? Thérèse was far too complacent, sitting there contentedly, gazing from the window at this bright sunlit city, thinking herself safely out of the way until it all died down.

As the months passed and no investigators came looking for them, Frédéric began to relax. During the hottest months the family took their siesta under the shade of trees on the hotel's patio, perambulated in the cool of the evening with other strolling citizens, enjoyed succulent meals with the opulent of society and delighted in an excellent social life that, with the cooler air of autumn, became even more pleasurable.

Christmas Eve in Spain would be a solemn affair, but once families emerged from the churches after evening mass, the streets would come alive with music and jollity as everyone celebrated Noël. With only five days to go until then, the family gathered for lunch in Thérèse and Frédéric's apartment, Thérèse dramatically raised her champagne glass. 'To the downfall of all who oppose us!' she toasted in her husky voice.

Their responding laughter was disturbed by an urgent rapping on the door of the suite.

Romain got up from the table to answer the summons, giving his sister a querying look as he passed her. At the sound of men's raised voices Thérèse stood up, as did the rest of them.

Moments later, Romain reappeared, accompanied by the hotel manager and several officials. Grim faced, his arms were held in the grip of two police officers.

'They've found us,' was all he said.

Crowds waited for the train to pull into the station.

'Do you think they'll prosecute her?' a woman said to her friend.

'I don't see why not,' said the other woman, her eyes on the approaching train, its engine puffing like some out-of-condition sprinter. 'After all it is fraud – and on a grand scale.'

'They've come so near to it in the past, but she's always wriggled out of it. Maybe she'll wriggle out of it this time too.'

'The whole family is just as bad. Rogues, all of them.'

'What I can't understand,' said her friend, 'is why the police have never done anything. Some say they're in her pay and God knows she's rich enough to pay off the whole government administration.'

'Well, I don't think she will be getting away with it this time. The papers are saying that this last trick of hers nearly brought down the whole judiciary.'

'If she does go to trial, I heard it said she'll be dangerous to a lot of those investors as much as to herself and a lot of *them* could be pulled down.'

She craned her neck over the heads of others as the train began to slow to a stop.

'That's why everyone is asking if she'll ever come to trial. The system is afraid of her. She could pull so many down with her that it might even end up being a national disaster, and if that happens—'

She broke off as the train finally jerked to a halt, the special carriage having come to rest abreast of the waiting crowd which surged forward as the carriage door opened.

Though the police tried to control the mob, it was impossible to smother the jeers of condemnation as the woman and her family emerged.

Her head low, her face hardly visible beneath the huge hat, she clutched her coat close to her neck, her muff dangling from one wrist, the other hand holding an umbrella as if to defend herself with it against attack.

But that was prevented by the two detectives each side of her roughly pushing away anyone who came too near. Behind her, the rest of the family were being similarly shielded but nothing could prevent the taunts and catcalls, deriding the once grand Madame Humbert, a wicked woman, a thief, and yelling for her to give back all the money she'd made from her wicked deals and that she should spend the rest of her life rotting in jail for duping and stealing from many who could ill afford it.

Outside the station, running the gauntlet of yet more jeering crowds, newspaper reporters and photographers blatantly obstructing their path despite all the police could do, the Humberts were bundled into waiting police vans outside the station and whisked off to be locked in separate cells in the Conciergerie.

A little removed from the others, Armand and

354

Catherine were also detained in separate prison cells until judicial inquiry commenced. With the Christmas season in full swing, this would not now happen until the New Year.

Outside, Christmas was being celebrated more for the arrest of the whole Humbert tribe than for any holy purpose, as if their arrest was the only one there had ever been.

While Thérèse hung on to her belief that soon they would be released and told it had all been a huge mistake, Armand prayed bitterly that no such joy would be hers.

From the moment Thérèse had fled, he and Catherine had borne the blame, reviled by public and press alike as hiding something when no trace of her and her family could be found. Each time he thought of how many times his wife had collapsed in tears on hearing herself spoken of as Madame Humbert's evil demon. Their apartment had been searched by the police and they were forced out, the house sealed up; even their daughter had been included in efforts to find incriminating evidence against them and the Humberts, her little hat shop and her husband's studio raided. Armand felt he could never forgive Thérèse for what she had done to them. And now they had been incarcerated in jail as common criminals.

Thérèse would wriggle out of this mess as she'd always done and no doubt he and his wife would be released too, but the stigma for him would never disappear – the humiliation of having to flee Paris, only to be kept under surveillance by detectives from across the street as they took refuge in their younger daughter's home. How they'd managed to live without an income had been thanks to the few paintings Henri had been able to sell.

It had been Henri who dealt with the press as his wife's parents were marched off to jail. At this very moment he was generously sorting out Armand's defence. Armand felt he had everything to thank him for. Certainly nothing to thank Thérèse for, whom he and his wife had served loyally all these years.

The magistrate's hearing came in January 1903. Armand hadn't set eyes on Thérèse since her flight last May, yet she had the effrontery to hold out a friendly hand to him as they came into court. It did him good to see her face flushed almost crimson as he turned slowly from the offered hand.

The gesture wasn't missed by the court, and a murmur of respect for him went around those there to watch the proceedings, who had expected a vicious exchange of words.

He sat quietly throughout the whole business, managing to hide his feelings of triumph when Thérèse's husband fainted while he was being cross-questioned, suffering the indignity of being carried from the court.

On the other hand Thérèse kept leaping to her feet to voice her disagreement with the magistrate, having to be told time after time to control herself. She didn't realize it but her behaviour was helping Armand to keep hold of his own self-control, his head high as proof of innocence.

That too hadn't gone unnoticed, he was heartened to see, but it was a gruelling time and he only hoped that Catherine too would keep a hold on herself.

To his relief and intense admiration she did just that, standing upright and dignified in her somewhat outdated attire, her hat small, head-hugging and old-fashioned beside the feathered and huge-brimmed hats of the women spectators. Armand felt that in a way it drew their sympathy.

Something must have drawn the sympathy of the magistrate, as they found themselves released on the last day of January.

'And Thérèse Humbert remains in custody,' he said triumphantly to Catherine as they walked away from the magistrates' court into the free, wintry air.

'Even though I hate what she did to us, somehow I feel sorry for her,' Catherine answered.

'I don't,' Armand said with certainty. Catherine didn't reply as she buried her hands gratefully in her cheap fur muff.

Half the world was following the proceedings that lasted so long into spring that they seemed to be going on for ever.

'You have to admire her,' Armand remarked begrudgingly in the comfort of his daughter's house, where they were now compelled to lodge with hardly any money to their name. The Matisses had been more than generous in opening their home to them and when this was all over, Armand intended to find employment and repay their hospitality. But until the date for the trial itself was set and finished with, he dared do nothing to bring attention back to himself. Lying low was best.

'You have to admire her audacity!' he expounded. 'She is purposely spinning things out as if it's some play she's in. How can she invent such outrageous excuses and have them believing her even after all she's done?'

It was true. The matter finally went to trial as summer arrived, witnesses seeming almost bent on absolving her, still mesmerized by her for all that they'd been defrauded by her over the years. One witness, having lost his reputation and every penny he had, as well as his law practice, excused his weakness with, 'I do believe she actually hypnotized me.'

'Do you know,' Armand said as he read to his daughter and son-in-law from the day's newspaper report, 'Even that fellow Schotmann, the Lille distiller whose brother was found shot after he'd told Thérèse he'd not loan her another sou – even he is saying that she persuaded him against his will to invest another two million francs.'

'Some people are such fools,' Henri remarked.

'He's saying,' Armand went on reading, 'she even persuaded him to impersonate some fictitious wealthy uncle of hers to give more credence to her inheritance. He was so dumbfounded by the request that he went along with it. He says that he now feels it was like playing a role in a play and still can't explain how it all happened. Can you believe it?'

'I can believe anything of that woman,' Henri said ruefully. 'I was almost duped by her when she paid for our entire wedding. No one asked her to and I admit I too was carried away by her apparent generosity.'

Armand gave a bitter laugh. 'She could be very generous when she wanted, when it suited her.'

'Well, we'd nothing to give,' Henri said truthfully. 'So I don't know why she should have been so generous to us.'

Armand bit his lip and said nothing. Thérèse could be all things to all people, had always been so. She would never change.

The trial was dragging on to a packed house, witnesses coming out of the woodwork like death-watch beetles. The court was in constant uproar; even the counsel for the defence found himself near on one occasion to being physically assaulted by a witness, while another's evidence brought shouts of 'liar' and 'crook' in the general hubbub as someone yelled out 'Master Blackmailer!' and the magistrate threatened to clear the court.

Armand read the newspaper reports avidly, but Catherine's state of mind had begun to worry him. Unable to sleep, at the smallest mention of Thérèse's name she would burst into tears. He knew how bitter she must feel at the way her once closest friend had treated her.

Thérèse was now referring to herself as a creature hunted, exposed by cold-hearted men of the law, but it was Catherine who was suffering.

He began to fear for his wife's sanity as the trial dragged on. Her health was suffering too. No longer the stern, no-nonsense person she'd once been, she refused to hear Thérèse's name mentioned, or anything about the trial. But what could he do?

Suddenly it was over. Photographs in all the newspapers showed the once great Thérèse Humbert sagging like a wet sack between her warders, far from defiant after hearing herself sentenced to five years' solitary confinement with hard labour in Rennes women's prison.

Frédéric too had been committed to five years' hard labour and solitary confinement at Melun, her brother Romain to three years and Emile to two. It did Armand good to see the family humiliated, brought down, though he was glad that Eve, Thérèse's daughter, had been released earlier. He wished the girl no harm. It wasn't her fault that she had such a mother.

Less so Thérèse's sister, Maria, who was also released. Though perhaps he was being unfair; Maria most likely had fallen under her sister's spell like thousands of others.

When Armand told Catherine the length of the sentence Thérèse and her husband had been given, her only comment was sour. 'It should have been triple that. Even penniless, she can still bend authority to her will.'

It was the only time Catherine spoke of it. She never referred to it again, but Armand knew she was bottling up her anger, letting it gnaw at her insides like a rat gnawing wood.

He kept the repercussions of the trial from her

as much as he could. They were virtually impoverished but he was determined not to let that conquer him. Many were broke because of Thérèse, some had even committed suicide, but most chose to keep their humiliation quiet. That was exactly how Thérèse had made her millions – knowing that those she duped and defrauded would keep the humbling fact from the ears of others; each followed the same path, not knowing that others felt exactly the same.

She'd implicated many people in her schemes, had implicated many during her trial, he and Catherine too. He'd kept his nerve but Catherine had gone under, the lifelong faith she'd had in her one-time friend utterly destroyed. It would take years for her to recover. He feared that what Thérèse had done to her would never completely leave her. For that alone he hated the woman and her family with all his soul, and nightly prayed she would rot away from boredom and isolation in her prison with no one to admire her any more.

# Twenty-Nine

Five years had meant five years. In that time she'd grown thinner. She felt aged beyond her years. Her hair was greying. The corners of her mouth sagged. One thing that hadn't changed was her indomitable spirit. Even as she'd raged against the injustice of her sentence she knew she'd never allow it to conquer her.

As finally they let her out through the great iron gates she was still Thérèse Humbert, in her mind the girl who had fooled a nation and not the demoralized creature they had tried to turn her into.

But even with her small bundle of belongings in her hands, all she now owned in the world – her wealth, her properties, even her cherished chateau on the Avenue de la Grande Armée, all confiscated – she lifted her head and looked out on that very world, compelling herself to ignore the fact that she stood here utterly alone as the great gates clanged shut behind her.

Where there had once been crowds to greet her, now there were only scraps of waste paper fluttering in the roadway. Seeing that, she felt a shiver run through her even though the September air was still warm with just this small breeze. Not one soul had come to see her emerge. She had never in all her life felt so alone.

Thérèse ignored the moisture that gathered in her eyes, and squaring her stooped shoulders, began to move off with no idea where to although in her coat pocket there was an address, given to her by the prison authorities, of near-by lodgings.

The rattle of a motor vehicle made her turn. As it came to a stop she saw the doors open and three men get out.

For one second they looked like strangers but in that second a glimmer of recognition dawned and with a cry of relief and gladness she ran towards them, her arms outstretched ready to embrace them, her pathetic bundle of belongings thrown to the ground.

'Frédéric, my darling, Frédéric! Romain! Emile!'

Held by each in turn, she stood back to look at them again.

They all looked so much older, but then no doubt she did too. Though Romain had hardly changed, if anything he had grown fatter. She could imagine him looking out for himself while in prison and also he'd already had two years on the outside.

Frédéric, himself not long released, looked pale and gaunt and oddly subdued from his prison experience. He seemed to have diminished in stature. Only Emile having enjoyed three years of freedom hadn't changed, that thoughtful expression of his still with him.

'It's so wonderful to see everyone,' she cried as if they were a crowd. 'You all look so well.'

She paused. How did she strike them? She supposed she too looked older, perhaps even more than her actual years given her time in prison. But she didn't care to think about that. It was behind her now. She drew herself up to her full small height to disguise any possible indication that age might have lost her a few centimetres in stature.

'How is everyone?' she asked formally as they began to move towards the waiting car. 'And Catherine and Armand?' she went on when told that everyone was fine. Frédéric's face dropped.

'Catherine's dead,' he said quietly as he came to put a comforting arm about her. 'She passed away in June.'

Thérèse felt a sob grip her deep inside. Catherine dead! That didn't seem possible. Her Catherine who had been with her since she was a child, Catherine in whose arms she had so often cried away tears of frustration or laughed with over some foolish prank. It was hard to take in. There was suddenly a strange emptiness to her surroundings. She clung to Frédéric in an effort to drive it away.

'Had she been ill?' she managed to get out.

It was Emile who replied, his tone seeming to her ears to bear a ring of condemnation. 'I don't think she ever really recovered from the humiliation of being arrested and having to appear in court.'

There was silence from them all for a moment.

'I'm sorry,' was all Thérèse could say. She would not be made to feel guilty by it. She had loved Catherine, but had thought her to be of

364

sterner stuff. After all she, Thérèse Humbert, had been the one who'd gone to prison, and it hadn't altered her, hadn't made her bitter. In fact it made her stronger. Lifting her head, she stood away from Frédéric and smiled up at them as they stood by the car, far more modern than those she remembered.

'But we have to look ahead now,' she said as cheerfully as she could. 'I can't let what's happened to us interfere with our lives. I have plans.'

They were looking at her bewildered.

'Yes, plans,' she went on, gathering her old self about her. 'What I did once, I can do again.'

For a moment she was really her old self once more, the young girl who had so confidently faced a hostile world.

Then as quickly as it had come, defiance faded on her face, seeing the expression on theirs.

'I can do it! I can!' she cried stubbornly as Frédéric opened the car door for her.

'Maybe,' he said quietly, but he did not mean it. It was over. Hopefully she would come to realize that, though he knew it would be hard for her to grasp.

Perhaps the two of them could retire somewhere, maybe in Portugal where no one knew them. Or maybe Spain or Italy...

Wherever, in his heart was a single dream – for him and his family to melt quietly away, leaving the world to forget them.